Advance Praise

"Paris's latest novel is a delightful blend of wit and heart, offering a refreshing perspective on self-love and self-discovery."

— The BookView Review

"*Eat Dessert First* is a novel replete with insights about a big woman with a big heart and baking skills that too often preclude finding a love who realizes her true value."

— Midwest Book Review

"This book was so good I could hardly put it down. Abbey had a lot going on in her life, but dating was the biggest obstacle. She meets a guy at her best friend's wedding and sparks fly immediately. But could this relationship workout or will Abbey's insecurities sabotage it? This book was funny, amusing, and endearing. This is the second book I've read from this author and most definitely not my last. She knows how to keep your attention all the way through. I highly recommend reading this."

— Linda Martin, Avid Reader and Reviewer

"Paris is a master at characterization, making it easy to adore Abbey and Jax. I cheered for Abbey's growth and ached for her all too real struggle with caring for an aging parent in this delicious story!"

— Kimberly Hunt, editor, *Revision Division*

"Michelle's second novel is a delightful, charming, sensitive and wonderful read."

— Elaine Lundberg, Humor Therapist and author of *No More Bummers*

"Readers will feel like best friends with the sweet and sassy main character, Abbey Reilly after devouring this novel (I read it in one weekend!) Abbey's life is a whirlwind of taking care of her ailing mom, coming to terms with her curvy shape, working at a super star bakery, and maybe even finding Mr. Right. Nudged along in the romance department by her boss/friend Caroline, an outrageous, witty woman of a certain age, Abbey opens herself up to finding love. Her efforts are thwarted when she discovers one suitor is hiding his marital status. The next handsome guy in her path unfortunately lives in another city. Can they overcome the distance? Told with humor and hope, Paris' novel will keep you believing in love, and maybe even boost your own self-confidence. It will also make you ravenous with descriptions of all the sweets Abbey bakes, so have a snack on hand while you read!"

— Cari Scribner, author of *A Girl Like You* and *A Place Like This*

"Lovelorn, full-figured Abbey Riley is Bridget Jones in a purple apron, a young woman searching for love and eventually learning to love herself. *Eat Dessert First* is the laugh-out-loud-funny story of a young woman who leaves a promising career as an architect in Philadelphia and returns to her hometown of Ellicott City, Maryland, to care for her ailing mother. To make ends meet, Abbey works at Sweet Caroline's Bakeshop, where her customers fall in love with her red velvet cupcakes, brownies, and chocolate chip cookies. Some of them fall in love with Abbey, too, but are any of them the right guy for her? From the zany cast of characters to the snippets of classic rock songs, from the charming small-town bakeshop to the hoity-toity Philadelphia social scene, *Eat Dessert First* is a sweet treat read."

— Dian Seidel, author of *Kindergarten at 60: A Memoir*

Eat Dessert First

Eat Dessert First

a novel

Michelle Paris

Apprentice
House Press
Loyola University Maryland

First Edition

Hardcover ISBN: 978-1-62720-510-8
Paperback ISBN: 978-1-62720-511-5
Ebook ISBN: 978-1-62720-512-2

Design By Lindsey Bonavita
Editorial Development by Abby MacLeod
Promotional Development by Molly Gels

Published by Apprentice House Press

Apprentice
House Press
Loyola University Maryland

Loyola University Maryland
4501 N. Charles Street, Baltimore, MD 21210
410.617.5265
www.ApprenticeHouse.com
info@ApprenticeHouse.com

Also by Michelle Paris

New Normal

This book is dedicated to anyone who has ever heard "you have such a pretty face."

1

Abbey's finger hovered over the little blue arrow on her phone—the point of no return. She read the text again.

How are you?!?! Been thinking of you. Then hastily added *Happy Valentine's Day!!* And immediately second-guessed the addition.

She had been plotting this day ever since New Year's Eve when Charlie broke up with her via text. So, this "make him want you back" text had to be just right.

Charlie was her last (okay, in truth *only*) long-term boyfriend. At thirty-three, Abbey was a late bloomer when it came to romance. But it had taken almost a decade for her to get up the courage to download a dating app. She set up her profile and carefully loaded cropped pictures only showing from the waist up. Within seconds, she got a match. He was a fitness model with glistening tanned six-pack abs and owned a business in Nigeria. They communicated back and forth for the better part of two weeks only using text because of the difference in time zones. And then, it all quickly fell apart when her fitness model crush asked her to text a photo of a hundred-dollar gift card with the pin numbers scratched off. *Hmm. Really?* Nudes she had expected and even planned for with dim lighting and a full-length, flesh-toned Spanx bodysuit. But she drew the line at his request for money.

Her boss, Caroline, explained, "Oh dear, I think you've been catfished. It happens to us all." And Caroline should know. At seventy-ish (she never divulged her age but mentioned she had thoroughly enjoyed Woodstock "back in the day"), Caroline had no trouble meeting men even if she did have trouble keeping them—not because they sent her breakup texts on New Year's Eve, but because she liked them older—much older. She tended to date men well into their later years in life. She had buried four husbands and was in hot pursuit of number five.

After Caroline's lesson on catfish red flags, Abbey was more careful with the suitors who seemed too good to be true and limited her search to within a thirty-mile radius from her home near Baltimore. Three months later, she'd swiped right so often she got a callous on her thumb. But her reciprocated response rate was in the .0001 range. She was ready to cancel her membership and assume she'd be the first Bumble subscriber to not get pollinated when a sandy-haired, pimply-faced computer tech named Charlie swiped right too.

It didn't matter that they had nothing in common. He boasted he could recite every word of every episode of the original Star Trek—a television show she'd never seen. And he played a lot of video games. Sadly, she found out on their fifth date his skills with the joystick did not translate to the bedroom.

Their romance lasted just a bit longer than her three-month Bumble subscription. His text to her on New Year's Eve was short and to the point: *I want to break up.* He was never the best communicator, but there was no way to misinterpret this message. Her venture into the world of dating apps had taught her one thing: Charlie was the only man in a thirty-mile radius of Baltimore who swiped right on her. For that reason, she'd let her plan to make him want her back play out, no matter how humiliating a plan it was.

She reread her text to him and removed one exclamation point. Two gave the appearance that she was shouting. Oh, but one seemed desperate. She changed the exclamation point to a period and hit send. Then she returned her phone to her coat pocket and began walking the few blocks to the bakery.

A few steps later, she retrieved her phone to see if he'd responded. Nope. Not even the three jumping dots indicating he was sending a text. Even though it was just before 5 a.m., she knew he was up. He was an early riser. She hesitated for a second or two before typing: *In case you were wondering, I'm doing great.*

Send. She walked a little further before looking down at her phone again. *Damn him!* Still no response. She moved to phase two of her plan. Her fingers glided furiously over the phone screen as she typed: *I've lost weight and am very happy now!!*

Even though the part about losing weight was an exaggeration, okay, maybe an outright lie, it still felt good to let him think about it. She read the text over and added the words *a lot* before weight.

She took a deep breath. Send. Any guy who breaks up with a girl on New Year's Eve—via text – and then cuts off all communication deserves the torture and mental image of his slimmed down ex. Surely, that'd prompt him into thinking he'd made a big mistake.

She put her phone back in her pocket and continued walking the two blocks down Ellicott City's Main Street to Sweet Caroline's Bakery. It was cold outside, but then again, it was February. She sank her hand deep into the pocket of her navy pea coat, checking for the telltale vibrating sign that she had a text message. Then a cringy thought crossed her mind. What if he does respond? What if he wants to get back together only to realize she lied about the weight thing? She bit her lip before deciding Spanx would have to work some serious magic and that she'd cross that bridge when and if she came to it.

When she reached the bakery a few minutes later, sleigh bells above the door announced her arrival to no one. It wasn't unusual to be there before Caroline. At this time of morning, the bakery was peaceful. It'd be at least an hour before the first customer would arrive.

She turned the lights on and headed to the kitchen, in the back of the bakery. A pink beaded curtain covered an open doorway that separated the kitchen from the bakery's small café. The kitchen was large and industrial. Caroline bought the building from an old Italian couple that had a small restaurant featuring authentic Tuscan cuisine for nearly fifty years. The building's thin wooden walls were steeped in so much history and, evidently, lots of garlic. On some days, the smell of garlic still lingered. On the plus side, Abbey and Caroline would be very protected if there were ever a vampire apocalypse.

Near the ovens, there was a small glass-enclosed office where Caroline would do bookkeeping, order supplies, and take naps. Abbey hung her coat on a hook on the back of the office door and put her purse in the bottom drawer.

Forty-eight freshly baked cupcakes to supplement what was in the bake case from the day before should do for the morning rush. As she tied her apron around her waist, she wished she could loop the tie around so that the bow was in front like all the bakers on the Food Network and Baking TV did, but the ties were never long enough. The bright pink apron sported Sweet Caroline's embroidered logo—the one with an icing and sprinkle-topped doughnut for the *o* and a red gumdrop for the *i*—the same logo that branded the front door and every napkin, bag, and box they put their goods in.

Abbey loved to bake. She always had. When she lived in Philadelphia and worked as an architect, her coworkers looked forward to Mondays when she brought in baked goods. Most, if not all, were derived from her grandmother Nona's recipes with a tweak here and there. She started working at Sweet Caroline's a year earlier, after returning home to care for her mother who was physically and mentally frail due to a stroke. In the beginning, Caroline was more involved with the day-to-day operations. "Men love my coconut cream pie," she'd say with a wink and a devilish grin. So, Friday was always "Eat Caroline's Pie Day." The not-so-subtle innuendo was intentional.

When she started working at the bakery, Abbey adhered strictly to Caroline's orders on what to bake and when because she really needed the job. A few months in, while alone in the bakery one afternoon, she made a batch of chocolate chip cookies. The distinct smell of melted chocolate combined with the sweet scent of creamy butter and brown sugar permeated through the bakery just as the courthouse next door was closing for the day. Soon there was a line of customers, and the cookies were gone. Word got around, and people started ordering Abbey's chocolate chip cookies by the dozen for parties and events. According to Caroline, sales were up more than 25 percent that month alone. With a handshake followed by a hug, Caroline gave Abbey full control over the bakery's menu, including daily specials. But Abbey drew the line on designating Mondays as "Eat Abbey's Cookie Day."

Once she was given more creative control, the job at the bakery became more fulfilling than she expected it would. When she moved back into town, she needed something to help make ends meet. The bakery was close and there was a help wanted sign. At the time, she shrugged and thought, why not? She had planned to put her promising career as an architect on hold temporarily. Sigh. That was a year ago. And a year ago was a lifetime ago.

Since today was Valentine's Day, Abbey decided weeks ago to make the daily special be red velvet cupcakes with cream cheese frosting sprinkled with little cinnamon candy hearts. Before leaving for work this morning, she had posted the recipe on her blog, The Baker Abbey, which now boasted twenty-seven loyal readers.

She made her way to the island in the middle of the kitchen, which had five-gallon plastic bins of flour and sugar stored neatly on the shelf below for easy access. She found a mixing bowl underneath as well and carefully measured the dry ingredients—flour, sugar, baking powder, salt, and baking soda. Baking was an exact science, one that made perfect sense to her. It was like architecture, methodical in an artful way.

Once the dry ingredients were thoroughly blended, she slowly poured the mixture into a larger bowl and, one by one, added eggs, oil, vanilla, buttermilk, and a touch of apple cider vinegar (her secret ingredient). It was an old family recipe. Growing up, Abbey and her family lived with Nona in the same old Victorian house that she lived in now. The house was often filled with the smell of sweet baked goods because that's how Nona showed love.

"One, two, three, four, five." She counted the drops of red food dye, mixing in between each drop until the batter became a rich red. To give the cake a bit of spice, she stirred in a handful of candy cinnamon hearts. She took a spoon and tasted the batter to make sure the cinnamons weren't too powerful. "Yum." The creamy batter was perfect. Working at a bakery probably wasn't the ideal job for someone who wasn't happy with their weight and loved sweets, but Caroline had hired her on the spot, with no experience other than baking at home, and the location was perfect in case she needed to go home quickly to tend to her mother.

While she was filling the lined cupcake pan, the sleigh bells on the front door jingled. The smell of stale Scotch mixed with a hint of White Shoulders perfume entered the kitchen seconds before Caroline sashayed in.

"Brrr. It's cold out there." She shivered as she spoke. "Animals have it right—fur is so warm." She tugged at her full-length hooded chinchilla coat, pulling it tighter around her chest. It didn't matter that several animals were now dead so Caroline could be warm, or that with the hood up, she looked like a striped yeti. The coat was a gift from her fourth husband whose name, Leo, was always followed by the sign of the cross and "God rest his soul" as if it were one long moniker.

Caroline was a striking woman. She had very blond hair that was slowly turning white, piled high in a perfectly messy bun and green catlike eyes made greener with the help of colored contacts and eyelashes that could swat flies. To Abbey, she resembled Doris Day, only a little naughtier.

Caroline hung her coat on top of Abbey's and tugged at the hem of her hot pink mini dress, which crept back up to her mid-thigh after she let go.

Abbey frowned. "Is that the dress you wore yesterday?"

"Why, yes, dear. I did the walk of shame. Or in this case, the drive of shame." Caroline winked. She took a tube of fuchsia-colored lipstick from her purse and applied an additional coat to her already caked-on lips. "Mwah," she said, puckering her lips together to ensure coverage. She didn't need a mirror. Caroline was quite good at applying makeup from memory.

"But you just met him," Abbey said, trying not to sound judgmental or even a slight bit jealous.

"No, it was our second date. I never kiss on the first date." Caroline grabbed her apron from the top of the desk and put it on.

"Silly me." Abbey raised her eyebrows in mock sarcasm. "I stand corrected."

"Darling, it was marvelous. Simply a wonderful evening. He invited me over to his house, and he made these little mini beef wellingtons that he bought online from some exclusive shopper's club. Mmm." Caroline seemed lost in thought from her date the night before. "They melted in my mouth," she said. "Then we ate some Duck à l'Orange that was to die for." Her long pink nails, with polish that matched her dress, made a clacking sound as she toyed with a strand of pearls that fell just below her neck on top of the apron. "After that, we retreated to his den, which has a fireplace." She raised her eyebrows. "For cheesecake—not as good as yours, by the way. And he opened a bottle of twelve-year-old Glenlivet, which we finished, of course."

"Of course." Abbey smiled, shook her head, and added, "You are too much." She carried the tray of cupcakes to the preheated oven and put them in. She set the timer for eighteen minutes, went back to the island, and began filling a second tray.

"Do I want to know more?" Abbey asked playfully. She never thought that the sexual escapades of a seventy-plus-year-old woman would be the highlight of her day. But, in all honesty, they were.

"Yes, of course you do. Who else can I tell? My kids?" Caroline made a snarly face. "They think I'm the Virgin Mary. So, anyway, we were just enjoying each other's company. He's very funny, you know. After an hour of chitchat and a little kissy-face, he says, 'I've got a rash on my back. Would you mind putting some lotion on the places I can't reach?'"

Abbey stopped filling the cups, tilted her head, and looked up at Caroline with disbelief. "Ew."

"Oh, no, it wasn't like that. It was sweet."

"Okay, if you say so. How old is he, anyway?"

"Eighty-five."

"Eighty-five?"

"Yes, but he's in great shape. He's got abs that look like Tarzan, I'll have you know." Caroline leaned on the table, probably to keep from falling over.

Abbey closed her eyes, trying to erase the vision from her mind. She took a deep breath and said, "Okay, is there more?" *Please say no. Please say no.*

"What? Of course, there is. Well, one thing led to another, and we ended up in his bed and made passionate love. He was a tiger, or maybe even a stallion, if you will. Very, very loving, and romantic." Caroline had a broad grin on her face.

Abbey stopped filling the cupcakes long enough to insert her fingers in her ears. "La la la la. I can't hear you. TMI. Okay? TMI."

"Oh, you prude. It's just sex. Old people like to do it too."

Sighing, Abbey said, "Okay, I can't believe I am asking this. But did he use protection?"

"Oh, silly you, I may look your age, but I can't get pregnant."

"No, I know that. But you need to worry about disease."

Caroline crinkled her nose and nodded. "Hmm. Hadn't thought of that."

"You need to think of that. When are you going to see him again?"

"Tonight, for Valentine's Day." Looking very coy, she added. "This time, I'm making *him* dinner." Caroline walked over to the large refrigerator and opened the door. "Do we still have any of that chocolate ganache and whipped cream you made Monday—when we had brownies as a special?"

"I think so."

Caroline stuck her head in the refrigerator. "Oh, good, there they are. Okay, then, I'll just make myself a note to take them with me tonight. I'll leave them front and center so that I don't forget them. I will be the dessert. He can lick them off me later."

Abbey put her hand up. "Okay, I get the picture. Please stop." She walked to the refrigerator and gave Caroline a gentle nudge. She took one of the bowls out of Caroline's hands and said, "This isn't whipped cream, it's cream cheese frosting I made yesterday for today's special. Here's the whipped cream." She handed Caroline a small plastic tub.

Caroline surveyed the contents and then looked her body over. "Hmm. Not sure there's enough."

"I'll make some more after the rush."

That seemed to satisfy Caroline. She stepped away from the refrigerator and said, "So, have you thought about my offer?"

"What offer?" Abbey downplayed the question.

"To be my partner and take over when I decide to retire or," she said with a shrug, "whatever happens."

"Caroline, I told you, once I figure out how, I'm going to get my old job back and move to Philly."

"Hmm," Caroline said, sounding disappointed. "I thought you'd reconsider."

"There's nothing really keeping me here—in Ellicott City— but my mom, of course."

Caroline nodded. "No offense taken."

"You know that's not what I mean. I like it here." Abbey pointed around the bakery. "And you are the best boss I've ever had."

Caroline batted her eyelashes. "Why thank you."

"It's just not a career for me. All my life, I dreamed about being an architect—creating skyscrapers that people will marvel over." She looked down at the bowl containing a sweet mixture of ingredients. "Baking doesn't fulfill me." She reached for Caroline's hand. "In the truest sense, it isn't you, it's me."

Caroline seemed a little dejected as she shifted her tone. "We have to get you a man."

Abbey looked up. In a matter of minutes, Caroline managed to raise the top two topics Abbey wanted to avoid—her career and her love life. She rolled her eyes and sighed loudly as if to say, *We aren't going to go there, are we?*

"Yes, that's what's missing!"

Abbey shook her head.

"Look at you, so young, and such a pretty face." Caroline cupped Abbey's face with her hand.

"Yeah, I know, and an ugly body." Abbey carried the bowl of icing to the worktable and glanced at the timer. Five more minutes in the oven, but then the cupcakes had to cool down.

"Oh, come now. It's what's on the inside that counts. Any man worth it will see that. If that weren't true, I'd be a lonely woman." Caroline swayed her ample hips.

Abbey swallowed hard. It was different for her. Caroline exuded self-confidence that Abbey couldn't muster. She knew Caroline meant well; everyone who said things like "You have such a pretty face," always did mean well—no matter how Abbey interpreted the comment to actually mean "You're fat, but..."

"Can we talk about this later? I want to get these cupcakes done before the rush." It was Abbey's not-so-subtle way of getting out of the conversation.

"Okay, but I won't forget. So, what can I do to help?"

"Go check the bake case and see what else we should make today. I was thinking some heart-shaped sugar cookies would sell."

"Oh yes, that's a great idea. Be sure to make extras. I'll take some to my man." Caroline winked and walked toward the front of the bakery.

• • •

By 8:30 a.m., the rush was over, and Caroline was sleeping soundly, swaddled in chinchillas in her office chair. Abbey went to the bakery case in the front of the store. She reached for the last red velvet cupcake, having thought about eating one all morning. The jingle of sleigh bells stopped her mid-reach. She looked up from the case to see Judge Henry Hammonds, a bakery regular.

"Good morning, Judge," she said. With the county courthouse next door, judges, lawyers, and Howard County residents called to perform their civic duty as jurors were often customers. Judge Hammonds had a reputation for being a tough jurist with a sweet tooth. Even though he was probably twenty years younger than Caroline, it didn't stop her from openly flirting with him. She would often say he was a very distinguished-looking man who was also easy on the eyes. She was like a Venus flytrap—enticing men with her sticky flattery and batting eyelashes, only to devour them when they were caught.

Abbey kept to herself that she was attracted to the judge. His short salt and pepper hair, deep blue eyes, and aroma of a wood-smoke fireplace enveloping his long camel-colored wool coat were all slightly alluring.

"Good morning, Abbey," the judge said. "What's the special for today?"

"Red velvet." She smiled as she lifted the cupcake from the case to show the judge. "You're just in time. Here's the last one. If that's not what you want, we also have chocolate chip or sugar cookies and some peanut butter fudge brownies," she said, pointing inside the case.

The judge bent to look carefully at his options. "If you were me, which would you take?" he said as he stood back up.

"Me? Hands down, this." She raised up the red velvet.

"Okay, then, that's what I want. Can you box it up?"

"Sure, can do." She lined a pink square box with tissue paper and slowly placed the cupcake in, careful to make sure the icing didn't touch the sides of the box. "That'll be three fifty," she said as she handed the box to the judge.

He pulled four dollars from his wallet. "Keep the change," he said, and took the box. "Here," he said, handing the box back to her. "It's for you. Happy Valentine's Day."

2

After her shift at Sweet Caroline's, Abbey walked the few blocks home—all the while cradling the pink box with the red velvet cupcake. She let the feeling of being special linger. It was very flirty of him to buy the cupcake and hand it to her in the way that he did. *Did it mean more because it was Valentine's Day? Could Judge Hammonds be interested in her?* Caroline, who is an expert in those things, even said so.

Just a few hours earlier, she was obsessing over Charlie. In retrospect, thankfully he did not respond to her barrage of pitifully desperate and embarrassing texts. What a difference a few hours make. After the judge gave her the cupcake, she spent a good part of the morning worrying about what to say to Charlie if he did respond. Ghost him? No, that didn't seem appropriate, especially since she had been the one to reach out. Text back a simple, *Thanks. Take care,* and be sure to include a smiley emoji or winky face. That response made her cringe. She even toyed with the truth. *Thanks. But when I texted you, I didn't know Judge Hammonds was going to flirt with me. And I'm picking him over you.* Of course, she would never be so bold as to send that response. That was what she like to refer to as the "bubble over her head." And the bubble over her head was never, ever spoken out loud. As usual, she was overthinking a situation that hadn't even happened yet.

She approached the old Victorian house at 36 Main Street. The house—once touted as the grandest estate in Ellicott City, had been in the family since the 1920s and was now in need of repair. A few scallop-shaped shingles were missing from the roof, but it still kept things dry inside. The once bright yellow painted façade had faded to a dull light brownish tint. It was a "McMansion" before there were "McMansions," with cone-shaped turrets on both sides of the main entrance making it look like a medieval castle. It was too big a house for just Abbey and her mother—too big to keep clean, too big to keep warm, just too big in general. But selling it and moving would take emotional energy Abbey couldn't muster—not today, tomorrow, or probably anytime in the near future. Plus, the house had special meaning. Her grandfather, an amateur architect, had designed and built it. Her father grew up there, and so did Abbey and her sister, Penny. The house was a family heirloom of sorts full of sweat, tears, and happy memories.

At the sound of the heavy, old wood door creaking open, Figaro greeted her with a meow that sort of sounded like he was saying "momma." Abbey bent down to pet him as he wove between her legs. "Hey, buddy. How's it going?" Black and white fur flew in the air like dust bunnies. His winter coat was starting to shed.

She walked through the living room and removed her coat, carefully cradling the boxed cupcake from one arm to the other as if she were carrying a baby. She hung her coat on the banister post of the grand wooden staircase that led to a level of the house that hadn't been used in a few years.

She carried her prized possession into the kitchen and put it on the counter. How thoughtful. But why? More pointedly, why her? It seemed implausible that a tall, handsome man with a high-profile job who wore a tailored camel-hair coat would be interested in a frumpy overweight baker who spent lonely nights watching the real housewives of anywhere and reading.

From the kitchen, she walked into the dining room where a hospital bed took the place of the grand oak table that once hosted family meals. She stood at the end of the bed. Her mother, Millie, snored loudly. Millie was only in her mid sixties, but the stroke two years earlier had diminished her once vibrant spirit.

An older woman sat next to Millie's bed. "Hello, Miss Abbey," Betty said as she stood. Since Millie couldn't stay alone, Betty was hired by the state when Abbey got the job at the bakery a year earlier. Betty stroked Millie's hair as she spoke. "Mamma had a good day today. Didn't you?" Betty said in an accent as thick as Jamaican rum and just as soothing.

Abbey smiled faintly. "Thanks, Betty. See you tomorrow," she said as Betty put on her coat.

"Goodbye, dear," Betty said. "See you tomorrow. Bye, Mamma." She gestured with a wave directed at Millie.

Millie, awake by now, smiled and said, "Bye, bye." She pulled her hand from underneath the covers so that she could wave. "It was nice meeting you."

Betty didn't flinch. She was so kind to Abbey's mother—treating her like family—and Abbey was grateful. "You, too, my dear. I will see you tomorrow."

Shortly after Betty left the room, Abbey heard the front door shut. She walked over to her mother. "C'mon. Let's get up for dinner." Abbey used the electronic bed's controls to shift the mattress to an upright position. She helped her mother swing her legs to the side of the bed.

Abbey grabbed her mother's walker, which was folded and propped up against the wall. She unfolded it and put it in front of her mother, making sure the device was locked before she eased her mother from the bed. Millie stood, slightly bent over, and began to push her walker with the same ambition as a toddler. She took a few steps and stopped. "Where's Mickey?"

"Daddy's gone, Momma." Abbey walked slightly behind but

alongside her mother, keeping one hand on the walker and the other arm around Millie.

"Where'd he go?" Millie's face creased around her brow as a look of confusion set in. Her wrinkly skin was dull, and her eyes looked like a faded black-and-white photo.

"He's gone to heaven. Remember, we've been through this." It was a conversation they had nearly every day.

"Oh, that's right." Millie continued to shuffle slowly. "Did I ever tell you he was hung like a horse?"

"Yes, you have. Many times." Abbey said the last part under her breath. That, too, was a conversation they had over and over. She walked with her mother to a La-Z-Boy chair in the living room. Millie backed into the chair and flopped down, letting out a big breath of air when she did. "Penny called."

"She did?" Penny, Abbey's younger sister by ten months, rarely called just to chat. The two sisters could not be more different. Penny was wound as tight as the scrunchie that held her ponytail high on top of her head.

"I think she said she was coming over and bringing the children."

"Tonight?" That was strange. Penny *never* came over on a weeknight—her late afternoons/early evenings were filled with ferrying her children to soccer and dance.

"No. Soon, I guess." Millie thought about it some more. "I'm not sure."

Abbey handed her mother a multicolored granny square blanket Abbey had crocheted when she was a kid. "Here," she said, and tucked the blanket around Millie.

"Penny's the pretty one," Millie said, as if she were stating the one fact she was positive about.

"Yes, I know." Another comment that was often repeated.

"Penny's the pretty one—" as if there was more to the statement, and Abbey's the fill in the blank one. Abbey believed it was a code conversation that her parents had, but she was too afraid to ask her mother to fill in the blank. She assumed the adjectives were—fat, homely, not pretty—all bad.

Abbey handed her mother the remote to the TV and within seconds, the Game Show Network appeared on the screen. Six in the evening meant it was time for a Jeopardy rerun. The TV blared with the volume about four or five notches higher than it needed to be.

"I'm going to go make dinner," Abbey tried to say above the noise of the TV. She got no response from her mother.

Before the stroke, Millie had a thriving practice of dispensing alternative medicine and advice. She treated patients suffering from varying ailments, from migraines to joint pain. By creating a personal elixir, which included a bit of homegrown marijuana from the makeshift greenhouse on the sunporch of the house, along with a soothing neck and shoulder massage, most of the people were temporarily cured of their chronic pains. Sadly, there wasn't an elixir or concoction to cure what now ailed Millie.

Abbey went into the kitchen and opened a can of Campbell's tomato soup. She poured the contents into a pot and placed the pot on the stove. She looked at her watch as she stirred the soup until it began to boil.

A muffled meow sound came from the dining room as Figaro walked toward the kitchen carrying his emotional support (stuffed) cat, SuzyQ—an homage to the delicious Hostess chocolate cake with fluffy white icing—in his mouth. Figaro did not adjust well after the move from Philadelphia and suffered terrible separation anxiety when Abbey was at the bakery. Once she came home to him having scratched off most of the fur above his left eye from over-grooming while she was gone.

At first, she got him a companion, a sweet and fluffy orange tiger-striped foster kitten. But Figaro soon became codependent on the foster—carrying the kitten around by the scruff of his neck from room to room. Occasionally, the foster would escape Figaro's grip and hide behind the couch, striking with razor-sharp claws any ankle that walked by. There was a look of relief in the foster kitten's golden-green eyes when a mother and young daughter came to give him a fur-ever home.

So, the vet suggested a doll or stuffed animal that he could cuddle with during the day would help ease his emotional state. For Figaro, it was love at first sight. And now he transferred his love on to SuzyQ, and the two rarely could be separated.

As he approached Abbey, he backed up at an angle, took a few more steps, and backed up again before taking a few more steps in a move similar to that of a three-point turn that they teach in driver's ed and you use nowhere else. He was very conscientious not to bang SuzyQ's head or any other part of her body on the cabinet or sharp corners of the stove. Walking right up to Abbey, Figaro dropped SuzyQ at her feet.

"Really?" Abbey said with a sigh as Figaro straddled the stuffed cat and began to hump it while making loud purring sounds. "Do you have to do that here? In the kitchen?" Abbey picked up SuzyQ by pinching her ears, not wanting to touch any other areas. She carried it out in front of her like a stinky diaper and took it to the dining room. Figaro let out a ferocious, almost primal meow, and then followed her.

"There you go," Abbey said as she put SuzyQ on the floor. "Go have at her. After all, someone other than Caroline should be getting laid tonight." It was almost comical, and just as tragic, that a seventy-year-old woman and a cat had more sex than she did.

Without needing any encouragement, Figaro jumped back onto the object of his affection and went to town like an oversexed teenaged boy.

Abbey went back into the kitchen to check on the soup. Noticing the rapid bubbles forming around the edges, she turned the burner down and stirred the mixture. Reaching for two bowls to put the soup in, the pink box with Sweet Caroline's logo on it caught her attention.

Opening the box, she smiled as she swiped her finger along the icing edge. What did it mean? "Happy Valentine's Day." His words echoed inside her mind as the scene played and replayed. Her reverie was interrupted by her phone chime. *Shoot!* Maybe Charlie had texted back after all. Or maybe, just maybe, Judge Hammonds got her number from Caroline? *What? No!* Caroline wouldn't give out her number without permission. Her overactive imagination continued. He's a judge, surely he has ways of getting contact information if he wanted to. She quickly swatted that thinking down as probably illegal.

Her heart thumped in her chest as she removed the phone with lightning speed only to be slightly disappointed to see the text was from Camille, her best friend.

Can't wait to see you Sat!! xoxoxox The text was followed by a smiley face emoji, kissy-face emoji, and two pink heart emojis.

Camille and Abbey met ten years ago when they were both junior architects at Allen Anderson & Associates in Philadelphia. Two years ago, Camille started dating Allen Anderson, Jr., the firm owner's son. Camille and "Skip," as he preferred to be called, were now engaged and getting married in a few weeks. Camille asked Abbey to be her maid of honor. Saturday was the combined bachelor and bachelorette party.

Ugh! The party was an event that was taking nearly as much planning as the wedding. Camille and Skip had rented out the entire first floor of a two-story brownstone that housed Philadelphia's newest and trendiest bars. The bride and groom-to-be invited *seventy* of their closest friends to have fun before the wedding.

Abbey secretly did not want to go. A true introvert who suffered from an occasional bout of social anxiety, the thought of making small talk for several hours with mostly strangers was painful.

She stared at the cupcake like it was a fierce enemy taunting her with its sugary scent and sweet lusciousness.

It was nearly six weeks before Camille's big day. Abbey did quick math in her head. Six weeks was plenty of time to lose twenty-five pounds—if she starved herself. Twenty-five pounds, while not even close to her goal weight was marginally better than her current weight. When Camille first called a year earlier to tell her she was engaged, there was less desperation in the weeks-to-wedding to weight-to-lose ratio. Abbey was confident she had enough time and motivation to finally get to the elusive goal weight she'd carried in her head for years. She envisioned a new slimmer and sexy body that would look amazing in any bridesmaid's dress. With the weight loss would come new confidence. She would spend the night of the reception on the dance floor, showing off her new body with moves like Beyoncé. One by one, the single men attending the wedding would line up and ask her to dance. They'd politely tap the shoulder of one another to cut in. It was a dream she'd had since middle school when she'd watch that scene play out with the thin girls, but not her.

She stared at the cupcake again. Approximately three hundred fifty calories or ten Weight Watcher points—she knew every diet calibration by heart. Would eating it be so bad? Would it set her that far back?

For as long as she could remember, food had controlled her.

She had this love-hate relationship with it.

Be strong. She took a deep breath and reached for the cupcake. She walked the short distance to the sink. One flick of the switch, and the disposal would do away with it.

Her finger grazed against the rich cream cheese frosting that she loved so much. She put her finger to her mouth. A lick won't hurt. She felt confident after licking the icing off her finger she'd have the strength to dispose of the cupcake.

But she was wrong. Once the sweet confection touched her lips, she instantly wanted more. Sugar was her kryptonite.

3

Train #103 pulled into Philadelphia's 30th Street Station just past 3 p.m. The ninety-minute ride was uneventful, with the exception of a wailing child two rows behind Abbey's seat. Since a nap was out of the question, she spent most of the ride trying to rid her jeans of the flour dusted on them.

Once outside of the station, Abbey hailed a cab to take her to Camille and Skip's apartment in Center City. When the cab dropped her off in front of the building, a doorman dressed in a long red coat and white gloves tipped his hat as he opened the door. "Hello, ma'am," he greeted. "Is someone expecting you?"

"Yes," she answered. "Camille Ritter. Apartment 2207."

The doorman walked to his desk, picked up the phone, and punched in a few buttons. "Hello, Ms. Ritter." He covered the phone receiver with his hand. "What did you say your name was?"

"Abbey, Abbey Reilly."

"A Miss Reilly is in the lobby. Should I send her up? Thank you, ma'am." He hung the phone up. "This way, Miss Reilly." He pointed toward the elevator.

Twenty-two floors later, she got off the elevator. The minimalist Northern European style that plagued the lobby didn't look any better on this level. She turned the corner and knocked on the door marked 2207.

"Hi-yee!" Camille greeted Abbey as she opened the door. Camille's voice was as bouncy as her highlighted blond hair. "So good to see you." She hugged Abbey for a long time, her chin and nose nestled in Abbey's frizzy yeast doughnut-scented hair. "Come on in."

When they met, Camille was fresh out of Dartmouth, and the kind of girl Abbey avoided in high school and college—a perky cheerleader-type that screamed of old money and things always going her way. But soon after meeting Camille, Abbey realized *she* was the judgmental one. Camille was warm and friendly and would frequently stop by Abbey's desk and engage in conversation. They had only known each other about a month when Camille invited Abbey out for happy hour with her Dartmouth friends. Abbey quickly declined. The next month, Camille asked again and added that she was going to ask until Abbey relented. Her cheerful pout was impressively endearing. Abbey went with Camille and her friends that night and actually had fun.

After that night, they became great friends, and at one point, even roommates. When they lived together, they would spend hours talking about each other's dreams for the future, so it came as no surprise when Camille asked Abbey to be her maid of honor.

"Skip! Skip! Look who's here!" Camille called to her future husband.

"Hey, there, Ab. How ya doing?" Skip kissed Abbey on the cheek. He was a tad shorter than Camille. He always wore docksiders and Bermuda shorts even in the wintertime and had perpetually tanned skin. His mousy brown hair was shorn close on the sides, and he used product to make the hair on top of his head spiky.

"Doin' okay. Are you sure you don't mind if I stay here tonight?" Abbey asked.

"What? No. Anytime." Skip took Abbey's quilted Vera Bradley tote bag from her hand. "Here, let me put this is in our guest room." He walked down the hall toward a spare bedroom.

Camille and Skip's apartment was small but expertly decorated.

With an overstuffed leather sectional sofa taking up most of the living room and throw pillows propped just so, it looked like a spread in *House and Garden Magazine*.

"Come. Sit." Camille walked toward the couch. The couch sat a mere few inches away from a floor to ceiling window that featured a bird's eye view of the city. Beautifully embroidered rust-colored drapes framed the window with elegantly pleated swags on the top and a gold tasseled trim tie-back. Camille always did have good taste and didn't mind spending money on things like home décor. Camille sat down, and Abbey sat next to her.

"How's your mom?" Camille asked.

"Um. Okay." Abbey shrugged. "You know. The same, I guess. Thanks for asking."

"Of course." Camille's voice was full of compassion. "How do you do it? Work and take care of her?"

"Dunno. I just do it, I guess," Abbey said, hoping Camille would get the subtle hint to change the subject.

"It must be hard to see her that way. Your mom was always so much fun."

Abbey shifted in her seat. The conversation made her slightly uncomfortable for reasons she could not articulate. But she allowed Camille to go on without interruption.

"Remember when she came to visit when we lived on Washington Avenue?"

"Yes. I do" Abbey thought back to the time about three years ago when her mother came to Philadelphia to attend an herbalist society conference.

"She slept on this couch. And I remember thinking 'Abbey's mom is so cool. My mom would *never* sleep on the couch.'"

The contrast between Camille's mother and Abbey's mother was stark. Abbey had met Camille's mother, Katherine, "call me

Kate" a few times. She spoke with a thick Boston accent and wore expertly tailored navy-colored woolen suits with big gold buttons and white rickrack trim that smelled of Chanel perfume and cigarettes.

"Your mom read my tea leaves and said I was going to meet someone very special within six months," Camille said with a raised eyebrow. "I'd say she hit the nail on the head." She smiled as she looked toward Skip, who had just reentered the living room. She turned back toward Abbey. "Okay, changing the subject. Have you heard from Charlie?"

And just like that, the conversation shifted in a direction that made Abbey even more uncomfortable. "No," Abbey said in a voice barely audible. Inwardly, she cursed herself for sharing too much with Camille. "This is your weekend. Yours and Skip, I should say. Let's not talk about me and my failed relationships." Luckily, she had not mentioned the cupcake from Judge Hammonds. Camille would have been all over that. "How sweet," Abbey could hear her saying before launching into a well-meaning litany of questions to determine whether he's worthy. The thing with the judge, whatever it was, needed to stew a bit in Abbey's own mind before she would share.

Camille frowned. "You know, it's his loss, don't you?"

"Yeah. Sure."

Camille gave her a knowing look. "Abbey," she said with eyebrows raised. "You know I'm right."

Abbey did not protest, even though she didn't agree.

"Well, don't you worry," Camille said. "Skip has a lot of fraternity brothers that will be at the wedding, don't you, honey?"

Skip nodded. "Sure."

"Some of them may be here tonight."

Skip's look changed to one of horror, which Abbey read as

Whaaat? None of my fraternity brothers would date a fat chick.

"What about Bernie King? He's not dating anyone, is he?"

"Actually, I think he is."

"He is?" Camille looked confused. "Oh, I'll have to update the guest list so that he can bring her."

"Yeah, I'll tell him he can."

She turned back toward Abbey. "Don't worry. There will be single guys there tonight. You scope it out and let us know which one you're interested in. Pinky swear?" Camille locked her perfectly French manicured pinky around Abbey's.

"Pinky swear," Abbey said out loud, while on the inside she thought *hell no.*

The doorbell rang. "Oops, I almost forgot," Camille said. She got up and walked toward the door. "I hired a hair and makeup artist to do a test run for the wedding. I thought it'd be great for you and me to get all dolled up tonight. I'll bet that's her."

There was no time for Abbey to hide from Camille's ambush.

"Hi-yee!" Camille said as she answered the door. "You must be Meegan. Did I say that right? Meee-gan."

"Yes," said a young woman with bright orange hair and a small hoop in her nose.

"C'mon in."

Meegan strolled in wheeling more luggage than Abbey brought for her overnight stay. "Where should I set up?" she asked.

"We can do it in the bathroom." Camille led the orange-haired woman down the hall.

After a brief moment of silence that seemed like an eternity, Skip cleared his throat and said, "So, Abbey, Camille says you're working at a bakery now?"

"Yeah."

"Do you ever miss it? Miss being an architect?" He sounded

sincere.

Abbey twisted a lock of hair and remembered how she'd had a crush on Skip when he first joined his father's firm. She told no one, not even Camille. She had butterflies in her stomach the time Camille said he would be joining them for happy hour. She allowed herself to fantasize that he'd walk into the happy hour, pull her aside, and profess his undying love for her that night. And that basically did happen, but to Camille, not Abbey. After the happy hour, when Abbey got home, a pint of ice cream soothed her feelings and helped her accept that guys like that never fall for girls like her.

"Yeah. I do miss it, actually," she said.

"You were really good at it. Being an architect."

"Thanks."

"My dad used to say you were one of the best."

For an instant, Abbey wondered what her life would be like if she didn't return home to care for her mother. If she were still working with Camille and Skip at Allen Anderson & Associates, would she be happier? Maybe. When she worked there, she liked what she did, but her social life was no different from what it was in Maryland—lonely and alone. But at least in Philadelphia, her career made her proud. And the desire to be on the fast track to partner could always serve as an excuse as to why she wasn't in a relationship.

Camille entered the living room without the makeup artist. "Okay, she's ready for you," she chirped.

Abbey stood and walked to the bathroom.

Inside the cramped room, Meegan had spread out her goods. A bevy of brushes, in order by width, lay on the counter next to the sink. And a black bag similar to a doctor's kit appeared to have every hue of eye shadow to match a large Crayola crayon box.

Meegan looked Abbey up and down. "Red hair, green eyes, fair complexion ... perfect canvas!"

Abbey was taken aback by the comment and wasn't too sure if Meegan was being sarcastic or truly complimenting her features.

"Have a seat." Meegan motioned for Abbey to sit on the commode. Abbey complied.

Once Abbey was seated, Meegan took Abbey's chin in her hand and tilted it slightly. "Do you moisturize?" she asked, inspecting Abbey's skin carefully by running her hand over a few dry patches on Abbey's cheek. "You should always moisturize. The sun really does a number on us fair skinned girls." She rubbed some white cream over Abbey's forehead, nose, cheeks, and chin. "The skin likes to drink as much as we do." Her hands massaged the cream into Abbey's skin, making it tingle.

For the next three-quarters of an hour, Abbey became Meegan's canvas as the makeup artist mixed colors on her palette and painted Abbey's face. Occasionally, Meegan would step back, squint, and nod her head.

Abbey was seated in a way that she couldn't see her reflection in the mirror, she could only imagine all the gobs of makeup were making her look like a drag queen.

"So, for your hair," Meegan said. "I'm thinking of a little updo." She pulled Abbey's long hair and piled it on top of her head. "No, I changed my mind. Beautiful curls shouldn't be wasted, they should be highlighted." Meegan sprayed a mist onto Abbey's hair and used her hands to scrunch curls all over. "Do you know how many people would kill for this hair?" She then pulled a little hair back on both sides and secured the strands in the back of Abbey's hair with two bobby pins. She stood back and looked again. "There," she said with a satisfied look on her face.

Abbey stood and turned toward the mirror. She stared at the

face she didn't recognize. Hair pulled out of her face and makeup contouring all the right places, mauve eye shadow made her eyes look deep set and catlike. From the neck up, she liked what she saw. A lot.

"Is that okay?" Meegan asked.

Abbey smiled. "Yes. Thanks." She hugged Meegan before walking out of the bathroom. When she reached the living room, she said, "Okay, it's your turn."

"Wow! Ab, you look beautiful!" Camille said.

Skip, who was sitting on the couch, turned to catch a look. With his eyebrows raised and mouth agape, he did not mask his look of shock. "Yeah, you sure do," he said.

• • •

After Meegan finished Camille's makeup, Camille, Abbey, and Skip Ubered to One-Eleven arriving just before seven, thirty minutes after the party started. "Hi-yee! So nice to see all of you!" Camille greeted her guests like a queen would her court, inclusive of the royal hand wave.

An immediate glass of pinot calmed her social anxiety enough to walk over to the only two people she recognized in the room— former coworkers, Sondra White and Betsy McNeil.

"Hi," Abbey said.

"Oh, hi, Abbey," Sondra said. She hugged Abbey. "How have you been? We've missed you."

"Okay. I'm good. I miss you, too."

"Camille said you were coming," Betsy said. "So, what's new with you?"

Abbey filled them in on the reason she left Philadelphia. She didn't go into great detail about anything else. The two women ticked off how wonderful things were for them—Betsy had a five-year-old wunderkind who was 'simply brilliant.' And Sondra's husband had just been named partner at Philadelphia's largest law firm. The conversation eventually came to an awkward grinding halt with each party having nothing more to add.

"So, Abbey," Sondra said, tapping Abbey on the wrist. "Let's catch up later tonight."

Strange, that's what we just did. "Of course," Abbey said. "Let's do." She tilted her glass of pinot and saw it was empty. "I think I'm going to head over and get another glass of wine."

She turned and walked to the bar. After getting her wine, she took a sip and scanned the bar. Camille was nowhere in sight. Not normally a drinker, Abbey's head felt light, and her cheeks were on fire. Darn tannin allergy always made her look like a red-faced clown. She maneuvered through the throng of guests to the side of the bar with an outside patio area.

Once outside, she found a far corner of the patio to gaze up at the twinkling lights of the Philadelphia skyline. It was a beautiful and clear night. She stared admiringly at the JPL building—one of the city's tallest. When she lived here, she'd been fascinated with that building because it was so modern. Long clean lines and forty-four floors of tinted mirrored windows and a spire on top jutted toward the sky like a pointy sword. But the coolest aspect of the building was how the bottom part was so different. The first four stories were brick.

"What are you looking at?"

"What?" Abbey was so lost in thought she hadn't noticed that a man was standing next to her. She turned toward him. She was sure she let out an audible gasp. The light on the patio was bright enough for her to see a most handsome man. He was about her age, mid-thirties, she guessed, and tall and lanky with thick dark brown hair that curled just below his ears and deep dark brown eyes that matched his hair. He used his hand to brush his hair off his forehead. Abbey did a double take; he was a dead ringer for a young Paul McCartney.

"Which one are you looking at?" He pointed toward the buildings as he leaned closer to her to get her exact sightline. His scent, a mixture of some sweet and musky cologne and sandalwood soap, was intoxicating.

Abbey's heart beat a little faster than it had a moment ago. "You see that building ... the one with JPL on the top?" She pointed and hoped he couldn't see that her finger shook slightly.

"Yeah," he said.

"I like the mixture of styles—you have modern and brick in one building. I think it's genius," she said.

"You're correct. They are two buildings in one. They say, the older building, the one to the left..." He leaned in even closer and pointed. "You may not be able to see it from here, but the brick part—"

"Yes."

"It's haunted."

"What?" Her eyes widened. "No!"

"Yes, they tried to tear it down years ago, but weird things started happening—"

"Like what?"

"Like screams would come from nowhere. And the day before it was set to be demolished," he said as he tapped her lightly on the forearm, "the crane that was positioned right next to the building went missing."

"Wow! Oh my gosh." Abbey covered her mouth as she took it all in.

"Do you know how much those things weigh? Not to mention how hard that would be to move a crane," he said.

"Are you serious? I can't believe I never knew this." She was fascinated not only by this gorgeous man standing next to her, but by the story about the old building.

A smile crept across his face and his eyes twinkled when he said, "No, I'm just kidding. It's not haunted—at least I don't think it is. It was an inn where the founding fathers would get liquid courage before determining what's best for our country. So, it's a historic landmark."

"Oh," Abbey chuckled. "I think I like the ghost story better."

"Atta girl." He winked. "Me too." He held out his hand. "I'm Jackson Lawrence. My friends call me Jax."

"Nice to meet you. I'm Abbey Reilly. My friends call me, well, um, Abbey. They just call me Abbey." Oh God, the two glasses of wine were talking. That was not a good thing.

"Okay then, that's what I'll call you. Nice to meet you, Abbey." She put her hand in his. His handshake was firm.

"I saw you come in with Skip and Camille. I assume you know them?" He looked at her sideways and rubbed his chin. "Or maybe a crasher?"

Abbey let out a loud laugh that was almost a snort. She covered her mouth in an attempt to muffle the over-the-top and unfortunate reaction. "Camille's my best friend. We work—worked—together at Allen Anderson. I'm the maid of honor," she said with pride.

"Oh. The honorable Abbey Reilly." He mocked a curtsy.

Who was this charming man? "So, are you here for the bachelor-bachelorette party, too?"

"Yep, Skip and I went to college together."

"Harvard?" she asked.

"Yeah. Don't hold that against me."

"I'll try not to." She pointed to herself. "UPenn."

"I see. So, the honorable Abbey Reilly of UPenn, since you worked with Camille at Allen Anderson, and you were staring so intently at that funky building, I'll bet you're an architect."

"Wow. You're good, Harvard." Feeling quite cheeky, and rather enjoying the exchange, Abbey followed her playful comment with a wink. And she made sure not to correct him. He didn't need to know that she had traded in blueprints for recipe cards.

"So, would you like a tour of the building? I work there, so I'm pretty familiar with it. It's actually pretty cool how they joined the two buildings together. And it has one of my favorite spots in the city." He pointed his finger at the top of the building. "I don't think you can see it from here, but on the top there's a nice garden with a koi pond. A little oasis in the middle of the city. I often have lunch up there."

Abbey was in slight disbelief. "Tonight?" she said. She looked over her shoulder toward the entrance of the bar and was about to agree when she heard him chuckle.

"No, not tonight." His laugh was sweet and not the least bit condescending. "Why, I'd think the honorable Abbey, fair maiden of honor's presence would be truly missed from this fete. I was thinking maybe tomorrow."

Tomorrow? Shoot! She had to get back home by noon to relieve Betty. She took a sip of wine. Looking up, she caught his beautiful brown eyes that resembled two melted Hershey Kisses. She put her hand on the bottom of her chin to ensure her mouth was closed. Was this perfect specimen of a man actually flirting with her? Then a sinking feeling crept inside of her. The judge with the cupcake, Meegan transforming her into a person she didn't recognize, and now this encounter with this smoking hot charmer of a man—only one explanation made sense—she must be in a coma. Yes, that had to be it. When her father drifted into a coma during his last days, he had the most beautiful smile on his face, like he had suddenly found intense happiness.

She felt a soft but firm hand on her shoulder. "Are you okay?" he asked.

His touch sent shivers through her body. Would a coma feel this real? No, she reasoned, this was really happening. The pinot was screaming *Do it! DO IT! You may never get another chance.* "I'm fine," she said, clearing her throat, grateful this was really happening. "I'd really like to see *yit.*" Her brain mashed the words you and it. "It. I'd really like to see it. Can we do it in the morning? I have to be somewhere later." She held a breath as she waited for his response.

A crooked smile slowly appeared on his face. "I'm a morning guy myself. How about nine?"

She nodded as she mentally calculated the timing. The JPL building was within walking distance of the Amtrak station. It'd be close, but she could pull it off. "Okay," she said. "See you at nine."

4

Abbey looked at her watch for probably the hundredth time. Ten after nine. Standing outside of the JPL building, she was nervous, but she wasn't sure why. It wasn't a date. She wouldn't let her mind go there. It was just a nice guy showing someone he thought was an architect bricks, mortar, glass, and maybe some ghosts, she repeated to herself.

Did he say to meet in the lobby? She couldn't remember. She tugged on the front door handle. Locked. It was now eleven after nine. How long should she wait? Had she been ghosted? She laughed as she said the word out loud. After all the talk about ghosts, wouldn't it be ironic if he ghosted her?

But why? He'd seen her in all of her voluptuousness—her ample form out on display and he didn't run. At the end of the bachelor-bachelorette party, he'd even sought her out to say he looked forward to seeing her the next day. He seemed genuine, but then again, Abbey detected alcohol on his breath. He probably woke up with a hangover and a vague memory of talking to Camille's big friend at the party, thought to himself *WTF was I thinking,* and then decided to blow her off.

After all, this wasn't a date. This wasn't a date. She repeated over and over.

She rechecked her watch again. Nine thirteen. If she left now, her self-respect could be in tow. Only Camille knew. And when Abbey told her, she was careful to downplay any hint of excitement by leaving out names, places, and any identifying characteristics that could be traced back to the handsome stranger. She didn't want Camille to become overly involved. Camille was great at being a cheerful, supportive best friend. It was just too embarrassing to admit when things didn't go well.

At exactly nine fourteen, she declared defeat. She turned away from the building entrance and started the short walk to the train station. A few steps in, she looked up and saw a familiar face: a man smiling as he quickly approached the building. Excited, her arm shot up, and she gave him an enthusiastic wave—which she immediately regretted. That is, until he waved back.

"Hi," he said, when he was near. He seemed out of breath. "I am so sorry. I got stuck on the El. And this was useless." He gestured with his iPhone. "Not because I didn't have cell reception—because last night, I forgot to get your number. So, I ran the two blocks." He pulled a handkerchief from his back pocket and wiped his brow.

Abbey was somewhat relieved. His explanation was plausible. They turned and walked to the building entrance.

"Here, let me get that." He reached in front of her and used an electronic key fob to unlock the door. "After you," he said, motioning her to enter.

"That's okay, I just got here myself," she said. He held the door open for her. She looked up to see his expression. Their eyes met. His smile was warm and inviting. Embarrassed, she looked away. She hoped the makeup she caked on under her eyes covered the dark circles. He didn't need to know that she barely slept the night before, or that she carefully plotted her morning—thoroughly estimating subway train arrival times within a five-minute margin of error. She had her plan all thought out before deciding SEPTA was too risky and opted for an Uber to the Amtrak Station, rented a locker for her suitcase, and then took an Uber to the building. Neurotic overthinking, as usual. No biggie.

Her two-inch sandals clopped like horse hooves as they walked into the marbled-floor lobby. But they were the only shoes she brought. She briefly thought about running to Torrid—the one on Market Street that she knew so well—and buying a whole new outfit, but the store didn't open until noon. So, she was stuck with the oversize navy-blue silk-blend tunic, with long cuffed sleeves and an open neckline, and white leggings that she had packed so she'd be comfortable on the train ride home. There was no way she could fit into anything Camille wore, so she didn't even bother asking. Although Camille graciously draped a pink cashmere pashmina around Abbey before she left. It was Camille's subtle way to improve Abbey's style without appearing to be judgmental. And since today was marginally cooler, the pashmina was welcomed.

A security guard clumsily took his feet off the desk. "Oh, Mr. Lawrence." He stood. "Hello, sir. Sorry about that. You know, Sundays are pretty uneventful around here."

"No, it's okay." Jax waved a dismissive hand at the guard. Abbey felt the guard's stare linger as Jax put a gentle hand on her back, guiding her toward the elevator. "This way," he said.

When they got to the elevator, Jax pressed the up button. "This is original brick," he said as he pointed with his free hand to the exposed walls that surrounded the four elevators. "See?" His finger stroked the groove in print of a brick that read: 1770.

"Wow," Abbey ran her fingers along the numbers. "That's really cool." When her fingers touched his slightly, she got nervous and pulled her hand away.

"Yeah, this side is the original building, and where Rodney the guard was, is part of the new building."

"When was the newer part added?" Abbey asked.

"Well, the old part sat empty and dilapidated for years—probably decades. A real eyesore for the city. About thirty years ago, there was an effort to gentrify this area, so it made sense for JPL to buy this building and develop it."

The elevator door opened, and the two went in. Jax reached in front of Abbey to select fifty-two, the top floor. With his arm stretched, Abbey saw the initials JPL embroidered on his shirt sleeve peek out of his overcoat. JPL, the same letters on the building. JPL, only the most prominent commercial real estate company in Pennsylvania. When she was an architect, she often did projects for clients moving into JPL-owned and managed buildings. But she remembered from her research that the company was run by a man much older than Jax ... whose last name was, of course, Lawrence. Could it be? Could Jax be of *the* Lawrences? No. Her imagination was getting away from her. Lawrence was a common name.

The penthouse of the building was enclosed with two glass doors with gold accents and the words "Executive Suite" stenciled in block script. Jax swiped his fob, and as if on command, the door swung open. "This way," he said, leading her down a hallway with floor to ceiling glass-enclosed offices on one side and cubicles on the other. They reached the end of the hallway and an office with the name Jackson Lawrence, CEO, stenciled in the same gold block script that appeared on the front door of the building.

Abbey became flushed. The guard's reaction, JPL on the sleeve. She looked at him. "Is this *your* building?"

"Um, technically, it belongs to the bank, but yes, this is my company's headquarters. We're in commercial real estate. But since you're an architect, you probably have heard of JPL."

She nodded. She knew JPL had owned many buildings in Philadelphia and had offices in Beijing, Singapore, London, and Dubai. "Forgive me, I should have known."

"Known what?" Jax seemed confused.

"I didn't know you were—" She couldn't quite get the words out. "It's just I thought—" She realized she was stammering. "I thought the CEO was older."

He laughed. "My grandfather built the company in the 1960's before handing it over to my dad in the 1990's. He retired last year—my dad, that is. Well, sort of. He still likes to tell me what to do." He chuckled. "When he was in charge, I tried to stay behind the scenes. You know, I didn't want to be seen as the boss's son—the guy that got everything handed to him."

Abbey thought about how Jax must have been raised—a privileged life, no doubt, with nannies and summer homes. Far different from the nomadic hippie life her parents provided her and her sister.

He pushed the door open to his office and flicked a light switch next to the door. Her jaw dropped. Towering over much of Philadelphia, the view was magnificent. It was as if they were high in the clouds. She walked toward the window to get a closer look. Jax strolled behind. He lightly touched her shoulder and pointed with his free hand. "See that glass building? The one with the pointy top?"

Abbey was afraid to move. She was enjoying feeling his closeness. She looked in the direction that he was pointing. "Yes. I see it," she said.

He leaned in even closer. "That building was only thirty stories, but then we built this one, and they added that thingy on the top so they could say they were taller." He said with a hearty chuckle.

The building had a thin column of glass panels that stretched a few stories high. It resembled the eye of a needle and seemed to be for aesthetics, not office space. "A nonfunctioning point—I gotta hand it to the architect that came up with that design," Abbey laughed. "Pretty clever." And then the most unfortunate thing happened—she let out a god-awful snort—something she was often prone to do when laughing. She covered her mouth with her hand, hoping he didn't hear the sound that was now echoing inside of her head like a gong. She looked up at him, expecting to see a look of disgust. Instead, she saw the gorgeous chiseled clean-shaven chin and a smile that was punctuated with the cutest dimples.

"I know, right?" Jax said in a reassuring way. He turned away from the window. "I have something here that might interest you," he said as he walked toward a tall cherrywood stained cabinet behind his stately matching wooden desk. He opened the cabinet and took out a long thin tube and walked to the glass table near the room's entrance. Abbey followed every step of the way like a puppy, staying close, but not too close.

Jax removed the cap of the tube and brought out thin rolled papers, which he spread out on the table. He pressed his hands on both ends to prevent the papers from curling back up. "These are the plans for when the building was renovated."

"Wow." Abbey said when she saw the neat block letters of an architect's pen: 1800 Broad Street and Avenue. Est. 1995. "This is so cool." She knew from her studies that the computer-aided design software, or CAD, was not commonly used back then, and many architects drew designs freehand.

"So, you see," Jax said. He lifted his hand, and the paper curled. "Would you mind holding this end?"

Abbey got closer to Jax. Close enough to smell that intoxicating scent. She dutifully placed her hand on the flimsy paper.

"See here? This is the line where the new building met the old one." His finger traced a hard line in the middle of the plans.

"Oh, yes, I see." His body leaned against hers ever so slightly. She could feel her heart beating up through her neck, and her palms began to sweat. For a moment, she allowed herself to fantasize about what it would feel like to be in his muscular arms. Then she instinctively retracted her abdomen, hoping it made the rest of her body firm and not so fleshy to the touch.

"It was my grandfather's idea—to join the two buildings together. We owned the old building, and the city declared it a historic landmark, thus, it couldn't be torn down. But we needed more space because the business was expanding. I was a kid then, but I remember the conversations he had with my dad."

"Wow." She was in awe.

Jax looked at her and said, "So, tell me about some projects you're working on now."

"Me?" Abbey was flattered that he'd asked but embarrassed by the answer. "Um, nothing interesting, really." She didn't want to say the most interesting part of her day or week was baking a batch of chocolate cupcakes filled with peanut butter centers and cream cheese icing.

His brow knitted as his eyebrows raised and nearly touched. His eyes were so brown, warm, and caring. She knew she was staring a little too long, but so was he. She didn't want to turn away, and maybe, just maybe, he didn't either. A curl sprung loose from her tightly wrapped ponytail and bobbed in front of her face.

She was about to tuck it back into place when he said, "You have such pretty hair. You know, red is a recessive gene. That means that both parents have to have it in their bloodline."

His gaze was penetrating, something she wasn't used to. She straightened her body from the leaning position. Leaning one hand on the building plans, she stood. "I'm not sure where I got it. No one else in my family has red hair."

"Like a rare gem—truly special," he said, his voice becoming very sensual, or maybe it was her overactive imagination.

Abbey always felt like an outcast; she had red hair and fair skin with freckles, while the rest of her family had an olive complexion and dark hair—or in Penny's case, very bleached blond hair. She lifted her hand and tucked the curl in. "Thank you," she said, her freckled cheeks on fire.

Jax rolled the building plans back up into a tight scroll. She held the tube as he glided the plans in. "Would you like to grab some coffee? There's a great little place right down the block."

"Yes." She cleared her throat, trying to mask her enthusiasm. But then her enthusiasm deflated like a helium balloon. "Wait. What time is it?"

He tilted his Movado watch to read the dial. "It's about quarter to ten."

"What?" Her facial expression probably said it all. "I gotta go." She had promised Betty she'd be home by noon so that Betty could attend her church picnic. Betty had been so wonderful, and Abbey couldn't let her down. "I'm sorry, it's just—I really have to go."

Something held her back from telling him the truth even as she saw a feeling of rejection wash over his face. "Can we do it some other time?" she said, not exactly sure when that would be. "I'm sorry, I have to be somewhere by ten o'clock."

"Of course. Rain check then," he said.

"Rain check."

Then he said, "I'm going to stay and catch up on some work then. But let me walk you out."

"Oh, no need." Panic had set in. She was very worried she was going to miss the train. "Please, stay here."

"Okay. I will." He walked her to the elevator bank and hit the down button. If he wasn't standing there with her, she would have hit it over and over about one hundred times. As the minutes ticked, she really needed to get out of there.

When the elevator came, she got on. "Okay then, rain check on coffee," she said.

"Rain check," he said and added a wink as the elevator door shut.

When she was out of the building, she ran as fast as she could the two blocks to the train station. She had just enough time to pick up her luggage before she heard the loudspeaker blast, "Last call for train number one hundred ten."

Once on the train, she found a seat in the third car. Sinking into the stiff leather, she struggled to catch her breath and cursed herself for being so out of shape. Could he be the one dreamy guy who can see past her curves? Just when she allowed herself to believe it could happen, a sick feeling overwhelmed her. She realized, once again, they didn't exchange phone numbers.

5

As the new week began back home at the bakery, Abbey was still disappointed by the way things ended the day before. She hadn't heard from Jax, nor did she expect to. Could she get his number from Camille or Skip? Probably, but in all honesty, he could get hers in the same way ... if he really wanted to.

The sleigh bells above the front door jingled, and a waft of cold air blew in. "It's cold out there," Judge Hammonds shivered as he entered the bakery. "How did we go from the seventies on Saturday to the fifties yesterday to thirties today? What's tomorrow going to be—in the teens?"

"Hope not," Abbey said.

He dusted some snowflakes off his shoulders. "It's just enough snow today to be annoying. You know what I mean?"

She did indeed. Snow during rush hour would lay a thin coat on the sidewalks and roads enough to make the commute a little slippery.

"Probably will delay the trial before me by half an hour. You know how people react to a dusting of snow around here. Not the best drivers, if you ask me." He raised an eyebrow.

True, but with the snow as infrequent as it had been in recent years, Marylanders were definitely the best at being prepared. Whenever there was the slightest hint of snow, schools would close and toilet paper, bread, and milk could not be found at any grocery store.

The judge's presence distracted her from the day before, but not necessarily in a good way. Her heart pounded. Should she say something about the cupcake? Should she say something flirty like, "Don't you look handsome today?" Ew, that even sounded terrible in her head. She went with what was most comfortable for her. "So, Judge," she said. "What will it be today?"

"Henry. Please call me Henry," he said.

Henry, did he say call him Henry? Her heart was beating so loudly she wasn't sure exactly if that's what he said.

"Hmm. Let me see." He bent down and inspected the bakery case. "Are those seven-layer bars?" he asked, pointing to a pedestal of square confections loaded with coconut and chocolate chips covering a graham cracker crumb and melted butter base that Abbey had made Saturday, just before leaving for Philadelphia.

"Yes. Seven-layer." She nodded.

"I love them. They remind me of my mother."

"Well, these are my grandmother Nona's recipe," she said.

"Sold! No bag. I'll eat it here. And can I have a cup of coffee? Black."

Abbey sized up the pedestal tray of seven-layer bars and selected the largest square. She put it on a white china plate and poured some fresh brewed coffee into a mug. If she hadn't just brewed a fresh pot for herself, she would have made one for him— there's nothing worse than bitter coffee that has sat on a burner for too long.

Henry walked to one of the small, round café tables and sat down.

With the plate holding the seven-layer bar in one hand and the mug of coffee in her other hand, Abbey walked slowly—careful not to spill or drop anything along the way—to the table where he was now seated.

He stood and removed his overcoat—a beautiful camel-colored

one that fit him perfectly—folded it lengthwise with the swift motion of his hand making a perfect pleat and then in half before placing it on the white wrought iron chair next to him.

Abbey put the mug of coffee and bar on the table in front of where Henry was.

Before sitting back down, Henry reached into his pants pocket and took out a wad of bills held together by a silver money clip with the initials HHH engraved in large letters. He peeled off a twenty and handed it to her. "Keep the change," he said.

"What? No. That's too much."

"I insist." He waved a hand before putting the bound wad of money back in his pocket and sitting down.

"Okay, thank you. But it really is too generous." The twenty would be more than a 100 percent tip, which didn't happen that often—well, actually, it never happened before. And, of course, she could use the money, so she didn't protest too hard. Abbey took the twenty and put it in her apron, planning to ring up his order when she got back to the counter.

"Can you take a break and join me?" Henry asked. He motioned to the other chair—the empty one next to him. He had blue-gray eyes that always looked serious.

She looked at the clock on the wall. Nine sixteen. Then she looked around the empty bakery. Before the afternoon rush, which usually started around eleven thirty, she needed to bake a tray of brownies and three dozen chocolate chip cookies. She already felt pressed for time. But she smiled and said, "I can take a few minutes."

"Great," he said in an even but authoritative tone. He motioned for her to sit.

The wrought iron chair had uneven legs and made a loud noise when she dragged it on the tiled floor to give her enough room to sit. Once seated, she knitted her fingers together firmly and placed her hands in her lap so that Henry wouldn't see her hands shake as she tried to get over her inner thoughts screaming about how ridiculous this was. Just the day before, she was dreaming about a life with Jax, only to have that encounter fizzle to a dead end. She had to be careful not to expect anything from this either.

Henry blew on his coffee as he brought the mug closer to his lips. He took a sip. "Ah, that's good." He put the coffee mug on the table. "So, Abbey, did you have a nice weekend?"

"Me? Um, yes, I did." She wasn't sure why the familiar and casual words coming from him caught her so off guard. She used her hands to smooth her apron in an attempt to hide the bounce of her foot tapping on the table pedestal. "How about you? Did you have a nice weekend?"

"I did. I finished reading Michael Lewis's book—about two Nobel Prize-winning scientists. *The Undoing Project.* Have you heard of it?"

"I'm embarrassed to say, no, I haven't."

"Don't be embarrassed. The truth is never a wrong answer." He had a charming way of making her feel at ease. "What do you like to read?"

"Me?"

He nodded.

Abbey thought hard about how to answer his question. In her case, the truth could be a wrong answer—admitting she had a stack of romance novels piled high on her nightstand would probably be a turnoff to a real learned man like Judge Henry H. Hammonds. "I don't have much time for reading these days."

Henry seemed content with her answer. He took a bite of his seven-layer bar and thankfully changed the subject. "Oh, this is good." He used a napkin to wipe a few graham cracker crumbs from the corner of his mouth. "How did you become a baker?" he asked.

"Well, it's a long story. I'm not sure you want to hear all the gory details."

Judge Hammonds looked at his watch and said, "If it doesn't go past ten, I'd love to hear all the gory details." His smile displayed a row of perfect white teeth.

Abbey clicked her tongue against the roof of her mouth. The whole "I'm really an architect" seemed like she was making excuses. He was a regular who seems to enjoy what she made. There didn't seem to be a reason to back into the story. She cleared her throat. "Well, growing up, we lived with my grandmother, Nona. And she liked to bake. At first, I liked to just watch—and of course, lick the beaters."

Henry let out a slight chuckle and nodded. "Go on."

"So, it wasn't long that I started helping too. She had this small card file box" —she placed her hands about five inches apart— "about this big where she put recipes. All filed in categories like cookies, cakes, pies. All sweet things. The card box was full. I don't think she could have added one more. She'd write these little notes on the cards like, 'good, make again' and 'good, but kids didn't like.'"

"That's charming," he said. "It sounds like your grandmother was just what you'd want a grandmother to be."

"Yeah. She was."

"I take it she isn't around anymore."

"No, she passed away when I was ten." The more she shared, the less nervous she became. "In her will, she left everything—the house, her car, and what was in her bank account to my father, her only child. Everything except..." She raised one finger for emphasis.

"The recipe box?" he asked.

"You got it. I still have it. And I still use it."

Henry smiled. "Well, here's to Nona, is it?" Before putting a bite of seven-layer bar in his mouth, he raised it in a cheers motion.

"Yes, Nona."

He wiped some crumbs from his mouth all the while staring at her intently. "Did you get those beautiful green eyes from your Nona, too?" he asked.

Abbey's cheeks blazed like a five-alarm fire. She did not respond. Or, more accurately, she could not respond. She was too stunned.

"I've noticed your eyes from the day I walked in here. They are very expressive. Like two of the most beautiful emeralds in the world."

She diverted her newly acclaimed most beautiful emeralds in the world around the bakery. Anywhere but in his direction. She tugged a curl at the nape of her neck and felt it spring back into shape in her hand.

"Am I embarrassing you?" He looked surprised. "Surely men tell you how beautiful you are all the time."

Was he joking? She looked at his expression to see if he was. Sure, she'd heard "You'd be pretty if only you lost weight" more often than she could count. But he wasn't saying the "if only..." part. Most men didn't even acknowledge her existence. In middle school, she got the dreaded nickname of "Peppa Pig," and her class-mates—mostly male—would make oinking pig sounds whenever she walked by. She never really got used to it. She learned to endure it by pretending she didn't hear them, giving no reaction at all to their hateful chants while holding back a dam full of tears until she was alone. And secretly, each summer, she'd try every fad diet, hoping earnestly that she'd return to school in the fall a slimmer, trimmer version of herself that would get a different response from her tormentors. But the pounds would not budge, because her commitment to the diet would never last more than a day or even a few hours.

When she was in college, her roommate, Martha, showed her how she could eat whatever she wanted—cookies, chips, a whole pint of ice cream, and then stick her index and middle finger down her throat until it touched just the right spot, and the entire contents of her stomach would come back up. That semester, she got down to close to a "normal" weight for the first time in her life. It felt good, but weird to see boys do a double take when she walked by. But the new Abbey didn't last long. Just as she wasn't very good at dieting, she wasn't very good at purging either. She decided having bulimia was too exhausting. She kept up the bingeing part, but not the purge. And soon, she gained the weight back and some more. But the bigger she got, the more invisible she became. No one shot a single glance her way.

Henry took the last bite of his seven-layer bar and wiped his fingers carefully with a napkin. "Did you go to culinary school?"

"What? Me? No. I went to Penn."

Henry looked confused. "I'm sorry, I'm not connecting the dots, but I'm sure there's a story there that I do want to hear." He looked at his watch. "But I have to go. Can't have a trial without a judge." He took the last sip of his coffee and said, "That hit the spot." He crumpled up his napkin and put it in the mug. "Abbey, forgive me for being forward, but can we continue this conversation over dinner? I'd love to learn more about you."

What? Did he just ask her out? She paused before responding, even though her brain was shooting off confetti cannons. If she blurted out yes too quickly, he'd probably think she was desperate—even though she was—and be turned off. *No, play it cool,* she told herself. Was it possible that this suave, distinguished-looking older man—a district court judge—was asking her out? In her thirty-three years on the planet, this had never happened. She only had two boyfriends—Charlie and Will, her study partner in college. Will spontaneously started making out with her during a study session and then broke up with her after three weeks of wild sex and a B- in Ancient Roman Cathedrals. Neither Charlie nor Will had asked her out on a proper date.

"I'd love to go to dinner," Abbey heard herself say in a voice she didn't recognize—it sounded high-pitched and squeaky like helium being let out of a balloon—nerves and the belief in fairy tales and unicorns had overcome her body and mind. Maybe he didn't notice that a munchkin from the Wizard of Oz had hijacked her voice.

His knitted brows let her know she sounded as off-putting as she thought. And then he smiled broadly. "Good," he said. "When I get back to the office, I'll look at my calendar. Can I text you then?"

Afraid to speak, Abbey nodded.

"Are there any nights this week that won't work?"

She shook her head. Technically, this response wasn't true. While she was free every night, she would have to check to make sure Betty could stay with her mother. But Abbey chose not to mention this detail. Why complicate things? Besides, the cynic in her was already doubting the date would ever happen.

"Okay, let's exchange numbers, and I'll be in touch later."

After they exchanged numbers, the judge stood up and put his coat and hat on. He reached deep into his pockets and pulled out a pair of black gloves that smelled like expensive real leather.

Caroline emerged from the kitchen behind the beaded curtain. "Oh, hello, Judge Hammonds," she said.

"Hello, Caroline." He turned toward Abbey. "Abbey, I'll be in touch." And then he walked toward the door. "Good day, ladies." He lifted his hat as a goodbye gesture and walked out of the bakery.

"Goodbye, Henry," Abbey said.

Caroline turned to Abbey. "Henry?" She mouthed. Once it was clear he'd left the bakery, Caroline said, "Okay, spill it. My spidey-senses are telling me I interrupted something good." She added a wink.

"No. Nothing, really." Abbey picked up the mug and plate from the judge's table and walked toward the kitchen.

Caroline followed her. "Oh, come on now, I know better than that. When you aren't here, he always asks 'Where's Abbey today?' And I tell you, until just now, I don't think I knew his first name. I know a crush when I see one."

"Yes, he did ask me to dinner. But..."

"But what? But nothing. That's wonderful. Tell me all the details."

"No details yet. He's supposed to text me when and where. But I don't know."

"What?" Caroline approached Abbey. "Don't know what?"

"I don't know. I'm scared, I guess."

"Of what?"

Abbey shrugged. "It just doesn't make sense. What does he see in me?" She gestured toward her curves. "No one in their right mind would say that this is beautiful."

Caroline frowned. "Didn't those hippie parents of yours ever teach you self-love? You are beautiful. I know it, and he knows it. It's time you believe it." Caroline took the dishes out of Abbey's hands and put them on the counter. She reached for Abbey's arms. "Look at me." Caroline stared straight at Abbey. "You've got to take chances in life for it to be fulfilling and rewarding. Could you get hurt? Yes, of course. But maybe you won't. If I didn't take a chance,

I'd never have been with husband two, three, *or* Leo." Caroline let go of Abbey's hands and made the sign of the cross. "God rest his soul," they said, in somber unison.

Caroline continued. "Maybe, just maybe, it will be something wonderful. Isn't that worth taking a chance?"

Abbey's phone vibrated in her apron. When she took her phone out, she noticed there was a text from the number she had just entered into her contacts list as Henry.

How about dinner Thursday, 7 p.m., Main Street Grille?

"Well, I guess I'm going to be taking a chance," Abbey said, smiling.

6

During her lunch hour, Abbey went to the dry cleaners to pick up the dress she'd dropped off the day before. She was planning to wear it when she met Henry for dinner the next night. Once he asked her out, she raced home and found it in a wad of neglected clothes on her closet floor. She found the perfect choice—black was slimming and the wraparound style gave an illusion of a waist that would be enhanced by body-shaping undergarments. The last time she wore it was to her father's funeral a year earlier. The cleaner promised they could get out the blotchy stain on the skirt that resembled bird droppings but was actually the result of over-loading a pita chip with too much artichoke dip.

When she got back to the bakery, it was almost two in the afternoon, enough time to make a few batches of cookies for the evening rush. Before taking off her coat, she inspected the case to see what needed to be replenished. She felt her phone vibrate in her coat pocket. Removing it, she read the text. It was from Henry.

Confirming our dinner tomorrow night. Looking forward to it.
HHH

She smiled. How sweet. The fact that he reached out to con-firm their dinner plans briefly relieved some of the pressure she was feeling because evidently, he was, as he put it— "looking forward to it."

She texted back, *I'll be there. See you tomorrow.* She contem-plated adding "looking forward to it too," but then decided against it because she still had nagging doubts that he could actually be into her. Her overactive imagination wondered if this was just a ruse and he was going to ask her to make a cake for a work party or for a special occasion like his birthday. She envisioned showing up at the restaurant tomorrow all goo-goo-eyed only to be completely wrong about his intentions. Like the time in high school during seventh period algebra when Jimmy Erickson—a boy she had a secret crush on—asked her what she was doing on Friday. She had excitedly replied "nothing," only to have him ask her to cover his girlfriend's shift at Target where all three of them worked, so he and his girlfriend could go to a concert. She'd learned a valuable lesson that day—it was better to keep her hopes at a minimum.

The bells above the bakery front door chimed. Abbey stood and saw an elderly gentleman dressed like Sherlock Holmes—wearing a tweed full-length cape and matching hat.

"You must be Abbey," he said. He approached the bakery case where she was standing.

"Yes, I am. And you are?"

"I'm Dwight, Caroline's—" He cleared his throat seemingly with pride or perhaps phlegm. "I'm Caroline's gentleman friend."

"Oh," Abbey said with a bit of wonderment. She looked him up and down and instantly wished Caroline hadn't shared so much about their intimate moments.

"Is she available?" he asked.

Abbey stood motionless, trying to erase her mind of the bawdy tales Caroline had told of her oversexed octogenarian "gentleman friend," including the little red bikini underwear that made him look so "sexy." She turned to walk toward the kitchen, but before she got very far, Caroline sauntered out.

"Well, Dwight, I thought I heard your sweet voice." She walked over to him and kissed him on the lips. "What a wonderful surprise. And look how handsome you are in your man-cape."

Caroline stroked the front of the tweed garment near Dwight's barrel-shaped chest.

Did she just say "man-cape?" Two words that should only be spoken in the same sentence when talking about a superhero.

"I brought the baby," Dwight said.

"Oh, the baby!" Caroline raised an eyebrow. "Goody."

Abbey looked around, but she didn't see an infant.

"I thought we could go for a ride."

Was Caroline planning to go for a ride in the middle of the day with this Sherlock Holmes character and his great-great-grandchild? Abbey was very confused.

Reading Abbey correctly, Caroline explained, "*The baby* is what he calls his car. It's a Bentley," she said with a wink.

"Oh," Abbey said. The scene was still weird—man-cape and all—but less weird since there was no baby.

"Oh, how special. But I can't just leave in the middle of the day. I'm not like you. I'm not retired. I have a business to run," Caroline said. She wrapped her arm around his. "I can't possibly leave Abbey here alone. We get so busy in the afternoons." She continued to stroke his chest, petting him like a puppy.

"Please, Caroline, go. I'll watch the store. Go and have fun," Abbey said.

"You sure?" Caroline asked.

"Of course. Go. I'll be fine."

"Well, okay then." Caroline blew an air kiss toward Abbey and mouthed, "Thanks. I owe you," before grabbing her chinchilla coat and walking out the door arm-in-arm with her new beau.

It was okay that Caroline left Abbey in charge—she did it with more and more frequency. It could be a not-so-subtle attempt to get Abbey on board with becoming a partner. But Abbey saw the bakery job as a temporary thing—something to hold her over until her mother got better and could live on her own. Then she'd move back to Philadelphia, get her old job back and do what she was supposed to do—design buildings.

Occasionally, she still thought about Jax even though Henry had asked her to dinner. Caroline had said having to juggle two suitors was never a bad thing. "Let it play out and see which one *you* like best." At this point, the judge was in the lead, because it had been a few days and she hadn't heard from Jax—nor did she have his contact information. Henry was very handsome and eloquent. He was exactly the man she'd dreamed of when she was a little girl, sort of like Cary Grant in *Bringing Up Baby*, a little stiff—but in a good way—older, suave, and debonair. He seemed like a solid man. It felt amazing that he noticed her.

But what if Jax did get in touch? Could she actually juggle two men? That thought made her laugh, and to think that a little more than a week ago she'd sent a pitiful text to Charlie. What a difference a week made.

After the late evening rush, Abbey closed the bakery and stopped by the mini mart on her way home. The plastic bag of fresh produce and half gallon of milk grew heavy as she slowly walked up the hill toward her house. She shifted the bag from hand to hand every minute or so, careful not to let the dry-cleaned garment draped over her arm drag and graze the patches of ice that hadn't melted yet from the bit of snow a few days earlier.

When she reached her house, she had energy she hadn't had in a while. She abandoned her rule about not building her hopes up too high. The excitement about meeting Henry the next night built along with the possibility of what could be. She had played her future in her head over and over. They would hit it off. Date for a few months before he'd get down on one knee and propose. He'd tell her he loved her just the way she was. But she would still lose weight before the wedding so that she wouldn't feel self-conscious and burn all the wedding pictures. Mrs. Henry Hammonds. Judge and Mrs. Henry Hammonds. Abbey Hammonds. Camille and Caroline would be her attendants. But she knew she was definitely getting ahead of herself. That was nothing new. It didn't hurt to dream, did it?

She opened the front door to her home and walked in. In the living room, her mother was seated in her usual chair. The TV was on. And of course, it was loud. Betty was seated next to Millie.

Betty took a tassel from her Bible to mark the page, closed the book, and stood. "We had a good day, today, didn't we, Mamma? We ate a good, healthy lunch and played some cards. Good day." Millie smiled and reached for Betty's hand, cupped it in her own hands, and brought it to her cheek.

"Thank you for staying a little late tonight, Betty. And thanks for agreeing to stay tomorrow so I can go to dinner," Abbey said. Since once again, she could not rely on her sister's help.

"No problem, Miss Abbey." Betty walked toward Abbey. "Is this the dress you're wearing tomorrow night for your big date?" Betty reached for the dry-cleaning bagged garment and rolled the plastic up to get a better look. "Mm-hmm. Pretty."

"It's not a date, not really. It's just dinner." Abbey felt her jaw tighten and her face redden.

"For *just* dinner, the black dress is nice." Betty nodded her approval. "Tomorrow, I'll stay as long as you need. You need me to stay all night—" she winked— "I'll stay all night."

"No, that won't be necessary, but thank you."

"Goodbye, Miss Millie. I'll see you tomorrow." Betty put on her coat. She walked to the front door and waved as she opened it. Millie smiled and waved back.

"Okay, I'll get dinner going," Abbey said. She hung the dress over the banister and went to the kitchen. She took from the grocery bag a bunch of carrots, still with their greenery attached, a stalk of celery, a big red beet, a cucumber, and a bag of spinach. After washing all the produce, she peeled the carrots and the beet and chopped them into big chunks. Removing the juicer from a cabinet above, she placed it on the counter. It had been a few months since she had tried the juice diet. This time it would work and render her slimmer and attractive, she thought to herself confidently.

She put a glass at the spout, gathered a handful of chopped vegetables, tucked them in the machine's compartment and turned it on. The machine whirred, spit, and sputtered before finally emitting about two inches of greenish-gray slime. She picked up the glass and looked at its contents—a thick green blob that resembled more like guacamole than a smoothie. She put the glass to her lips. As soon as the liquid touched her mouth, she immediately spat it out. It tasted like a dirty garden—too earthy. The only thing super about this so called "super drink" was that it was super bad. Some Google research was necessary because a tweak or two to the recipe was definitely in order. The liquid diet would have to start the day after her dinner with Henry.

7

The sun was just setting when Abbey approached the restaurant. The Main Street Grille was across the street and only a few blocks down from the bakery, but her feet ached in four-inch shiny black heels she hadn't worn since her architect days. She used the bathroom in the back of the bakery to shower and change. And Caroline was nice enough to blow dry Abbey's curly and frizzy hair into a stylish straight bob and put on her makeup in between customers so that Abbey didn't have to run home. She crossed the street only when the flashing WALK sign was lit, and after looking both ways three times. All day long, she had avoided doing anything risky for fear that one wrong move would elicit a meteor of fate that would ruin her evening plans. As silly as that thinking was, it made perfect sense to this Chicken Little glass-half-empty kind of girl.

Once she crossed the street safely, she hesitated before entering the restaurant. She had been there so many times before, but never on a date. The restaurant had been on Main Street—hence its name—in the old part of Ellicott City for as long as she could remember. Its stone-covered building used to be an old mill that was deemed too precious to tear down by the town's historical society. It was the restaurant Nona would take them to on special occasions—birthdays, anniversaries, and even a Thanksgiving or two, when they could get reservations. So many wonderful memories, and she hoped tonight would be memorable in a good way too.

When she entered the Grille, a young woman with a nose ring and pink hair pulled high in a ponytail greeted her. "Table for one?" she said.

The hostess's blatant assumption was not lost on Abbey. "No, actually, I am here to meet someone. Judge Henry Hammonds." Abbey smiled. Her chin jutted up, and she puffed out her chest just a little as the words came out of her mouth.

The hostess looked Abbey up and down, in a way that oozed both judgment and curiosity. "He's over here," she said. She turned and started walking to the main dining room, and Abbey followed.

The main dining room was dimly lit. The walls were painted burgundy, and the floors were covered with dark stained oak panels. The room was filled with square and rectangle tables with long white tablecloths that came close to touching the floor and Williamsburg-style chairs with low, rounded backs and that had six spindles each.

Abbey nearly stumbled when she saw Henry seated in the far corner of the dining room near the stone fireplace that glowed with logs and burning embers. A smile lit his face when he saw her. She regained her composure enough to return the smile. He stood as she and the hostess approached.

When they got to the table, the hostess grunted something inaudible before walking away.

"Abbey," he said. "Thank you for coming."

Abbey shrugged. "My pleasure."

He helped her off with her coat, which she hung on the back of her chair. She caught his gaze on her ample cleavage like a bullseye and instantly regretted how revealing the "perfect" dress was. Before sitting down, she ran her hands down the jersey knit fabric of the skirt of the dress.

His arm lingered on the small of her back as he leaned in and said in a hushed voice, "You look lovely."

"Thank you." She hoped he couldn't hear her heart, which was beating through her neck, or see the beads of sweat that were now forming on her forehead.

She sat down and so did he.

"Have you been here before?" he asked.

"No." Nerves had gotten the best of her before she could correct her answer.

"Their steaks are delicious."

She moved the leather-bound menu to the side so that she could put her cloth napkin in her lap.

A server approached the table. "Good evening, Judge."

Henry nodded acknowledgment.

"What can I get you?"

"I'll have a Macallan 18, neat," he said, in a commandingly confident voice. A confident man was very sexy.

The waiter turned to Abbey. "And you, ma'am?"

So many thoughts were running through her head. She didn't drink that often, so she wasn't sure what to order. Wine? No, that made her rosy cheeks even rosier. Gin and tonic? Um, no, not since she drank one too many in college and emptied the contents of her stomach—several times. Pina colada? No, too many calories. Rather than wimp out and order a Diet Coke, she said, "I'll have the same."

When the server left the table, Henry said, "I didn't know you were a Scotch connoisseur. Good choice."

Ugh. She wasn't a Scotch connoisseur. It was a terrible choice! Macallan was a Scotch? Of course it was. The name was a dead giveaway. The only time she had Scotch was when she and Penny snuck a sip from their parents' bar in the basement. Abbey hated the taste so much; she spit it out as soon as it touched her mouth.

"It's the only brand worth fifty dollars a glass—in my opinion."

Fifty? Did he say fifty dollars a glass? She tried not to give away the full panic that had set in. Hopefully, her palate had matured. And, hopefully, she wouldn't spit it out like she did when she was ten. And then another horrible thought entered her mind—what if dinner were Dutch treat and they would split the bill? Fifty dollars was what she had set aside in her head in case that was the case. She couldn't decide what would be more embarrassing, spitting out the Scotch, having it hit Henry's fine silk Italian suit, or having her debit card declined when the bill came. Both scenes were pretty awful. Only two minutes in and she was already making cringe-worthy mistakes.

The server returned with just one glass of the brown liquid. "I'm sorry, Judge. But this is the last of Macallan. It's been on back order."

Abbey seized the opportunity. "Please," she said, "I insist you take it." She motioned for the server to put the drink down in front of Henry.

Henry shook his head.

"No, I'm serious," she said. "You know"—*think fast, think fast*— "I, um, I just remembered. I shouldn't drink since I'm on antibiotics." *Good.*

Henry looked concerned and a bit confused. "Oh, dear."

"Oh, it's nothing. Female stuff." As soon as the words tumbled out of her mouth, she wanted to take them back. "Female stuff" was what she'd say when she didn't want her father to ask for additional details. But in this case, "female stuff" could be confused with something awful—like herpes. "It's not herpes," she blurted, making it exponentially worse. *Sigh.* "A yeast infection. I have, had, had—it was weeks ago—had a yeast infection. Down there. But it's gone. Now." She willed herself to stop talking. When she was nervous, she tended to overshare.

"Oh. Okay. I hope you're better."

"Yes, I think it's from all the baking." Of course, that wasn't true. But the judge seemed satisfied, albeit a little grossed out. The server, however, seemed mortified. *TMI. TMI!* And it wasn't even the truth. In her head, Abbey coined a new acronym—*TMFI*. The "F" stood for fake or something a little more rated-R. She took a deep breath to try to calm her nerves. "Can I just get a Diet Coke?" she asked.

The server nodded and hastily left the table.

Henry took a sip of his Scotch. "Oh, that's good." He put the glass back down on the table next to his place setting. "So," he said, "I invited you here to learn more about you. Who is Abbey Reilly? What makes Abbey tick?"

Good question. But she wasn't sure how to answer. The truth seemed so pathetic. But she didn't want to make up something either—not again. That had gone so well just a minute earlier. Her inner voice dripped with sarcasm. Instead, she said, "I'm just me. What you see is what you get."

Henry leaned in a little. "I very much like what I see."

Was it the Macallan talking? She studied his expression. He didn't seem drunk or glassy-eyed. She had seen that look on Caroline enough to know when it was the alcohol doing the talking. Was it possible that he thought she was attractive? She clung to examples of very handsome men dating—even marrying—plus-size women. She had seen pictures of Ashley Graham—big, beautiful, and proud, with her very handsome, thin husband. The only thing she and Ashley had in common was the first letter of their names. But still, it could happen—a thin, normal, hot, sexy man could fall for an overweight, okay-looking woman. She told herself it does happen—rarely—very rarely, but there wasn't some rule that it couldn't happen. Why couldn't she be the unicorn? Why couldn't she be the everyday version of Ashley Graham?

She took in his words, his smile, his dreamy eyes that looked like Nona's five-carat aquamarine ring and swooned out loud a little. In the novels she loved to read, this would be the part where he would lean in and kiss her passionately.

The server returned with Abbey's Diet Coke, interrupting what could have been a very intimate moment. "Have you decided on what you'll be having tonight?" he asked.

Abbey hadn't even looked at the menu. She quickly perused the prices of entrées and felt intense dread—*thirty-five, thirty-eight, a pork chop at forty-two?* Her eyes scanned the left side until she found salads. "I'd like the Field of Greens with grilled chicken, please. Ranch dressing." At twenty-two dollars, it was within budget and wouldn't make her look like a glutton. Normally, she would ask for extra ranch, but instead, she said, "Dressing on the side, please." On the side, but she'd probably douse the salad with the entire contents of the side container. It was her way of showing some restraint and to appear dainty.

Henry didn't even open his menu. "I'd like the filet—ten ounce—medium rare. I'd also like a side of sautéed mushrooms and a baked potato with sour cream and butter. What's the vegetable of the day?"

"Asparagus."

"No." He frowned. "That'll do. Just the steak and potato."

After taking copious notes on a small notepad, the server clicked the pen before putting it in the pocket of his long black apron. He picked up the menus and left the table.

Henry raised his glass. "Here's to getting to know each other."

She raised her glass and clinked it against his. "Cheers," she said.

He took another sip of his drink and let out one of those drinking "aahs." And licked his lips. "So. Where were we?" he asked.

As far as Abbey was concerned, there were so many questions.

Was this a date? Did he like *like* her? She bit her lip and finally said, "Are you from Maryland?" It seemed like a good way to break the ice and get to know someone. Personal, but not too personal.

Henry tilted his head and shook it slightly. "No, I'm from California. I went to Georgetown Law School. That's how I ended up on the East Coast. And you?"

Abbey paused. Did she want to go into the vagabond lifestyle her parents had subjected her and her sister to when they were very young? No, she decided against it. "I moved here when I was five."

"The other day, in the bakery, you started to tell me about how you became a baker. I've always assumed you went to the world famous culinary institute in New York or Le Cordon Bleu." He spoke with a perfect French accent—his *r*'s and *l*'s were lyrical.

"Me?" Abbey pointed to herself. She chuckled lightly. It felt good to have someone say such flattering things. "Up until a year ago, I was happy being an architect. I thought I'd be one forever. That is, until—" She shrugged. "That is, until my dad died. Then I moved home to take care of my mom. She had a stroke."

Henry nodded. "You know, that speaks volumes about the kind of person you are. But I kind of thought that already."

Abbey felt the tension she'd been holding in her shoulders ease up. She toyed with a curl that had formed at the nape of her neck. "I'm no hero," she said, slightly uncomfortable talking about herself so much. "My sister is married—with small children. So, I was the logical choice."

"Yes, but you could have said no."

That thought had never entered her mind. She felt a duty and an obligation to take care of her mother after her father died. "I suppose. But my mother can't live alone."

"There are places—homes—assisted living facilities," he said, demonstrating his knowledge as a lawyer. Abbey imagined he was probably very adept at making arguments. Did she want to go into the whole story—that she had promised her father, on his death-bed, no less, and the clunky part that her parents lived every day to the fullest and never saved for retirement. Decidedly, she did not. She shrugged. Changing the subject dramatically, she said, "Enough about me."

He raised an eyebrow. "Oh, I see, it's my turn."

"Yes. What makes you tick, Henry? Turnabout is fair play."

He took another sip of his Scotch, which was nearly all gone by now. "I prefer to be an enigma."

"Well, that's not too fair." Her boldness surprised her.

"Maybe." He had a very calculating look on his face. "All I know is that right now, I am sitting in front of one of the most beautiful and intriguing women I have had the pleasure of being in the company of in a very long time. And for me, that's all that matters." His gaze and words made her feel special—like she was the only woman in the room, and her guard tumbled.

Midway through the meal, she had told him about Charlie. Henry agreed a text on New Year's Eve was a dastardly (or maybe he'd used the word bastardly) way to break up with someone, but that she was much better off. Near the end of their dinner, the restaurant had gotten a little noisy and hearing every word was a bit challenging. And he even said—at least she thought he said, maybe she had imagined it—that Charlie's loss was his gain.

When the bill came, he waved her off and insisted dinner was on him. That was a good sign, she told herself. And he walked her to the door, guiding her with his arm gently on her back. He offered to drive her home, but she said no for no particular reason other than she had read an article on dating that said you shouldn't do that on the first date.

On the brief walk home, her feet didn't hurt at all. She knew now what it felt like to walk on air—to be so happy that you wanted that moment in time to stop.

The next morning, after a sleepless night due to dreaming of Henry holding her and kissing her, Abbey was in the kitchen baking a batch of carrot cupcakes when Caroline walked in. Abbey was still on cloud nine—giddy from the night before and basking in the newness of the feeling that something wonderful was about to happen.

Abbey stopped working on the cupcakes and quickly walked into the office behind Caroline. She couldn't wait to share how the evening with Henry had gone. Caroline took her coat off and threw it on the couch.

"Well, aren't you going to ask?" Abbey said. She didn't give Caroline a chance to respond. "Oh, I can't wait to tell you," she blurted. "Here's the Cliffs Notes—it was wonderful, spectacular, better than you could even imagine."

Caroline sighed. "Sit down, sweetie. I have to share something with you."

Caroline looked serious—in a way Abbey had never seen. "What is it?" Abbey sat down next to the chinchilla coat, careful not to sit on it.

Caroline took her phone from her purse. "I googled him."

"Who?"

"The judge," Caroline said. The mood in the room turned very serious.

"Oh." Abbey wasn't sure she wanted to know what Caroline had discovered.

"It's not good."

Abbey felt the balloon inside of her burst along with all of her hopes.

8

"Married?" Abbey said faintly. "He's married?" She looked down at Caroline's phone in disbelief. On the screen was an article from last Sunday's *Baltimore Sun* that had a picture of Henry with a striking dark-haired woman. The caption read: *Board member and Howard County Circuit Court Judge Henry H. Hammonds and his wife, Louise, attend The Walters Art Museum annual gala*. "He's married?" Abbey repeated, as if saying it over and over would make it not so.

Caroline nodded.

"Last night was so wonderful. He was kind and attentive. He never mentioned a wife." Abbey thought back to the conversation of the evening. He had avoided really saying anything about himself. Was he wearing a wedding ring? No, of course he wasn't. That was always the first thing she checked. Surely, she would have noticed one last night or when they sat together the other day while he ate a seven-layer bar. "Why would he do this to me?" She wiped a tear from her eye and tried hard to keep the dam of tears on the inside from busting.

Caroline got up and walked to where Abbey was sitting. She moved the chinchilla to the arm of the couch so that she could sit close to Abbey. She reached over and stroked Abbey's hair. "There, there," she said. "I know it hurts. And I'm sorry to be the one to tell you, but I didn't want you to get sucked in and then find out. It's better that you know now."

Abbey nodded and sobbed. "I thought he really liked me.

How could I be so stupid? Why did I let myself think that he'd be interested in someone like me?"

"Oh, his interest was genuine." Caroline broke the embrace and cupped Abbey's chin in her hand. She stared directly into Abbey's eyes. "This has nothing to do with the way you look. You know that, don't you?"

Abbey looked away. Her throat felt tight. She didn't know that, and no one could convince her otherwise. Was it so much to ask that a handsome man with a good job and promising future would want to date her? Of course it was. Like it or not, her weight was an issue. Attraction mattered, and let's face it, men were not attracted to her because of her body. And, if they were, it came with strings—like a wife.

"Listen to me. Some men are two-headed snakes. They often think with the wrong head. I've heard it all before. I'm sure he will say he's in a loveless marriage, but a divorce will wipe him out." She rolled her eyes. "Oh, he'd probably whine a little and get you to feel sorry for him. Lord knows I've known my share of married men. If that's what you want, no judgment here."

Abbey shook her head.

"You are a beautiful woman. Don't settle for someone who doesn't treat you the way you deserve to be treated. You deserve to be someone's one and only." Caroline's words, however wise, did little to comfort Abbey.

Caroline stood and walked to her desk. She picked up her apron. "Why don't you take the day off?" she said as she looped the belt around, tying a large bow in the back. "I've got this. Go on."

"No, I'll be okay."

"No, you won't. Besides, he may come in to see you."

Abbey hadn't thought of that. She felt a little nauseous.

"Go on now," Caroline said with a shooing motion. "I got this."

"Okay," Abbey said weakly. She took off her apron and threw it in a heap on top of the desk.

When she got home, all she wanted to do was crawl into bed and maybe never get out.

"What is it, Miss Abbey? You forget something?" Betty greeted her as she made her way to her mother's room. "Why are you home so early?"

"I'm not feeling well."

"Poor thing." Betty reached for Abbey's forehead. "No fever." She looked into Abbey's eyes, and, as if she could read her mind, she said, "Go lie down. I'll stay and take care of Mamma."

Abbey went to her room and lay on her bed. She nuzzled her face in her pillow and felt the moisture of her tears. Was there anyone out there who would love her? Why was finding love so difficult? She felt bitter that people judged her on her body size. But no one judged her more than she did herself.

She was about to doze off when her phone pinged.

She picked her phone off the nightstand. "Meet Magda (dressmaker) for fitting," read the appointment reminder on the calendar app. Sigh. With all the drama, she'd forgotten about the dress fitting for Camille's wedding. And now, she had fifteen minutes to get to the dress shop, which was, at the very least, a fifteen-minute brisk walk from her house.

Can this day get any worse? And just like that, it was about to.

• • •

"Hmm." Abbey felt the bridesmaid dress constrict as Magda struggled with seemingly great effort to get the zipper up beyond Abbey's waist. "The bride no like you?" Magda said in a thick Eastern European accent.

"What? Yes, she likes me. Why?"

"I don't know, this pink, it is, hmm, how do you say? Unflattable. Pink is not good for red hair." Magda's words were muffled as she talked with long straight pins in her mouth. "Black would be better, yes. Sometimes bride think of self only. Not how others look. And this." Abbey watched in the mirror as Magda tugged at the short flared and gathered piece of fabric that encircled Abbey's middle. "This is no good."

"Actually, she let me pick out the dress myself. My friend, Camille—the bride, just said wear pink." When Abbey saw this dress online, she thought the peplum would hide things she wanted to keep hidden." Abbey tugged at the flaring piece of fabric. She had to admit she looked like a marshmallow Easter Peep that had been blown up in the microwave. The peplum hid nothing.

"Hmm. No. Is bad choice. Not just peplum. Color. Color is bad. I used to dress Bolshoi dancers. This pink is no good. Even on dancers are not flattering." Magda stared intently at Abbey. She tapped a finger on her chin. "Don't worry. I'll fix. Now, suck in," Magda commanded with the authority of a Russian general. "On the count of three...one, two, three." Abbey held her breath and heard Magda let out a loud sigh. The zipper didn't budge.

Magda tilted her head from behind Abbey until she was visible in the mirror. She looked like a little wood nymph, tiny in stature and almost pointy ears sticking out beyond her overdyed jet-black hair. "You said you were size sixteen, no?"

Abbey nodded. Magda put her reading glasses on, which were hanging from a beaded chain around her neck. Checking the dress label, she said "Sixteen. Yes. Hmm." She inspected the dress seams and then took the tape measure coiled around her neck like a boa. "Hold tight," she said as she placed Abbey's hands on each side of the unzipped zipper. Abbey felt Magda's calloused fingers fumble on her back as she imagined a gaping valley where the dress did not fit.

"Okay, let me think." Magda said as she appeared in the mirror again, she removed the pins from her mouth and put them in the bun in her hair. "When is wedding?"

"Um, April fourth."

"We need an eighteen or twenty. April fourth?" Magda asked and appeared to count the weeks in her head. "No time to place order for new dress."

Geez, eighteen or twenty? A size sixteen was mortifying enough. The thought of wearing a double-digit size starting with a two caused Abbey instant shame. "I'm planning to lose weight," Abbey said in a voice barely audible. "Before the wedding," she added.

Either Magda did not hear Abbey's comment, or she did not believe her because she had no reaction. Instead, Magda stood in a very pensive pose—chin in hand—for what felt like several minutes. Neither spoke. Abbey tugged at the peplum, wishing the ground beneath the dressmaker's shop would open up and swallow her.

Finally, Magda raised a finger in the air and said, "I got it! Stay here. Don't go anywhere. I will fix," she said confidently and left the dressing room.

Eighteen or twenty? Eighteen or twenty? The words cut through Abbey like a sharp knife. All this time, she had worn sweatpants and stretchy jeans to work, she really didn't know what size she had become. Never in her wildest nightmares had she realized she gone up a size or even two.

When Magda returned, she had two dresses in fuchsia-colored silk. "Ten plus eight equal eighteen. No?" Magda said with pride as she held the two bright pink dresses made of chiffon material up to Abbey's body. "I'll take these two dresses and make one more flattering. Yes!!"

Abbey swallowed hard through the lump forming in her throat, hoping Magda wouldn't notice her pain and embarrassment. Just when she thought it wasn't possible, sewing two dresses together to make one had made the experience even more humiliating. Just a few hours earlier she was on top of the world. Now, she was definitely near the bottom. The emotional swing was exhausting.

Magda hung the two dresses on a rack in the dressing room and helped Abbey pull off the one that didn't fit. Then she used the tape measure to measure Abbey's thighs, hips, waist, chest, and arms—being sure to write down each number on a small notepad she kept in her pocket. Before putting the tape measure back around her neck, Magda did one last measurement from Abbey's shoulder to her ankle. "Okay. Done." Magda made a head-tilting gesture toward the clothes Abbey wore to the shop.

As Abbey got dressed, Magda methodically measured the size eight and size ten pink dresses and wrote down those numbers as well. When that task was completed, she draped the dresses over her arm.

Before leaving the dressing room, Magda reached up and cupped Abbey's face with her hand. "Such beautiful face. Don't worry, I make rest beautiful too. In Russia, they call me Magda the Magician." She smiled as she patted Abbey's cheek. "Don't worry. Our secret," she winked toward the two dresses draped in her other arm.

As she was leaving the dress shop, Abbey felt her phone buzz.

Stopped by but you weren't there. Had a great time last night. Hope we can do it again soon. H.

Great. Just great.

9

When Abbey got to work the next day, Caroline was already there.

"I'm surprised to see you," Caroline said after she gave Abbey a big hug. "How are you feeling, dear?" She brushed Abbey's hair off her shoulders.

"Okay," Abbey muttered.

"You sure you feel like being here?"

"Better than home."

Caroline nodded in a knowing way. "Why don't you stay in the kitchen, I'll take care of the counter."

Abbey shook her head.

"Yesterday, he came in here looking for you, you know. The judge, that is." Caroline looked at Abbey for a reaction. "I told him you went home sick. Which was kind of true—sick of him, that is."

Abbey put on her apron and mixed dry ingredients for lemon cupcakes. "When life gives you lemons, make lemon cupcakes," she said, only half joking.

"Have you thought about what you'll say to him? Boy, I wanted to tell him off." Caroline balled her fist. "I was going to tell him his money was not good here." She huffed. "I still can."

"No, I'll handle it," Abbey said, not sure she knew what exactly she was going to do or say when she saw him.

About ninety minutes later, the morning rush was in full swing. Abbey carried a tray of freshly baked lemon cupcakes piled high with a vanilla frosting swirl to the bake case. She looked up and saw him enter the front door. He walked toward her.

"Hi," he said with a broad smile.

"Hi," she said back in a low voice.

"Are you feeling better? I hope it wasn't something you ate," he said with concern. "I've been worried. You haven't answered any of my texts."

Abbey swallowed hard. She didn't want to announce to a bakery full of customers what she knew. "Can we talk after the line dies down?" she asked, hoping he'd just go away.

"Sure." He stood to the side of the counter with a confused look.

As she served customers, she could see him standing there. He was not getting the hint. He removed his hat and ran his hand along the brim. He's nervous, Abbey thought to herself.

After what seemed like an eternity, but was probably only ten minutes, the morning rush died down. Abbey walked from behind the counter and toward the judge.

He reached out for her hand. "I've missed you," he said in a smooth voice.

Abbey kept both hands in her apron.

"Is everything okay?" Henry asked.

"When were you going to tell me?"

"Tell you what?" He appeared genuinely surprised.

Abbey wasn't sure she would have the courage to continue the conversation. She looked behind the counter toward Caroline who nodded her head telling her to go on.

"I know you're married," she said. The words did not come out easily.

Henry looked shocked. "What?" What is it with married men posing as singles? Are they all good actors?

"I saw a picture of you and your wife in last week's *Sun*. At the Walters gala."

His expression fell. It was true. "I'm sorry. I, I—"

Abbey wanted to cry. No, she wanted to sob. Somehow, she managed to keep the tears from flowing. "So, it's true," she said. Her voice was noticeably cracking.

"Yes, it's true."

"Well, I'm not sure what you had in mind." She looked straight at him and summoned courage she didn't know she had. "I am so mad at you. You made me think you liked me."

"I do like you. I like you very much."

She looked at him with disbelief. "I don't know if this was your idea of some sick joke."

"No, I can assure you it wasn't. I had good intentions." He reached for her hand. "Abbey, please, hear me out."

She pulled her hand away. "At least tell me you're separated."

He shook his head. "Not legally. Let me explain."

"There's nothing to explain. You're married, and I don't date married men."

"Yes, but we, she. Listen, I'm sure you won't believe me, but we really don't have a marriage. We haven't for quite some time."

"What does that mean? Haven't for quite some time." She repeated his own words back to him.

"It means that are we legally married. Yes. Are we in love? No. I stopped loving her years ago. But she never had a job. If we got divorced, she'd get all of my money. So, this is what we do. We live together as roommates." It was just as Caroline said. He reached for her hand again. Again, she did not accept it.

"What did you expect me to do? What did you expect me to say?" Her hands shook so badly, she put them in her pocket.

"Really, I hadn't thought things through. Look Abbey, I never wanted to hurt you. You have to believe me. The truth is, I find you very intriguing. You made me want to get up in the morning. I couldn't wait to see you. I just thought we could see where it goes. Our dinner was wonderful, wasn't it?"

"Why didn't you tell me then? Were you ever going to tell me? Were you going to wait until I was hooked and then tell me?"

"No. I would have told you. I just didn't know how. Or." He cleared his throat. "When."

"You work on this very block. Did you not think we'd run into a coworker? Even at dinner."

"I admit there was no grand, well-thought master plan. I wasn't even sure you'd say 'yes.'"

She willed herself not to cry again. "I've got a lot going on. I don't need to be someone's mistress."

Henry nodded. "I understand," he said. "Look, I hope one day I get the courage to leave my wife."

"Don't think she'll wait around for you!" Caroline yelled from behind the counter. She started walking toward Abbey and Henry. When she got to within inches, she waved a finger in Henry's face. "Abbey's not going to wait for you to get your act together. She's too much of a class act for that." Caroline let out a "Huh" and muttered "Smug prick" loud enough for Abbey and most definitely Henry to hear before backing down. Her stare was icy, and her growl was not unlike a momma bear protecting a cub.

Henry put his hands up in a surrender pose. "I am sorry. I never wanted to hurt anyone." He put his hat back on and tipped it to Abbey. "Good day, Abbey. You are a very special lady."

"You got that right. Judge, I'm going to ask you to leave. Now. And please don't come back," Caroline said.

"I understand," he said. And he left the bake shop.

Abbey ran into the kitchen. She began to hyperventilate. The smell of the sugary baked goods was intoxicating, but not in a good way. Her head was spinning as the scene that just happened swirled around inside. She steadied herself on the counter and took deep breaths before the sobs came. She hated him. She hated that she liked him. She hated that she let her imagination get away. But most of all, she hated that hope was gone.

She eyed a pecan cinnamon ring that she had baked as a special order for a woman coming in at ten to pick it up. It was still warm from the oven. Cinnamon wafted through the air. Twelve plump yeasted rolls perfectly proofed and layered with cinnamon sugar and topped cream cheese buttercream icing. She picked up a fork and dug in. She closed her eyes as the warm cake met her lips. For an instant, she felt good inside. For an instant, she could forget.

Caroline came into the kitchen. "No, no, no!" She waved her hands in the air. "Don't do that."

Abbey put the fork down.

Caroline ripped an entire roll off the ring and handed it to Abbey. "Use your fingers," she said. "It's more efficient this way."

10

Caroline graciously gave Abbey the weekend off. Abbey made it through the following Monday afternoon but just barely. Her heart and head just weren't in it. With three more hours left on her shift, she didn't want to leave Caroline to hold the fort again, so she toughed it out.

"You look deep in thought," Caroline said as she entered the kitchen. "What's on your mind?"

"Stuff."

Caroline touched her arm gently. "Listen, sweetie, somewhere out there, there is a wonderful man that deserves you." Caroline had this uncanny skill of reading minds. "You got to let these things play out the way they are supposed to. The universe has a plan for everyone."

Abbey nodded. Inside, she was already dismissing Caroline's cheerful "just hang in there" speech.

The jingle bells above the door announced a customer. "I've got this," she said to Caroline and left the kitchen. When she arrived in the front of the bakery, she gasped. She'd recognize that tall, lanky, hot hunk anywhere. It was Jax. She abruptly turned around and went back into the kitchen.

"What's wrong?" Caroline asked. "You're as white as a ghost."

"It's him," she said in a whisper, trying carefully not to speak so loudly that he may hear.

"Who? The judge? Why I told him—" Caroline's voice was raised.

Abbey motioned for her to lower her voice. "No, not him. It's Jax. The guy I told you about from Philadelphia."

"Oh," Caroline mouthed. She peeked through the beaded curtain. "Cu-te!" She flicked her hand. "Hubba hubba."

"What am I going to do?"

Caroline looked confused. "About?"

"I never told him I worked here."

Abbey's response did not erase Caroline's look.

"I told him I was an architect in Philadelphia. Well, actually, I let him think that."

"So, what if you work here? What's wrong with that?"

"Nothing," Abbey said, knowing she'd offended Caroline. She made a mental note to deal with the fallout later. "There's nothing wrong with working here. I just wasn't forthcoming is all."

"Oh, it's fate. I know it's fate. What are the odds that he'd find you?" Caroline said.

Yes, how did he find her? Good point, Abbey wondered. "Maybe he's a stalker."

"Hmm. Hadn't thought of that." Caroline looked pensive. "Would that be so bad? I mean, it's thoughtful that he tracked you down."

Abbey felt queasy. She stuck her head through the pink beaded curtain. He was bending down inspecting the bake case. Good, he hadn't seen her. She quickly turned around. Her face ran smack into Caroline's chest. The momentum of Caroline's forward motion pushed the two women to the ground and through the beaded curtain and into the front of the bakery. There they lay with the upper part of their bodies sandwiched together in a most intimate way—Caroline on top facing Abbey.

Jax ran over to the two women. He stopped short as the look on his face changed from concern to surprise. "Abbey?" he said.

Abbey stared up into his beautiful and soulful eyes and almost swooned. And surely forgot about her current predicament—getting her boss off her. With a slight push, Abbey helped Caroline roll to her knees.

"Are you okay?" he said. He extended a hand to Abbey.

"Oh, hi. Jax, isn't it?" Abbey said. She tried to play it cool by blowing a strand of hair that had fallen over her eyes. She rolled over till she was kneeling. If ever there was a time to not look like a beached whale when getting up from the floor, now was the time. She took a deep breath and with his assistance and trying not to put most of her weight on his outreached hand, she heaved her body to a standing position—albeit a little wobbly one.

Jax then reached his arm out for Caroline and Abbey took the other side. After the count of three, Caroline was standing as well.

"This is Caroline." Abbey pointed to her boss. "Caroline, this is Jax. He's a friend," she raised an eyebrow, "of Camille and Skip." She gave Caroline a look that encouraged her to read her mind by not divulging anything too embarrassing, like how she pined for him, or how much she really liked him, or the fiasco with the judge. Caroline, always the best at reading the room, just smiled and said, "So nice to meet you."

Once assured of no obvious broken bones, Caroline said, "While you visit with your friend, I'll wipe down the tables." It was Caroline's way of protecting Abbey, and Abbey appreciated it.

Abbey stood and turned to face Jax. They smiled at each other, and she wondered if he felt as uncomfortable as she did. The silence was getting more and more awkward, so Abbey blurted out, "How did you find me?"

"Find—?" He laughed. "Wait? What? Oh, no, I'm not a stalker."

Phew! She was both relieved and slightly dejected and a lot embarrassed.

"I came to Ellicott City to look at a property, and I saw on Yelp this place had the best cookies. I've got a real sweet tooth."

Sweet tooth—could he get any better?

"You work here?" he asked. "I thought—"

She sighed. "It's a long story."

"Well, I've got about an hour before I need to catch my train."

Abbey reached into the bake case and pulled out a chocolate chip cookie and handed it to Jax.

He reached for his wallet, and she waved him off. "On the house," she said.

After giving Jax the cookie, she told him the whole story—that she was an architect in Philadelphia, but she'd returned home to care for her mother. "I'm sorry I didn't come clean when we met. I think I'm still getting used to my shift in responsibilities."

He lightly tapped her shoulder. "You are a good daughter. You should feel proud."

His words were warm and comforting.

"And, Yelpers are right, you do make the best chocolate chip cookies in the area." He raised the last bite of cookie in the air in a cheers motion. "Another reason to be proud."

He had this way of making her feel special—looking past the things that most people would judge—and that was nice.

"So, I believe you owe me a rain check for coffee? Do you have time now?" he asked.

Abbey looked over at Caroline, who was nodding enthusiastically. "Go ahead, dear. I'll mind the shop."

Abbey took off her apron, folded it neatly, and placed it on the counter. "Are you sure?" she whispered as she brushed by Caroline.

Caroline whispered back, "Never been more sure."

Before leaving the bakery, Abbey went behind the case. She

took a chocolate chip cookie and put it in a small wax paper bag. She handed the bag to Jax. "For the train ride home."

He put the cookie in his backpack. "Thanks. I doubt it will make it all the way home."

As Abbey and Jax left the bakery, Caroline yelled, "Have a good time!"

Once out on the sidewalk of Main Street, Abbey said, "So, there's a little coffee shop over there." She pointed across the street to Perks. Her curls danced in the light spring breeze. "Or, if you want, we could just walk around." It was a nice sunny day, but it was a little on the chilly side. Abbey instantly regretted not bringing a coat.

Ellicott City was an old mill town only twelve miles or so from Baltimore but felt like a world away. Main Street was lined with storefronts that had been in families for generations. The wooden-framed buildings were mixed in with brick ones, and they all had one thing in common—they hadn't changed much in nearly a century. Small houses shared the short street with storefronts. It was the quintessential small town, even with white picket fences. The art of parallel parking was alive and well on Main Street as cars lined the street with barely inches in between.

"I'd be up for a walk." He looked up and down Main Street. "It looks like a postcard," he said, which were the exact words Abbey liked to use about her hometown. After a few steps, he removed the cookie from his backpack. "See, I told you it wouldn't make it all the way home." He took a bite and stopped in his tracks. "Oh, wow." With a mouth full of crumbs, he moaned slightly. "So good." They walked a few more steps, and he said, "So, from an architect to a baker of delicious chocolate chip cookies? You never cease to amaze me."

Abbey felt embarrassed, but in a pleasant way. "Baking is kind of like building—you know?"

Jax said, "Tell me more."

"Well, everything is precise. There are layers in flavors. The measurements for both need to be precise. And building a cake takes the mind of an architect to give it a solid foundation." She wrapped her arms around her body and tried to warm her exposed upper arms.

Jax stopped walking. "You must be freezing," he said. He took off his backpack and removed his coat—a short black wool one with large black buttons. Abbey feared what he was planning to do next. Surely the coat of a tall, lanky man would not fit properly over a short, fat girl. She tried to wave him off. Too late. He draped the coat over her shoulders and tugged at the lapels. "There," he said.

She took hold of the lapels and instantly drank in his sweet scent.

He put his hands firmly on each of her shoulders. "Better?" he asked.

"Yes," she said truthfully. "Thanks."

He picked up his backpack, and they continued their walk. "Of course. Now, where were we?" he asked.

To be completely honest, she had lost track of the conversation.

They took a few more steps, and he said, "So, you were telling me about how baking is like architecture. I've never thought of it that way. How did you get into it? Baking, that is?"

A calmness came over Abbey. She was typically shy and fearful of judgment, but Jax made her feel so at ease. "My dad used to have this saying: 'life is short...eat dessert first.' So, that's what we'd do. Every Wednesday night, we'd eat dessert first." She had only shared that story one other time, when she was in college, and she and her best friend, Sarah, were telling wacky stories about home life. When Abbey divulged her secret, Sarah's eyes instantly went to Abbey's waist. Sarah's "Oh, I see" said it all. Abbey looked at Jax for a reaction. And the judgment she feared was not there. So, she continued.

"My grandmother, Nona, would bake cakes, cookies, pies— something different each Wednesday, and I would help her. We'd sit around the dining room table and have dessert first. Most of the time, we wouldn't have room for a traditional dinner. We'd just have dessert."

His eyes lit up, and he said, "That must have been awesome."

"I guess it depends. My parents were pretty unconventional."

"In what way?" He seemed interested.

"My dad was an artist—he painted big canvases and murals. There's actually one here on Main Street, not too far from here." She pointed down the block.

"Really? I'd love to see it." Jax said as they strolled.

Abbey remembered when her father painted the mural. He looked like a homeless man, disheveled, specks of paint splattered on his long graying beard like a Jackson Pollock canvas. She was overweight and shy in high school at the time—a terrible combination at a time when most young girls craved attention. In home-room, Ben Dorham, who she had known since first grade—nearly all her life, turned to her and said, in a voice loud enough for the whole class to hear, "Does your dad have a ladder?" Once he had commanded everyone's attention he added, "my parents' house could use some painting." A chorus of laughter followed, and Abbey felt instant shame and humiliation.

"Your dad must have been talented and creative," Jax said.

"He was pretty special," she said, wishing she would have defended her dad the many times kids teased him. "My dad never cared about stuff. You know, material things. Once, we lived in a tent for a year." It took many years, but she had grown to appreciate what a great man and father he was. "He wanted to teach us how to survive with only a knife, water, and fire."

"That's fascinating. I don't think I've ever met anyone who did that. How'd that go over?"

"As you can imagine, at first, it was really fun. I was four, and my sister was a year younger. It was like a game—we were camping. But then we missed playing with other kids, and it got boring. Not to mention, uncomfortable. We were normal, whiny kids—not these selfless mini-me's that he thought he had created. We had been poisoned by capitalism. We wanted stuff!" She raised her finger in a mock symbol of protest.

Jax looked deep in thought, as if he was trying to imagine the family living off the grid. This eased her worry that she may be divulging too much.

"After the year was up, we moved here. I think our complaining got to him. That and my Nona's house had air conditioning. She convinced my dad to move us in with her. I think she was worried because it was time for me to start first grade. But, let me tell you, while I may have missed out on kindergarten, I can catch a trout that could feed a family of four." She pointed to her chest with her thumbs and said it with an air of pride.

There was no judgment in his broad smile. "How refreshing. Sounds very different from my childhood. I had the typical, traditional, boring family. I cannot catch a fish big enough to feed a cat."

"I know." Abbey nodded. "You always want what you don't have. As much as you think you'd like to have parents that had no rules, I grew up craving structure. I'm guessing something like your childhood," she said. "I'll bet you grew up in a family where your mom was a homemaker—" She looked him over carefully. "And president of the PTA. You had pot roast on Sundays, went to summer camp and had to be in bed by eight—in the winter months, that is. Am I right?"

"Very good. But you left out the part about the time I got the family's one and only B. It was a B plus in history when I was in middle school. My mother wouldn't leave the house for a week. She was afraid 'people knew.'" He put air quotes around the last part. "I like to refer to that as the dark ages. Shameful." He shuddered in a playful way.

Abbey laughed again. "My parents never even looked at a report card. Grades were society's judgment and oppressive means of controlling the masses." She rolled her eyes. "Whatever that means."

"What *does* that mean?" He laughed in a way that she took meant he was delighted to be in her presence and that they shared an inside joke.

Abbey stopped next to a brick building with the words "Historic Ellicott City" spray-painted on the side. "Well, here you have it. A Mickey Reilly original," she said. The mural depicted the history of the city, from its origin as a mill in 1766 to its modern-day likeness. Main Street was the exact point where the Tiber and the Patapsco Rivers met. The street's steep incline made it prone to flooding. Her father painted it as a tribute to the town and its resilient residents and business owners who had rebuilt time and time again after several floods.

Jax took it all in. "That's impressive," he said after a long and thoughtful pause.

"Yeah, I've heard they're going to tear the building down because it's been vacant for years. It used to be a bookstore, but now everyone buys books online."

The two of them walked to the front of the building. Jax peered in through the dirty glass windows. "Tear this down?" he said, as if in disbelief. Inside, you could still see the shelves where books used to be. They walked back around to the side of the building with the mural. Jax touched the old bricks. "It looks like it's still in good shape. Good foundation."

"Yeah, I know, it'd be a shame to see it go. But I hate to see it vacant too."

They made their way back to the bakery. "Thanks for showing me around," he said.

"Of course. It was my pleasure." She had never uttered a more truthful statement. She handed him his coat back, and he put it on.

He laughed slightly. "You know, when I woke up today, I had no idea I was going to see you, but I'm glad that I did."

"Yeah, me too."

He looked at his fancy watch with the smooth leather strap. "As much as I hate to say this, I've got to go. Before I go—" He took out his phone. "Let me get your number. Don't want to make that mistake again."

The two typed in each other's phone numbers into their respective contact lists. Abbey was extra careful when she did so.

"Oh, wait," Abbey said. She went to the bake case and took out a chocolate chip cookie, bagged it, and handed it to him. "One for the road."

"Thanks." He winked. He started walking away and when he reached the door, he turned toward her and said, "I'll be in touch."

There was no underestimating how much Abbey wanted to believe he was telling the truth.

• • •

When Abbey got home, she fed her mother and took her plate with microwaved frozen pizza to her room. She sat on her bed and opened her laptop. Going to Google, she typed Jackson Lawrence.

More than fifty-five million hits came up. She needed to narrow it down. Jackson Lawrence Philadelphia. Bam. Up popped pictures of an older version of Jax. Must be his father, she thought.

A headline read: "Jackson and Bunny Lawrence donate one million dollars to the Philadelphia Children's Hospital's Cancer Ward." *A million dollars, holy crap.* She clicked on the article and skimmed through it. It was from five years ago. Jax's parents, "Philadelphia's prominent couple," were the kind benefactors of state-of-the-art diagnostic phlebotomy testing equipment to aid in detecting leukemia early. She read further: "The Lawrences lost a son, Harold, to the disease in 1998." After reading the rest of the article, Abbey did the math. Jax's brother would have been thirty-three had he lived.

She went back to the search engine and typed Jackson Lawrence III Philadelphia. An image with a familiar face filled her screen. She gasped when she read the headline from last summer: "Jackson Lawrence III to wed Philadelphia Socialite Elle Franklin Thompson." Elle, with her bleached blond hair piled high on her head, sharp cheekbones, and long eyelashes, looked every bit the part of upper crust uptightness.

Abbey's heart sank. She let out a loud sigh. *Here we go again.* She took a bite of pizza. There was a numbing buzz inside her head, and her throat ached from the lump that was in it. Why did she let herself think it could happen? She looked down at her stomach, so big it stretched her sweatpants. No one will ever love a fat girl, she said to herself. As contradictory as it might seem, knowing full well that food was the enemy and that too much food had made her this way, too much food was to blame for the loneliness and low self-esteem, she kept eating—pizza slice after slice. When she was on her fifth and last piece, tears formed. Food made things better. Even if the feeling was fleeting.

She remembered the time her mother's mother, Gigi as they called her, and her dad got in a big fight. It was the summer before Abbey was to enter eighth grade. She had put on some noticeable pounds. She had puffy cheeks and dimpling skin on her thighs that were pinched by shorts that no longer fit. The family went to dinner at La Pomodoro for pizza. And Abbey had reached for the last piece of pizza only to have Gigi take her plate from her. "Haven't you had enough?" Gigi was a force to be reckoned with. Even though she stood only about four feet nine. What she lacked in height, she made up in attitude. She rarely kept her thoughts to herself. She had no filter and "spoke the bubble above her head," as her father would say. Her skin was brown and leathery from too many cigarettes and too much sun. She wore bright pink lipstick and had white hair that gave her the look of a blacklight poster.

Abbey's father took the plate from Gigi and slid it back to Abbey. "Here, eat whatever you want," he said while looking Gigi straight in the eye. Gigi then said, "You do realize you're ruining her life. Look at her." A tug-of-war ensued. Her father said, "A piece of pizza will hardly ruin her life." And then her grandmother said, "She'll get to be as big as a house. Is that what you want? You want her to be a sad, lonely girl that never gets a date?" Her father then said, "Any man worth something will love her because of her heart." And Gigi said, "Why do you let her believe in that fairy tale? It's not true, and you know it." Abbey's father's eyes grew dark in a way she'd never seen. He pounded his fists on the table. "Enough!"

They never saw Gigi after that, but her words hung around in Abbey's head forever.

While she contemplated what to do with him, her cell phone pinged, indicating she had a text. It was from Jax with two simple words: *sweet dreams.*

11

It was half past nine the next morning when Caroline sashayed into the kitchen. She walked over to the counter where Abbey was and said, "So, what do we have here?"

"A special order—chocolate on chocolate for Timmy Reynold's eighth birthday." Abbey picked up a plastic Tyrannosaurus Rex. "Dinosaurs." She put the T-Rex next to the three other plastic creatures she had bought to decorate the cake. "They are picking it up at two."

"Oh. Good." Caroline yawned as she put on her apron. "I'm getting too old for these all-nighters," she said.

Abbey tapped each round pan lightly on the counter. Satisfied the air bubbles were gone, she carried the pan to the waiting oven.

"So, did you hear from Mr. Philadelphia after he left?" Caroline walked over to the counter where Abbey was working.

"Yeah," Abbey walked back to the counter and wiped off the flour and cocoa powder that had flung out from the mixer.

"Yeah? Just Yeah? What did he say?" Caroline was acting like a giddy schoolgirl ready for the gossip.

"Sweet dreams. He texted sweet dreams." Abbey said flatly as she shrugged her shoulders.

"How sweet."

"Yeah, I guess." Abbey tried to telepathically tell Caroline to change the subject. But it wasn't working. She turned her back toward Caroline and returned to her task of baking.

"I knew it was just a matter of time before a smart fella figured out what a catch you are."

Abbey shrugged again.

"Why, I thought you'd be a bit more excited." Caroline put her hands on Abbey's shoulders and turned her around so that they were facing each other. She cocked her head and looked at Abbey. "Okay, what gives? If a man like that sent me a text like that, you'd have to pry me off the ceiling."

Abbey broke free from Caroline. "It's just..." Abbey took a deep breath. She sighed and brushed her hands of the flour into the sink. Using her apron, she wiped her hands. "I think he's engaged."

"What?" Caroline scowled. "No way. I know when a man's interested. He was *very* interested."

Abbey took her phone from her apron pocket. She typed Jax Lawrence into her search engine, and the engagement article popped up because she had looked at it so many times. "Here. See for yourself."

Caroline took the phone from Abbey and looked closely at the screen. "This doesn't mean anything." Her nose crinkled like she was smelling something bad as she read the post.

"Really? You think it doesn't?" Abbey held her hand out to take her phone back.

"There's only one way to find out." Caroline stepped away from Abbey. "Let's see here. Ah, here we go." Abbey could hear the phone dial. Before she could protest, she heard Jax's voice on the other end say, "Abbey?"

"What are you doing? Give it back." Abbey whispered, reaching for Caroline.

Caroline was just quick enough to get out of Abbey's reach. She hurried into her office. "Hello. Jax? No, it's not Abbey. It's Caroline. We met..." Caroline's voice trailed off as the office door closed.

Abbey could see into the office through a window that was open to the kitchen. Caroline's expression was very animated, and Abbey heard laughter. Abbey felt the blood leave her body. She walked to the office door and turned the handle. Locked! She knocked lightly on the door. Inside the office, Caroline waved her off before pulling the window blinds down.

Abbey stood next to the door. Her heart pounded through her neck. She pressed her ear near the door's edge, hoping to hear something but only could hear muffled sounds. Within minutes, the doorknob clicked, and Abbey pulled away. Caroline walked out of the office. "What a charming gentleman."

"Well?" Abbey asked. Not sure she wanted to know the answer.

"Well, what?" Caroline looked confused.

"Is he, or isn't he?" Abbey barely had the courage to ask.

Caroline still looked confused.

"Engaged? Is he engaged?"

Caroline bit her lip. "Oh, that." She paused. "I forgot to ask."

"What? I thought that was the reason you were calling him."

"Yes, it was, but he's so charming. I got distracted. You should hear what he had to say about you."

"Me?" Now Caroline had Abbey's full attention. "What did he say?" Abbey's emotions fluctuated between being excited and worried.

"He said he really enjoys talking with you. Said he feels like he could talk to you for hours."

Abbey's heart beat faster as her guard softened. "He said that?"

"Yes. I think he's really smitten." Caroline handed the phone back to Abbey.

Abbey was relieved, but the worry wouldn't go away. "How do we find out if he's still engaged?"

"Maybe you can ask him. He'll be here for dinner Friday."

"What?" Panic set in.

"Oh, you can thank me later."

"Wait a minute. What...how...? Give a girl time to prepare before you unload something like that." Abbey stared at Caroline in disbelief.

"He said he's coming back to Maryland to look at another building. And I said, 'Oh, well, you'll have to come for dinner.' That's what a proper lady would say."

"Is it really?" Abbey caught her breath. And then a terrorizing thought occurred to her. "He did know you were inviting him to have dinner with me ... not with you. Didn't he?"

Caroline laughed. "Of course! I said, 'Since you'll be so close, you must have dinner with Abbey.' At least I'm pretty sure I said you." Caroline looked like she was recounting the conversation in her head. "Listen, honey, I'm all about the girl code. I wouldn't steal your man. Besides, I don't think I could. He seemed thrilled. Like I said, he likes you." Caroline reached her arms out to Abbey, and Abbey allowed her to pull her close. "He likes you, and why shouldn't he?" She stroked Abbey's hair.

Abbey could think of a million reasons why he shouldn't. Her phone vibrated in her hand. Abbey pulled away from Caroline and looked at the screen. "It's him!"

"Okay, just breathe." Caroline coached deep breaths in and out.

Abbey tapped accept and put the phone to her ear. She smelled Aqua Net hairspray as Caroline pressed her head close to Abbey so that she could hear the conversation as well. "Hello," she said hesitantly.

"Abbey? It's me, Jax." His voice was smooth, like a radio announcer.

"Yes, hi, Jax." The two women with the phone between them

bobbed their heads in unison.

"I don't know if you heard, but I think Caroline invited me to dinner this Friday." He let out a little laugh.

"She was just mentioning that."

"Well, I hope it's okay. I don't want to impose. But truthfully, I was going to call you later today to see if you wanted to get together."

Abbey's insides felt like a bowl of soft chocolate mousse. "I'm so glad you'll be here again. I'd love to see you." She managed to say.

"Maybe you can recommend a place we can go for dinner."

Abbey thought hard about her response. There was little chance she could find someone to stay with her mother on short notice. Betty typically had plans to do karaoke at the Watering Hole on Fridays. And even if she didn't, she had been asking Betty to help out a lot lately. So, Abbey decided not even to ask. Her sister, Penny, yeah, right, sure. She'd never do it—not on short notice. Actually, probably not even on long notice. "How about you come to my house? I can cook." She worried that it seemed quite forward, and she didn't want to give him the wrong impression. "It's just that I have my mom," she added as she waited for a response.

"Oh, right, sure. I forgot you take care of your mom. That works for me. I'm not going to turn down a home-cooked meal."

Phew!

"So, what time works for you? I should have my site visit wrapped up by five-thirty."

"How about six?" Abbey bit her thumb nail as she spoke.

"Perfect. Text me the address." There was a pause, and then he said, "I'm looking forward to it."

A warm feeling came over Abbey. It was the feeling of hope.

Caroline peeled herself away from Abbey. "Yay!" she said, punching her fist in the air. She reached for Abbey's hand and jumped up and down, taking Abbey for the ride. The kitchen of the bakery turned into a dance-off as the two women shimmied and twisted.

Abbey was enveloped in a joyful feeling she did not recognize. And then reality set in. She let go of Caroline's hand and stopped dancing. "Wait, he's coming Friday? That's three days from now. What am I going to make?"

Caroline placed her hand up. "Just calm down. I've got a chicken pot pie recipe that is to die for. I'll find it for you. You use puff pastry on the top." She shifted to a sheepish look. "But be careful, he may want to jump your bones—it helped me get husband two and Leo." She made the sign of the cross. "God rest his soul," they said in somber unison.

"So, wear something that's easy to get out of," Caroline added.

12

At exactly five fifty-nine on Friday, the doorbell rang.

Walking to the front door, Abbey ran her hands down her skirt in an attempt to smooth out any wrinkles. She started to second-guess wearing her favorite boho-style tiered black maxi dress with embroidered hot pink trim and long pink tassels that hung from the collar to near her waist—the one that Caroline had once commented made her look thin. A quick check in the hallway mirror didn't increase her self-confidence as much as she'd hoped. But there was no time to change.

When she reached the door, she drew in a deep breath and slowly let it out. Her palm was so sweaty it was hard to grip the doorknob. She opened the door and saw the handsome man—as dreamy as ever—carrying a huge bouquet wrapped in twine ribbon, green tissue, and cellophane.

The sight of the flowers made her let out a long and audible swoon.

"These are for you," he said. He handed the bouquet to her.

Was that a little quiver in his voice? Or more likely a quiver in her hearing.

Abbey peeled away the tissue just enough to see that they were roses—too many to count quickly, but she guessed at least two dozen in many different colors—shades of pink, white, yellow, peach, white with red rims, light purple, and even red.

"I wasn't sure what color was your favorite, so I said, 'give me some of these and some of these, and some of these,'" he said, pointing to different flowers.

She swooned again even harder. Abbey lifted the bouquet to her nose and breathed in. They smelled like a garden on a spring day. "Oh my God. They are beautiful. Thank you so much." No one had ever given her flowers, let alone roses, before. It was a new and slightly uncomfortable feeling having someone pay this much attention to her, but a feeling she imagined she could get used to. Cradling the flowers like a cherished baby, she said, "Come on in."

They walked into the living room where her mother was sitting in her chair facing the TV. The Jeopardy theme was coming from the TV at least three levels louder than it needed to be. Millie did not take her eyes off the set when Abbey and Jax entered the room. Abbey walked over to her mother and took the remote that was in Millie's lap. With a swift move, she muted the TV. This got her mother's attention.

Millie looked up at her daughter, and her eyes widened. "Did someone die?"

"What?" Abbey said.

"Are those from a funeral?" Millie asked, looking directly at the flowers.

"These?" Abbey shifted her look to the bouquet. "No, he brought them for me. Do you remember I told you that a friend was coming over for dinner tonight? This is Jax Lawrence." Abbey smiled when she gestured toward Jax.

Millie let out an audible gasp.

Oh God. "Momma, what is it?

"You didn't tell me he was coming."

"But I did. Remember." *Oh, please don't do this. Not tonight.* Abbey bit her bottom lip while she decided how to continue.

"Sir Paul McCartney. It is a true honor and privilege." Millie reached for his hand and, staying in her chair, bowed.

"No, Momma, this is Jax, not Paul. Jax Lawrence. Remember the friend I told you about?" Abbey turned her attention to Jax. "I'm sorry."

He smiled and laughed a little. "No problem. I get that a lot." He turned his attention to Millie. "It's lovely to meet you, Mrs. Reilly." He took her hand and lightly kissed the back of it.

"Paul, do you know Alex Trebek?" Millie asked.

"I know he was the host of Jeopardy," he said, thankfully playing along.

Millie looked him up and down. "Have you ever met him?"

"No. I'm afraid I never got the chance."

"Oh, okay." Millie then turned and faced the TV again, which was still on mute.

"Dinner will be ready in a few minutes," Abbey said. She handed the remote back to her mother.

"This is the iconic building where John Lennon was shot," the TV shouted.

"What is the Dakota?" Millie said.

"Momma, listen to me." Abbey got very close to her mother. "Can you look at me when I talk to you?" Evidently, the answer was no, so Abbey continued anyway. "Dinner will be ready soon, so don't get too caught up in the game," she said. "I set the table on the sunporch. We aren't going to eat here." It was as if she was speaking a foreign language. She got no reaction from her mother.

Abbey turned to Jax and said, "Why don't you have a seat over there on the couch." She motioned to the couch next to where her mother was sitting. "I'll take these to the kitchen and check on dinner," she said.

"Okay, sure." Jax took a seat on the couch as directed.

"What are legumes?" Millie's voice trailed away as Abbey walked the short distance from the living room to the kitchen.

Once in the kitchen, she found a vase under the sink. She unwrapped the flowers from their twine ribbon and cellophane swaddling. A man had given her flowers. Not just flowers, roses. She let that sink in. Would an engaged man make such a thoughtful effort? She couldn't get that article out of her head. Or the picture of Jax, the same man that was now in her house, the same man that brought her these beautiful flowers, smiling widely with Miss Perfect Blond Cutesy face. She needed to find the right time to ask him and accept the truth, even if it was hard to hear.

While she was in the kitchen, she checked the pot pie in the oven. The golden-brown crust signaled it was done. With two mitted hands, she took the piping hot pie from the oven. She put it on the stove. It smelled divine, a mixture of chicken, peas, pearl onions, and carrots in a rich creamy sauce wrapped inside buttery crispy pastry like a delicious present. The pie glistened like the sun's rays melting on a lake at sundown.

Pleased with the bake, she carried it to the sunporch where she had set a table Martha Stewart would envy. She covered the glass top wicker table with a white tablecloth she crocheted in ninth grade Home Ec class—the only one she could find, and probably the only one they ever owned. She dug out her grandmother's bone china, the set with the purple and yellow pansy pattern, and carefully placed each plate next to matching yellow cloth napkins. The sterling silver place settings had taken nearly an hour to polish off the tarnish after years of hiding in the bottom drawer of the buffet sideboard. She wanted Jax to think she had some class because she believed it mattered.

She put the pie down in the middle of the table. She then filled the gold-rimmed crystal wine glasses with wine from a bottle of Grenache that Caroline gave her for Christmas and was being saved for a special occasion just like this. Tonight, she knew she needed a little wine to loosen up—tannins be damned. Satisfied, she believed she may just pull this night off.

When she returned to the kitchen, Jax was standing there, wedged up against the stove and sink. He looked so cool, one elbow leaning just slightly on the counter. "I came to see if you needed help," he said.

"Was Jeopardy too much?"

He laughed. "No. I really wanted to spend time with you."

Gosh. So sweet! Then reality would set in—the dreaded engagement announcement headline and photo were etched in her brain.

"Something sure smells good," he said.

"I hope you like chicken pot pie."

"Who doesn't?" he said. "I don't cook for myself much, so honestly, anything that doesn't come in a takeout container would be good for me."

Figaro approached the kitchen entrance with SuzyQ firmly in his jowls.

Oh, no! Abbey cringed on the inside and tried hard not to display what she felt on the outside.

"Oh, you have a kitty," Jax said. He appeared in awe as he watched Figaro maneuver carefully around the corner of the stove so as not to bash SuzyQ's head. "Impressive," Jax added.

Yeah, that's not the half of it. Abbey went on the defensive. There was no way a cat was going to ruin her evening. "Come on, buddy," she said calmly. She reached and tugged at one of SuzyQ's leg's trying to pry it away from Figaro.

Figaro did not cooperate. Instead, he tightened his clamp and let out a feral, yet muffled, yowl.

"Figaro, come on. Let go." Her voice was stern, like she was talking to a willful child. Figaro yowled louder, so Abbey decided on a different approach. She tightened her grasp on SuzyQ's paw and dragged Figaro out of the kitchen and out of sight. She then let go of SuzyQ and said through gritted teeth, "Knock it off." Figaro shifted in reverse, moved slightly forward at an angle before shifting in reverse again to avoid coming in contact with Abbey's reach.

Abbey returned to the kitchen. "He likes to get in the way when I cook," she said in an attempt to ward off any weird thoughts Jax had in his head—although, from his expression—it was too late.

She washed her hands and dried them on a tea towel before hanging it neatly back on the oven door handle. Then she turned to Jax, her gnawing need to know if he was engaged raged in her head.

Jax looked up at her and his smile faded. "What's wrong?" he asked.

"Are you engaged?" she blurted out. The comment fell hard and fast, like a missile.

"What?" He looked in shock. "No. Not anymore. How did you—"

"I googled you," she said. She was both relieved and nervous.

"Oh." He let out a loud sigh. "Yeah. The internet. Look, this is the truth. I was engaged—last summer. But it didn't feel right, so I called it off. There's way more to that story, but I'll save it for another day." He reached for her hand and locked his fingers in hers. "For now, just know, I'm glad I did call off the engagement. If I had gone through with it, I wouldn't be here. Now."

"I feel so stupid for asking. It's just—"

"You shouldn't feel stupid," he interrupted. "I'm the one who should feel stupid for not saying anything." His look turned sheepish. "I googled you too."

Oh. Dear. God. "You googled me?" The internal cringe factor she was feeling was off the charts. "I guess that's only fair." She felt sick inside, not sure what he'd find. Was her high school yearbook online? She hoped not. Frizzy mopped, braces-faced, flabby

Abbey. *Dear Lord, please, please, please,* she begged.

He looked her deep in the eyes and said, "I wanted to find out all I could about this amazing, beautiful, architect turned baker." One of his eyebrows raised. "Allen Anderson & Associates Junior Architect of the Year."

Phew!

"I'm sorry. I probably should have told you I was engaged. Emphasis on was. Believe me, I was planning to," he said.

She did believe him.

He continued. "You just don't know when's the right time to bring up that conversation. Seemed a little inappropriate when I was showing you the office—and when we went for a walk the other day."

Abbey nodded.

"You have to believe me when I say I will never hurt you intentionally. I'm not that kind of guy." He kept her hand in his, brought it to his lips. His kiss was light but meant so much. She didn't want to let go. Could they just stay like this, maybe forever?

Abbey wrapped her other arm around her waist and secretly pinched herself to see if she was dreaming. And was grateful to feel the pinches. "And I'm very glad Caroline called you and asked you to come to dinner. I don't think I'd ever get the nerve to do that."

Jax smiled. "I'm glad she did too. Remind me to thank her." As he let go of her hand, their eyes met, and their stares lingered.

Abbey leaned closer to him, closed her eyes, and puckered her lips.

"Where's dinner? I'm hungry." Millie's loud voice broke the spell. Abbey opened her eyes and saw her mother leaning on her walker and standing at the entrance to the kitchen. Sigh. Abbey smiled at Jax. And he smiled politely back. The kiss, if there was one, would have to wait.

"Dinner's this way," Abbey said, walking to the room adjacent to the kitchen. They called it the sunporch because it was encased in floor to ceiling glass windows on three of the four sides. Abbey led the way, being sure to walk slowly so that her mother and Jax weren't too far behind.

Upon entering the room, Abbey let out a gasp. "Oh, dear Lord, no!" she said. She covered her eyes and hoped she wouldn't start crying. There, sitting in the middle of the table, like a centerpiece, was Figaro. His pink tongue was lapping up the pools of melted butter on top of the pot pie.

Abbey removed her hands from her eyes. "Get down!" she screamed.

Figaro looked up at her. In an act of defiance, he licked his lips and began washing his face with a paw.

Abbey clapped her hands loudly. With gritted teeth, she said, "I said, get down!"

Figaro stopped licking. For a second, he stared back at Abbey in an incredulous sort of way.

Abbey lunged toward the cat. Figaro ran to the far side of the table just out of reach—knocking over two wine glasses in his path. He attempted to jump down and make a clean getaway, but instead his back claw got caught in the crocheted tablecloth. He let out a shrieking, "Meeeeow!" As he tried to free himself, he continued to yowl and hiss, sounding more like a feral cat than one that sleeps under the down covers of a king-size bed. Each move he took tugged the tablecloth a little more in his direction. One final tug freed his claw. A black-and-white streak raced past them and out of the room. The spilled wine puddled on the floor.

All the planning, thinking through every detail, and now dinner was officially ruined by a defiant, ill-mannered cat. *Don't cry. Don't cry.* It was too late. Tears streamed down Abbey's cheeks.

She turned to Jax and her mother.

"Where should I sit?" Millie said.

13

With her hands on her hips, Abbey assessed the damage. "It looks like a murder took place."

"Figaro in the sunporch with a sharp claw," Jax said with a hearty laugh and a nod to the guessing game of Clue.

Upon hearing Jax's reaction, the tenseness in Abbey's body melted away. Even Millie laughed.

He placed his hand lightly on Abbey's shoulder and rubbed it gently. "It'll be fine," he said in a kind way, as if he could read her mind. "It's not the end of the world."

Abbey sighed. "What are we going to eat?" She thought about what she had in the pantry—some popcorn, Cheez-Its, and a half-eaten bag of peanut M&M's.

"That's what Yelp is for." Jax pulled out his phone and selected the Yelp app. "Step aside." He spread his long, lean legs in a wide stance and shook his hand a few times, flexing his fingers. "I am an expert in Yelp. It was certainly right about your cookies."

Thank God.

A few clicks and a scroll later and he said, "The Great Wok gets an impressive four point six stars out of five and is within point two miles—1161 Main Street. *And* they deliver."

Abbey looked him in the eye and said, "Thank you for being so understanding."

"What?" He shrugged. "These things happen."

Abbey believed Jax was just being nice and that these things rarely happened in his world. But it didn't matter. All that mattered was that he didn't run for the door at the sight of a cat centerpiece. It would have given him an excuse, and she wouldn't have blamed him. It comforted her that he seemed to genuinely want to be there.

After placing an order for three egg rolls, shrimp fried rice, sweet and sour pork, and cashew chicken, Abbey helped her mother back to her chair in the living room. "Here, I think you can catch the end of Jeopardy until the food comes." She turned the TV on and handed her mother the remote.

Returning to the sunporch, she saw Jax stooping near the mess on the floor. He put a cautionary hand out. "Be careful," he said. "I don't want you to get cut." He was using a napkin to pick up the large pieces of broken glass and pile them into one area of the floor. "If you tell me where I can find a broom and a dustpan, I'll sweep this up."

"In the closet next to the refrigerator." She pointed toward the kitchen. "Here, I'll show you." Before walking into the kitchen, Abbey looked down at the dish of pot pie. There was a gash down the center of the flaky top crust where Figaro had tried to get to the chicken pieces below. "Well, by the looks of things, Figaro thought it was good." She picked up the pie plate, which was cool by now, and carried it into the kitchen.

Jax followed behind. "I don't think I mentioned this, but my grandmother would make chicken pot pie on Sundays," he said. "When I was a kid, we'd go over there, have a late lunch and watch the Eagles." With the broom and dustpan in hand, the two walked back to the crime scene.

"Was your grandma a good cook?"

"The best." A fond smile filled his face. He held the dustpan as she swept.

"What was the best thing she made?"

He laughed a little. "She could make mashed potatoes like no

114

one else. Hmm-mm. I get hungry just thinking about Sunday dinners." His smile told her his grandmother was probably just like her Nona. "I would take a mound this high"—he exaggerated with his free hand— "and my brother would complain that I wasn't leaving any for him."

Abbey hesitated before she said, "I read that you lost your brother. When I was doing my internet research." She hoped she sounded as full of compassion as she felt. "I'm sorry."

"Yeah, that was tough." He sighed loudly. "He was the kind of kid that could do anything. Much different from me. He played baseball, basketball, and was smart as anything. But then he got sick. And you know what? He was really brave. I was the older brother ... supposed to be the brave one. But I was a mess. Really scared. He told me it would be okay. And, for the most part, it has been."

Jax carefully lifted the dustpan full of broken glass so as not to let a shard slip out and followed Abbey into the kitchen.

She opened the cabinet door underneath the sink where there was a trash can. After he emptied the dustpan, she turned toward Jax and said, "Do you ever wonder what your life would be like now if that never happened?"

Jax smiled and shrugged. "If he never got sick? Yeah, sure, all the time. All the time." He seemed to be reminding himself of the what-ifs. "He would have taken over the business, and then I could have followed my dreams."

"And what would that be?"

He bit his lip. A smile filled his face, and he brushed his hair with his hand. "You're going to laugh."

She reached out a hand and touched his wrist. "No, I won't."

He looked at her again. "I've never said this to anyone."

She smiled back in an encouraging way. "Go on. I won't judge."

"I can't believe I'm saying this."

"Go on," she said.

He took a deep breath. "Okay, I've always wanted to open a record store. You know, one with old vinyl records—the kind that have grooves and sometimes skip. I love them." A look of pure pleasure filled his face. "Nothing beats the sound of an old record—no tinny auto tunes—just real talent."

Abbey smiled and giggled a little.

"See, I told you. You think I'm nuts."

"No, I don't actually." She took him by the hand. "Come with me," she said. They walked past the living room to the grand staircase. "Let's go upstairs."

"Oh," he said with a raised eyebrow. "I see talking about my failed ambitions is a real turn on."

Abbey blushed a little. She could see how he'd get that impression. It was endearing and a tad bit flattering he'd think she was leading him upstairs to rip his clothes off—even if the thought had occurred to her over and over. "While it is a turn on, that's not why I'm taking you upstairs. There's something I want to show you."

The old wooden stairs creaked as they stepped on each one.

The upstairs bedrooms weren't used much these days except for storage. She led him down a small hallway to what used to be her parents' bedroom. Flicking on the overhead light cast little more than a shadow in the dimly lit room.

In the center of the room was a king-size bed that hadn't been slept in since her father died a year earlier. The dresser next to the bed was made of light pine and one he'd built with his own hands and tools. Even though it was empty, it still served a purpose because it was a piece of him.

She pointed to the corner of the room where there were three gray plastic milk crates filled with albums.

"Is that what I think it is?"

She nodded. "My father's collection."

Jax walked over to the crates, and Abbey followed. The first record he picked up was *the Beatles White Album*. His hand ran along the smooth cardboard surface. "Wow," he said. "A classic. May I?" He gestured to removing the record from the cover.

"Sure," she said. Abbey remembered how her father treated them like treasures. He'd wear white gloves when he removed them from their protective sleeves, blowing off any dust before putting them on the turntable.

Jax took the record out and handed the cover to her. He held the record like he was looking at a rare gem, with the same admiration her father used to have. "Wow," he said. "I feel like I'm holding a piece of art." He took the cover from Abbey and carefully slid the record back inside. He put the White Album down and picked up the next one. His expression indicated he was familiar with the record as his hand ran over the back cover of *Abbey Road*.

"Abbey?" he said, slightly in awe. You could see he was putting it all together as he smiled broadly. "Ah, now I see. That's why you spell your name with an *e*."

She nodded.

"I take it your dad was a Beatles fan."

"You got that right. *Abbey Road* was his favorite."

"Mine, too." He ran his finger down the back of the album cover and along each song title. "And don't tell me your middle name is Road."

She laughed. "No. Close. It's Rose. I think my mom had some influence in that decision."

Jax picked up the record and flipped it over to the front cover. A look of astonishment crossed his face. "You've got to be kidding," he said.

"It's real," she said.

On the front cover of the album, in the bright blue sky, was the signature of Paul McCartney. "It was my dad's prized possession," she said.

"I'll bet. How'd he get that?"

"He was studying abroad at Oxford when Abbey Road came out. Sixty—" She thought, making sure she'd get the year right.

"Sixty-nine," Jax said.

"Yes, sixty-nine. Well, when the record came out, he played it over and over. And you know, the Beatles had broken up by then."

Jax nodded.

"So, he heard that Paul was recording a new record at Apple—"

"*McCartney*—his first solo," he said.

"Yes, exactly. And he skipped class for days just to camp out at Apple in the hopes of seeing Paul come or go. And one day he did see him. Linda too, actually." She shrugged. "My dad, well, you'd have to know him. He really wasn't afraid of anything. One day, a shiny blue-gray Aston Martin with tags that read: 64 MAC pulled up. My father recognized the car from seeing it in tabloid magazines. So, he positioned himself next to the door to Apple. And when Paul got out of the car, he just walked up to him, took the record out and asked him to sign it."

"And he did."

"Yep. He did."

"That's amazing." Jax shook his head in disbelief.

"Yeah. He wouldn't play this one"—she gestured to the record in Jax's hands— "after that...ever. And even bought another copy so that he could play it. It's down there in one of the bins."

He carefully put Abbey Road back in the crate. "Geez, you have a gold mine here." Among all the Beatles records were also The Who, Pink Floyd, Zeppelin—all of the great classic rock acts from the late sixties and early seventies.

The first album in the second crate—Springsteen's *Born To Run*—seemed to touch an emotion. He lifted the album and turned the cover toward Abbey. "The way your dad felt about the Beatles is how I feel about this guy," he said. "Philly's close enough to Jersey, you know?"

Abbey nodded. "I like him too."

"Have you ever seen him?"

She shook her head.

"Oh, you have to. His shows are amazing."

"I'll bet."

"I've seen him probably twenty times. Just amazing." He thumbed through the next several albums—all of them Springsteen—and looked Abbey in the eye. "To think, I almost didn't mention how much I love vinyl."

"Why?"

"I don't know. I guess I'm kind of embarrassed. Who aspires to sell something that has no real market?"

"Who says there's no market?" Abbey asked sincerely. She had grown up surrounded by an appreciation for music, and she heard lately, there was a trend toward vinyl records.

"Well, my parents, for one."

"Okay, and..."

"Look, I'm not kidding anyone, I make a very comfortable living running our family's company. I'd have to sell a ton of records to make a living."

Abbey nodded. "Happiness is worth something, isn't it? I mean, more than material things."

Jax nodded, but only slightly. "I guess." A look of sadness crossed his face. "I know me, I'm just not brave enough to pull the trigger." He returned to the record stack, thumbing through until he stopped. "Wait, what do we have here?" He removed a photo that must have gotten stuck between *Born in the USA* and Jimi Hendrix's *Electric Ladyland*. He looked down at the photo and over toward Abbey. A boyish smile filled his face. "Is that you?" He turned the photo around and pointed to a little girl, about four or five, with curly red hair, wearing a rainbow-colored tie-dyed shirt and clinging to a man with unkempt hair and a bushy beard wearing the same rainbow-colored tie-dyed shirt.

Abbey took the photo from him. It had yellowed with age. Taken with a small, square gray camera that had cubed flash bulbs that would blind her for a few seconds and make everyone's eyes red in the picture. She remembered how much she loved the photo, and in it, how much she wanted to be just like her dad. "Yeah, that's me. And my dad."

"Let me see." Jax reached for the photo and studied it. "What a cute little girl."

Abbey smiled. The little girl in the photo was round and had chubby cheeks and legs. Her memory flooded to a simpler time—before the bullying and before she learned how to hate her body. Young Abbey was carefree and happy, a much different version than the person she was now. As much as she wanted to go back and whisper in young Abbey's ear and tell her she was amazing, and to not let what others say matter so much, she knew she could not. Maybe that would have eroded the negative voice that plays in a loop in her head.

He looked at the photo some more. "Your dad must have been a great guy."

She nodded.

"I'm sure you miss him." She nodded again. Fearing she'd start to cry, she said nothing. Jax caressed her shoulder. "I'm sure you do."

There was a long, awkward pause where it seemed as if neither knew what to say or do next. Should she make the first move? She couldn't read his signals. She licked her lips in an effort to send him a signal, but it appeared to be too subtle for him. Abbey started to lean in and pucker up when the sound of the doorbell broke the mood.

She put the photo back in the milk crate. "Come on, seems that dinner is here."

"Good thing, cuz I'm starving," he said.

• • •

Two hours later, half empty carryout containers littered the sunporch table, and Millie was snoring loudly in the living room. Abbey reached for a fortune cookie. "Here," she said, handing it to Jax.

Jax took the cookie from the plastic wrapper. The cookie made a click sound when he snapped it in half and revealed a white strip of paper. His eyebrows arched, and his eyes brightened as he read the fortune. "Perfect." He folded the paper up and put it in his upper pocket.

"What did it say?" Abbey reached her hand out to request the fortune.

"I can't read it out loud, or else it won't come true."

"I've never heard that," she said with a frown.

"Oh, it's true. And I want this to come true, so I'm not going to ruin it. Okay, now, your turn. But keep it to yourself."

Abbey reached for the last cookie. Jax made a drumroll sound with his fingers on the table as she took the cookie from the wrapper and snapped it open. Inside the white strip of paper read: "Nothing is impossible with a willing heart." It was the hopeful news she wanted to hear. Instantly, she started to overthink it. Did it mean his heart had to be willing or hers? Hers certainly was. She sighed, "Okay this one is good."

Jax stopped his drumroll and put one finger to his lips. His smile made her want the night to never end. He reached his hand across the table and laced his fingers in hers. "This has been fun."

Abbey knew she was blushing when she said, "I'm so glad you came."

"Me too." He looked at his watch. "I hate to do this, but I have an early meeting tomorrow morning. Let me help you clean up... again," he said with a laugh. He stood up and started to clear the plates from the table.

Abbey stood and took the plate from Jax's hand. She placed it back on the table. "No, no. I got this. You go ahead. Let me show you out."

When she got to the front door, she opened it and said, "thank you for coming."

"Of course, it was my pleasure. But—" He raised an eyebrow. "You still owe me chicken pot pie."

"You got it. Next time, no paw prints." She opened the door.

He nodded. He had a satisfied look on his face. Before stepping outside, he said, "Here." He put a piece of paper in her palm and closed it. "Read it after I leave—but to yourself—not out loud." He put a finger to his lips and said the last part in a whisper. "Until next time..." He leaned forward and kissed her on the forehead. Even though it wasn't the passionate kiss she'd hoped for, she was not disappointed. It was a sweet and perfect gesture to end a sweet and perfect night.

She was sure she was going to go limp from melting on the spot. She savored the moment as long as she could without turning it awkward. He turned and walked onto the porch and down the steps toward his car. As much as she wanted to call out to him and ask him to stay, she did not.

Abbey shut the door and peered through the window until Jax's car backed down the driveway and out of sight. She unfolded her hand and revealed the white strip of paper that Jax had placed in it. It was his fortune from earlier in the evening, which read "All you need is love." It was as perfect as he said it was.

14

Abbey was still on cloud nine the next day after her shift at the bakery. She hadn't heard from Jax, but she had a good feeling that she would. Her fears were diminishing as she spent more time with him, but there still was some smoldering doubt that things would blow up in her face—and not in a good way. When she turned the corner of her street, she noticed her sister's car in the driveway. She braced herself even though she wasn't ready for Penny to ruin her mood for whatever reason. Before opening the door, she decided to keep the news of Jax to herself. She turned the knob and heard the screams of Brandon and Kayley, her nephew and niece. "Aunt Abbey!" Brandon ran over to her and wrapped his little arms around her midsection. Abbey tussled his hair. "Hey, there, buddy. How's pre-school?"

"Okay," he said.

"You got a girlfriend yet?"

"Ew. No."

"Ew." Kayley scrunched her nose up. "Gross."

"Guess what?" Abbey said.

"What?"

"What?" Chimed in Kayley.

"I brought chocolate chip cookies from the bakery." Abbey raised a bakery bag high in the air.

"Yay!" Brandon jumped up and down.

"No cookies till later." Penny's voice was stern.

"C'mon, Mommy, please," Kayley whined.

"How about I wrap some up for you to take home?" Abbey said.

"Okay!" Brandon said cheerfully.

"But I want one now." Kayley rubbed her eyes as she started to cry.

Abbey mouthed "sorry" to Penny and then walked to the kitchen. She found two Ziploc bags and was about to put a cookie in each bag when Penny appeared. "Sorry about that. Hope I didn't cause too much trauma."

"You know four-year-olds. Everything is drama," Penny said.

Yes, indeed, but the drama wasn't limited to four-year-olds. At thirty-two, Abbey's sister Penny never grew out of her dramatic phase. Penny and Abbey were completely different, as if they had come from two totally different parents and grew up in two totally different homes. Penny had long perfectly straight hair dyed blond with dimensional highlights she touched up in the salon monthly so her naturally dark brown roots never showed. She was tall and slender and always dressed impeccably—everything was always matchy-matchy—the ribbon holding her ponytail always matched her clothing and jewelry would be themed depending on the color or style of her outfit. Today, Penny had on her uniform of a suburban Maryland soccer mom—a matching black silk-blend sweat ensemble with raised black velour leopard print that was only obvious in certain light, a big gold zipper and oversize big puffy cuffs at the sleeves and ankles which reeked of either expensive designer or trendy knock off. And was, no doubt, impractical for actually sweating in. The dangling gold leopard-shaped earrings with finely painted black splotches and eerie white fangs and her leopard-print patterned Kate Spade Keds were a dead giveaway that she was not planning to exercise today. Penny had inherited their mother's ability to eat anything and not gain weight. Metabolism, like everything else that was unfair in life, seemed to be inherited. Suffice it to say, Penny was the lucky penny of the family—pun intended.

"So, changing the subject," Penny said, "Mom said you had a friend here last night. A *guy* friend." She leaned in close on the kitchen counter. "Come on. Spill it."

"Yeah. A friend. Jax. Jax is his name."

"Well, so, what's the deal?" Penny eyed her sister to see if she could tell something that Abbey wasn't mentioning.

"He's a guy I met at Camille's bachelorette party when I went to Philadelphia a few weeks ago."

Penny frowned. "Philadelphia?"

"Yes. He owns a commercial real estate company there." Abbey was bragging, just a little, but she felt proud. And it was about time she had something to brag to her sister about.

"He lives in Philadelphia? Do you really think that's smart? I mean, dating someone that lives in Philadelphia?"

"We aren't really dating." Then she added in a faint, yet hopeful voice, "Not really. Not yet."

"Yet?" Penny scoffed. "What does that mean?"

"It means that maybe we will. I hope we will." Her voice trailed off at the end.

Penny looked at Abbey in disbelief. "Have you lost your mind?"

Abbey swallowed hard. "No. I haven't," she said—words she didn't even believe. As much as she hated to say it, maybe Penny was right.

"You have a job here." She motioned toward the living room, her ponytail high on her head bobbed when she spoke. "And, well, dating someone who lives in another state seems pretty irresponsible."

"Why do you have to do this?" Abbey asked. Penny's obnoxious and selfish protest about Jax was not a surprise. It was exactly how Abbey had played the conversation out in her head before she entered the home. Abbey thought back to a time when she and Penny were young. Penny idolized her. But that all changed in the cafeteria on Penny's first day of high school. Abbey saved her sister a place at the table where she was eating. "Over here," she called and waved to Penny, as she had done every year before. She knew how scary the first day of school could be, and the first day of high school in particular. Abbey could still remember the dismissive look Penny gave her before she joined her new friends. Penny joined the cool kids' club—a club that never offered membership to Abbey. After that, their relationship became more and more strained—maybe because Abbey was jealous and maybe because Penny was embarrassed—for whatever reason, Abbey was never again the idolized big sister.

Normally, Abbey would end the conversation by walking away, but this time was different. This time, Abbey was angry.

"Do what?" Penny said, full of indignation. "What exactly are you accusing me of doing?"

She turned to Penny and said, "Why can't you just be happy for me?"

Penny's lips formed a tight, thin line. "What? What do you mean?" she snarled. "I would be happy for you if you found someone. Here." She pointed her finger down to emphasize the word "here." "Nearby. Someone who didn't interfere with what you promised Dad and me." Penny had this way of looking even more indignant than she sounded. She crossed her arms. "I think it's a stupid idea—and pretty selfish, I might add—for you to date some guy who lives oh, let me see, more than a hundred miles away when you promised, promised Dad on his deathbed that you would take care of our mother because you ... you ... I have..."

"Just say it. You have a life, and I don't," Abbey said. She felt rage inside as the words came out.

"Stop putting words in my mouth. That's not what I mean."

"What *do* you mean?"

"All I'm saying is that you have a job here, and Mom needs you here. Someone has to do it." Penny uncrossed her arms and shook her finger in Abbey's face as she scolded. "This is your job, Abbey. You knew it when you agreed to it."

"Why does it have to all fall on me?" Abbey asked on the verge of tears. She hated confrontation—and most especially, fighting with her sister. But that's all they seemed to do lately.

"Because you're her daughter." Penny stated the obvious.

"*We're*—we're her daughters. Both of us." The words were coming out of Abbey's mouth faster than she could process them in her brain.

"Okay. Here we go. The guilt trip. Really, Abbey?" Botox had frozen Penny's eyebrows into a look of surprise no matter how red her face got. "Huh," Penny huffed. "I thought you were better than that."

"All I'm saying," Abbey continued, "is why does it all have to fall on me? Why can't you come over for more than an hour once a month."

"I am not having this conversation with you, Abbey. Not now. You play the victim so well."

"That's rich coming from you," Abbey growled back. Tears had given way to rage. How dare Penny? For a year now, Abbey had cared for their mother only occasionally asking for Penny's help.

Penny's eyes were dark and steely. "I'm not going to do this with you, Abbey, not now, not ever. If you need a break, hire a sitter. But don't put your problems on me. You see I've got my hands full. In case you thought of anyone but yourself for just one minute, I am raising two kids—just to remind you."

"Hire someone? With what?" Abbey's heart was beating faster and faster. "Look around, Penny. This is all there is. Mom lives off of social security. Betty gets paid by the state. Because we lived like a bunch of hippies, they didn't have any savings, let alone a retirement plan." Abbey took a deep breath before continuing. "Do you think I enjoy working at the bakery? No, I do it because we need money. *We* need money to eat and to keep the lights on." Abbey looked away. "Ungrateful," she muttered under her breath. She wiped a tear from her eye.

"What did you say?"

"You heard me. I said that you're being ungrateful." Abbey stood her ground.

"I'm being ungrateful? Oh, that's just like you, Abbey. Always needing a stroke on the back. Okay, here." She cleared her throat and bowed with a grand gesture. "Thank you. Thank you. Thank you, Abbey, for doing your job." Penny turned and stormed out of the kitchen. Abbey heard her say, "Kids, come on. We're going to go. Get your shoes on," she snapped at her children. There was an immediacy in her voice.

"What about our cookies?" Brandon said.

"Say goodbye to Mimi. We have cookies at home."

It wasn't too long before Abbey heard the door slam. She was overcome with a simmering cauldron of conflicting emotions. She felt shaken by the argument with her sister, but she also felt a little empowered. She had never stood up for herself like that. She took a cookie from the bakery bag and took a bite. As she was about to take a second bite, the phone in her pocket buzzed, indicating she had a text, and stopped her from an all-out binge.

She removed the phone from her pocket. *Been thinking about you a lot.* Her heart immediately calmed down. *Oh, that's so sweet.* His text had perfect timing. She clicked on the text and saw a conversation history. But her heart sank. It wasn't from Jax. She closed her eyes and said, "Charlie," with a heavy sigh. She hadn't heard from him in over three months. A month—even a few weeks ago, he was all she could think about. She fantasized about running into him at the grocery store, or he'd come to the bakery and admit he made the biggest mistake in his life when they broke up. Then she sent those stupid texts on Valentine's Day. Oh, darn it, why did she do that? She pounded a fist on her forehead. "Stupid, stupid stupid."

The three jumping dots at the bottom of the screen indicated he was still typing.

15

By ten on Sunday, Abbey assumed the morning rush was over. It was that sweet spot in between donuts for church coffee hours and grabbing a pecan ring for brunch. After wiping down the bakery case and tidying up the front area, she went into the kitchen. Her head pounded from lack of sleep and thinking too much. Should she take Charlie back, or should she see what's there with Jax? While she contemplated what to do, she put her head in her hands and collapsed on the kitchen counter. Caroline came over to her and wrapped her arms around her.

Abbey spent the morning filling Caroline in on her dilemma. "Oh, there, there. I've said this before, too many men—it's a good problem to have," Caroline said.

Abbey slowly raised up. "What would you do if you were me?"

"Hmm. Let's see." Like a detective trying to solve a case, Caroline's look got intense. "So, you dated Charlie until the end of last year?"

Abbey nodded.

"How long did you date?"

"About three months."

"Were you—" Caroline cleared her throat and gave Abbey a knowing look. "Were you intimate?"

"Yes." Abbey's face heated up. She knew that Caroline had no trouble telling her every gory detail about her own sex life, and even though Caroline was well into her seventies, she was a girlfriend. Girlfriends had this kind of candid conversation.

"Okay, inquiring minds want to know—was it good sex?" Caroline asked.

"Well, inquiring minds can continue to wonder because I'm not going there."

"Ooh. That bad." Caroline winced.

"I didn't say that. It was perfectly fine, if not necessarily bad, more like perfunctory."

"Perfunctory? Egads," Caroline's face was scrunched up like she smelled something bad, and she clutched her chest, mocking a heart attack. "Have you seen Jax naked yet?" Caroline's face became animated as she asked the question.

"What? No, of course not."

"Don't be such a prude, I'm just asking. The more information I have, the better advice I can give. Perfunctory doesn't sound great. You want a man to be skilled in this area, especially if it's a life partner. So, we don't know if Jax is—I'll use your word— 'perfunctory.'" She put air quotes around the word. "But let's assume he knows his way around the bedroom."

"Okay, let's assume that."

"Husband number two was *perfunctory*." She raised an eyebrow. "Good thing he died because perfunctory sex got old...fast. You think it'll be okay, until it isn't."

"I'll take your word on that."

"And you say Charlie broke up with you and not the other way around?" Caroline continued her investigation. "Why did Charlie break up with you again?"

"He didn't want something long-term."

"You haven't heard from him in how long?"

"About three months." Abbey paused. "Well...I should come clean—I sent him a text on Valentine's Day because I was mad that I was alone. It was kind of desperate."

"Oh, dear. How desperate?"

Abbey paraphrased the contents of the text to Caroline. "You know, trying to make him jealous. I mean, he broke up with me on New Year's Eve...in a text. What kind of guy does that?"

Caroline nodded. "Seems appropriate, given the circumstances," she said very matter-of-factly. "Did he respond to your text?"

Abbey shook her head. "Not until yesterday."

"So, these texts he sent you yesterday come out of the blue? This is the first you've heard from him?"

"Yep." Abbey popped the "p" in an overexaggerated way.

"What did it say, exactly?"

Abbey took her phone from her apron and pulled the text up. "Here," she said, handing the phone to Caroline.

She watched Caroline scroll to read Charlie's text. "The one that got away," Caroline repeated that part of the message out loud. She pursed her lips and raised her eyebrows. "Heard that before. Flattering." She handed the phone back to Abbey.

"Should I give him another chance, knowing that if I do, I'll ruin things with Jax?"

"Okay, so let's think this through. You had a wonderful time with Jax. Pro. He's dreamy and handsome. Pro. Pro." Caroline ticked imaginary boxes in the air. "He lives in Philadelphia. Con? Maybe?"

Abbey nodded. "Definitely."

"Charlie is local. Pro. You have a history with him. Pro."

"More of a con. He broke up with me."

"Yes. Commitment-phobia—a disease that often strikes twenty and thirty-something men. But he did say he made a mistake. Right? Maybe this time will be different? Did you enjoy being with Charlie?"

Abbey thought back to being with Charlie. He was a gentle man, passive and introverted. In many ways, the male version of her—a food lover with weight and self-esteem issues. She thought they were perfectly matched when she swiped right on his profile. "Yes and no. It was safe," she said. "Did he make my heart beat fast? At first, yes. It was fun. It was new. Toward the end, we both seemed like we were going through the motions."

"Oh, yes, perfunctory."

Abbey smothered her face in her hands again. "Oh, I don't know. Maybe I'm being too hard on Charlie because the stuff with Jax is so new—I'm jaded."

"Maybe. It could also mean that you're more interested in Jax." Caroline ticked another imaginary box in Jax's favor.

Abbey nodded. "Yes, I think you're right. With Jax, it's exciting, maybe because a lot of it is unknown. But, also because I really, really like him. When he came for dinner the other night, it felt so comfortable being with him. I felt like I could talk with him forever. The conversation was so natural." Abbey stood and sighed. "But the thought of putting it all out there and going for it is scary. What if it doesn't work out? I mean, at least with Charlie, he's making the move. I know where I stand."

"Yes, you could turn Charlie down, and your relationship with Jax could end for whatever reason—that could happen, but you never know if you don't go after it."

"With Charlie, it seems safer."

"Safer than what? Didn't he break up with you?" Caroline made a very good point. "I'd say there's risk there too. And, if I'm remembering correctly, you took that breakup pretty hard."

"Yes, I know I did. Charlie was my first boyfriend since—well, since forever." Abbey covered her face. "He was the only real boyfriend I've ever had." She never did count the college fling with a study partner as a true boyfriend because they never actually went on any dates. "I'm afraid I could turn Charlie down and end up with no one. Let's face it, we both think Jax is"—she cleared her throat— "out of my league."

"Poppycock. I'm not buying that." Caroline cupped Abbey's chin in her hand. "He's obviously interested in you. I see Charlie has thrown a wild card into the mix. Up until today, he wasn't even a factor. I would suggest you look at *all* of your cards. Why settle for a measly pair of twos when you could have a full house—with three aces?"

"It's not just that. Penny said I shouldn't even consider dating someone that lives out of state because I have responsibilities here. Maybe Penny's right. It's stupid to start something up with Jax."

Caroline did not hide her disdain. "Penny only thinks about Penny. Besides, Jax's got business here in Maryland now. Hasn't he come here twice in the past week? Besides, you said you wanted to move back up there."

"I did." Caroline was right. Abbey eventually did want to move back up to Philadelphia and resume her career as an architect.

"I think you are trying to talk yourself out of choosing Jax."

Abbey thought Caroline was making a lot of a valid points. "I guess you could be right. I'm pretty good at talking myself out of things. Do you think it's possible Jax could move here?" Abbey waved off the question. Forget it. I'm getting ahead of myself."

"Oh, I do think it's possible. And yes, you are getting ahead of yourself. But that's okay. Don't be afraid of the unknown. It's fun to plan and dream about the future."

"Okay, put down a half of a pro check for Jax." Satisfied with the research, Abbey said, "Now, where does that leave us? Who should I pick?" She never in a million years thought she'd be in this kind of predicament. And, moreover, she wasn't sure it was a good place to be.

Caroline looked confused. "Oh, dear," she said. "I guess I should have written it down. Let's recap..."

The bells above the front door jingled. Abbey started to go to the front of the bakery but stopped dead in her tracks. She could see through the beaded drapes that separated the front of the bakery and the entrance to the kitchen a familiar figure of a man. She turned around and edged backward a few inches so that she felt safe and out of sight. "It's him." She whispered as she pointed to the front of the bakery.

"Who?" Caroline mouthed.

"Charlie," Abbey said in a hushed voice.

"Oh, Mr. Perfunctory." Caroline got closer to the drapes and parted the edge of the beads enough to see but not be seen. Returning her gaze to Abbey, she whispered, "Do you want me to handle?"

Abbey thought long and hard. "Yes," she said. Then followed with a quick "No, wait a minute. Yes. Oh, I don't know."

Caroline took Abbey by the shoulders, spun her around so that she was facing the front of the bakery, and shoved her. The beaded draped clanged loud enough to stifle Abbey's whimpering protest.

Charlie looked startled, but then his expression melted into a smile. He was more cleaned up than Abbey remembered him being. Gone was the scruffy beard, and his normally bushy blond hair was slicked back with a gel and revealing a widow's peak she didn't even know he had. He even put on a khaki blazer that had sleeves about two inches too long and came to the base of his thumb. Abbey could see that he was trying to make an effort to impress her. "Hey, Abs," he said, waving his pudgy hand in the air. In what seemed to be an attempt to cover up nerves, he adjusted his belt and pulled his jeans a little higher. "I wasn't sure you still worked here. I thought I'd take a chance."

"Yes, I'm still here," Abbey said. She walked behind the bakery counter, and Charlie followed, but stayed on the other side. He looked down at the bakery case, sizing up the choices.

With one arm propped on the top of the case, he leaned in. "Oh, boy, I remember your snickerdoodles. Can I have two of those?"

Abbey felt the awkward tension between the two of them build as she bent down and selected two cookies. "For here or to go?"

"Here," he said.

She wondered if he was going to bring up the text. Maybe he was expecting her to. She put the cookies on a plate and handed them to Charlie. "That'll be four fifty-eight."

Charlie reached into his jeans pocket and pulled out a five-dollar bill. "Here. Keep the change." He reached for the plate and moved the cookies closer to him. "How's your mom doing?"

"You know, pretty much the same. Thanks for asking." Abbey rang his order up in the register and put the change into the tip jar next to it.

"You look great," he said.

"Thanks." She tucked an errant curl behind her ear. "Um, so do you. I like the jacket," Abbey said. Small talk was excruciating for her.

Charlie unbuttoned the blazer and revealed his favorite Metallica T-shirt underneath. "Some things never change," he said with a faint laugh. "I wore my lucky shirt today because—" He cleared his throat. "Did you get my text?"

And just like that, Abbey felt like the tension bubble was about to burst. "I did," she said.

"So, what'd you think? Um. About us?" He broke off a piece of the cookie and shoved it into his mouth.

"I don't know. It's been a while. You know?" She hoped he would not bring up her crazy series of unhinged texts to him a few weeks earlier.

"I know." With one hand leaning on the bakery case counter, he shifted his weight, looked down and then back at her. "I know I hurt you. I'm sorry about the way I ended things."

"A text on New Year's Eve? Really, Charlie." She wasn't trying to encourage any sort of charitable response from him. But rather she'd waited more than three months to say it to him.

"I know. That was bad. You deserved better." He looked again. "I got the text you sent." His eyes shifted up to meet hers. "On Valentine's Day."

She was afraid of that. "You did?"

"Yes. I was going to respond. Sooner. If anything, it did get me thinking about you again. I've drafted many texts in response— but I never hit send."

A few weeks ago, Abbey wanted nothing more than this scene to play out as it was right now. But a lot had happened since then. "Can I ask what has taken you so long to get back in touch with me?"

"I was afraid of getting close again. I'm kind of a commitment-phobe." He shrugged and seemed to get swallowed more in the tan blazer.

Caroline was right. A diseased thirty-something man stood in front of Abbey. "What makes you think you've changed?" she asked.

"I don't know. I just feel it. You have to trust me." He took the last bite of the first cookie. "Oh, boy. As good as ever." He wiped a few crumbs that were stuck on his chin. "Maybe we can do lunch or dinner sometime. You know, take things slow and talk it over?"

"Let me think about it, okay?"

Charlie took the second cookie and put it in his pocket.

"Don't you want a bag?" Abbey asked.

He shook his head and waved her off. "No, I'm good." He tapped a finger on the bakery case like a nervous drummer. "Okay. I'll give you some time. I promise, Abbey, things will be different. I've had lots of time to think about it. I know how much you mean to me. And I don't want to make that mistake again."

He walked toward the bakery front door. Before exiting, he waved. "You have my number," he said. Then he turned and left the bakery.

At the sound of the door chimes, Caroline came from the kitchen. "Well, how'd it go?" Her smiled faded when she saw the look on Abbey's face. "Look at you," she said. "You look like you just went to a funeral."

"He wants to go to lunch or dinner." The dread of that thought of accepting Charlie's offer to meet for lunch or dinner and losing out on whatever potential she and Jax had sank in.

"Abbey, I think you have your answer," Caroline said. "At least it's clear to me what you should do."

Abbey took off her apron and went into the office to get her jacket. "I have to go to my final fitting for the bridesmaid dress for Camille's wedding. I'll give it more thought, but I think you're right." She put her jacket on and put her hand deep into the pocket. Her fingers found the white strip of paper she was carrying around for good luck. She took the fortune out of her pocket. The words were beginning to fade from too much handling. "I'll admit, my heart does tend to lean in a certain direction." She read the fortune to herself once more. *All you need is love.*

She reached into her other pocket and pulled out the second fortune. *Nothing is impossible with a willing heart.* And was more confused than ever.

16

Sitting at a table in Perfect Perks, a coffee shop two doors down and across the street from the bakery, Abbey blew on the steam coming from a cup of hazelnut coffee—the flavor of the day. A cloud of steam lingered above her mug. At 2 p.m., the shop was nearly empty, and she knew it would be this time of day. Like Sweet Caroline's, Perks got its rush in the early morning, midday, and early evening.

The barista with dreadlocks coiled high in an impressive man bun wiped down the table next to her. Music blared from his AirPods loud enough for Abbey to distinguish it as techno, and that she didn't like it. It distracted her briefly from the reason she was there—Charlie. She promised to give his suggestion that they rekindle what they once had some thought—and she had. He'd accepted her text invitation to meet her today. She assumed he'd be here any minute.

To complicate things, it had been three weeks since Jax came to dinner. They chatted a few times on FaceTime after that, but then he seemed to vanish. And now, it had been a full eleven days, fifteen hours, and thirty minutes since they had contact—but who was counting? Thoughts of Jax filled every second of her mind, even though she willed herself to try to think otherwise.

He had seemed genuinely interested in spending time with her. She had lulled herself into believing that being in a long-distance relationship wasn't too bad after all, and that they could be the couple that defied odds and made it work.

Before the FaceTime "dates," she spent nearly an hour getting ready, flattening her unruly curls and putting on makeup. She even dressed up. She wanted to present the best image she could, knowing full well the small screen of an iPhone did nothing to enhance good features and did everything to spotlight the bad ones. Her worry had seemed for naught as the two quickly settled into a playful conversation about a shared interest in an obscure indie rock band named The Band's Mother that played in small dives between Baltimore and Philly. They may have even been to the same show a few years back. Kismet, Abbey had thought at the time.

Sitting in the coffee shop, waiting for Charlie, "Kismet," Abbey scoffed out loud. Maybe even too loud. She self-consciously looked over at the man-bunned barista, but he didn't even glance her way.

She returned to her obsessive recount of the days before her conversation with Jax came to a screeching halt. A day after the second FaceTime date, they had a nice and playful text exchange. While waiting for Charlie, she scrolled the messages. *I think Band's Mother is playing a show at the Ottobar in a couple of weeks,* he had texted. *We should go,* she bravely texted back. Her heart smiled when he replied simply with the thumbs-up emoji. The last text she received from Jax that night came at 10:30 p.m. He said, *It's late. Get some rest.* And then, he closed the exchange the way he always did—*Sweet dreams.* It was sort of his calling card. Two little words that made her smile and feel warm all over—and most of all—it gave her hope. That was the last time she had heard from him.

Eleven days without contact felt like eons. She felt consumed by the situation. Maybe she had been too presumptuous when suggesting they go to The Band's Mother show. Maybe he had realized she wanted more than he did.

She recounted all the special moments in her head. The fortune cookie? The kiss on the forehead? The sweet dreams texts? And then nothing. She assumed she'd have an answer in a few days—and it probably would not be good. Next weekend she was off to Camille's wedding, and she was sure that he would be there.

But she was getting ahead of herself—as usual. He may still contact her. Yeah, right. As the Magic 8-Ball would say if asked, "Outlook not so good." She sunk deeper into the comfy leather chair and sipped her coffee. She had to deal with Charlie first.

She wrapped her hands around the coffee mug, hoping the warmth of the beverages inside would relax her. She looked at her watch. "C'mon, Charlie," she whispered, while tapping her foot on the table pedestal. She knew she'd have to get back to the bakery soon. Then, as if on cue, Charlie walked in. He took off his sunglasses and propped them on his head before giving her a cheerful wave. "Hi," Abbey waved and mouthed back. He sunk his hands deep into the pockets of his cargo shorts before heading to the counter to order coffee. Abbey had second thoughts about what she was about to do. It was just like her to second-guess every decision. What-ifs played constantly in a loop in her head like one of her father's old records.

Dreadlocks man bun guy gave the table he was cleaning one last swipe with a rag. He stood up and slowly walked over to his side of the coffee counter. Abbey watched Charlie point to the menu, written in colorful chalk, and hanging high behind the counter. After a few nods, the barista packed some grounds into an espresso filter and began steaming hot liquid into a mug. He topped the drink with a several-inch-high cone of whipped cream before dusting the mountain with what appeared to be cocoa.

Charlie walked over to where Abbey was sitting. He pulled the chair out across from her and sat down. With a toothy grin, he said, "I figured it's good news since you decided to meet me in person."

It was not.

Abbey sighed loud and hard. She had put a lot of thought into her decision before concluding that she'd be settling if she gave her relationship with Charlie another chance. The only reason she considered it was because of her fear of having no one, which was more and more becoming a distinct possibility.

"Charlie," she said. Her foot tapped harder at the pedestal. She looked him straight in the eyes. "I've given this—you—us a lot of thought. And I don't think it's a good idea if we get back together."

Charlie's smiled faded to what could only be described as a look of indifference. "Okay," he said. He shrugged slightly as he stared at his coffee drink.

Abbey had seen more reaction from him when he lost a life trying to rescue Zelda on his Nintendo gaming device.

"It's not you, it's me," she continued, and he continued with a blank stare. "I've got my mom, my job..."

"Really, it's okay." He took a sip of his mocha, which left a dab of whipped cream on his nose. "It was worth a shot, right?" He tried to reach his tongue to lap up the whipped cream before using a napkin to get it.

There was a childlike quality to Charlie that Abbey loved and loathed—endearing and irritating at the same time. "Maybe we can be friends—you know, check on each other now and then?" she said. That should soften the blow. Even though the blow didn't seem to need softening in this case, she had rehearsed it this way, so she was going to get it all out.

He shrugged. "Sure."

Abbey wasn't sure if she was more relieved or hurt by his reaction, but she believed it was the former. It would have been harder if he would have begged her or gotten mad. It would have been harder, but she was prepared for that response. She had not rehearsed indifference.

There was a long, awkward pause where no one said anything. Charlie seemed more interested in his drink than her.

"Okay, then." Abbey stood and said, "Goodbye, Charlie."

He gave a light wave that resembled more of a salute. There were many ways she could have taken the gesture. She chose to take it to mean "Have a good life."

Abbey walked out of the coffee shop. And that was it. Just like that, it was over. A slight detour in an otherwise busy day, full of worry and sadness about her situation with Jax. She wouldn't even let herself call it a relationship. Who was she kidding? It was, at best, a dalliance at best—dare she say the dreaded "f" word—friendship. She had been right all along. There was nothing there. She let the fantasy of a smart, handsome, rich man wanting to be with her. It happened in fairy tales, not in real life.

Once outside, she took her phone from her pocket. Now, it was a full eleven days, fifteen hours, and forty-three minutes since her last text exchange with Jax. She thought about reaching out to him but then became paralyzed by the fear of receiving another humiliating breakup text.

With some trepidation, she selected Jax's contact information on her phone and selected edit. She knew once she did what she was about to do, there was no going back. She scrolled down. She hesitated a bit. And then selected "delete contact." And then she went to the text chain and swiped left before tapping the trash can icon. Their conversation was now gone, as if it never happened. Now if only it were that easy to erase the conversations from her mind.

The really tricky part was that she was sure that he'd be at Camille's wedding next week. After all, he was the groom's college friend.

Her brain was working overtime obsessing on the scenario of running into him at the wedding or reception. The way she saw it, she had several options, and none of them were good. Option number one—avoid him at all costs by hiding behind pillars or running to the ladies' room at any sight of him. Could happen, but she would have to be very stealth-like and make sure she saw him before he saw her.

Option number two—upon seeing him, start flirting and laughing with whatever male is closest to her. Off the bat option number two had flaws as all the groomsmen, except TJ, were married or dating someone else in the wedding party. And TJ, Camille's half-brother, was only eleven. Probably a few work colleagues from Allen Anderson & Associates would be there, but she wasn't sure who.

Option number three—feign an emergency and not go all together. She could certainly use her mother as a believable excuse. But that option seemed extreme and wouldn't be fair to Camille.

Of course, if she were a normal person who didn't have insecurity, there was option number four—not avoid him, and take the bull by the horns and talk to him. Maybe even confront him. Ask him why he hadn't been in touch, tell him she isn't interested in someone who plays games and walk off in a huff with her dignity intact. But she knew she was not a normal person, and she had definite insecurities.

Then a horrible thought crossed her mind. What if he was there with someone—a date? The perfect bleached blond ex. Oh, that thought caused her heart to race and nearly made her vomit. She covered her mouth with her hand and stopped dead in her tracks. She was not ready for that. Would he be that callous? No, during the brief time she spent with him, he was a gentleman. He didn't seem to be the type to play games. If he was, she couldn't wrap her mind around that scenario because, thankfully, her brain wouldn't let her mind linger there. With that in mind, option number one won by a longshot. Now it was just a game of wait and see.

17

Camille's wedding day fell on a sunny April Saturday during Easter weekend. As expected, Abbey was overly consumed with the thought of running into Jax. By now, it had been nineteen days, nineteen hours, and seven minutes since she'd heard from him. But honestly, who was really counting?

On the bright side, at least the dress Magda made for her fit perfectly. Made of bright fuchsia chiffon, it had a simple neck with a fitted top, short butterfly sleeves and a flowy floor-length A-line skirt that had a slit just up to above her knee. Magda was right, the bright pink color was better than the disastrous baby pink one Abbey had chosen herself.

She got through the ceremony without picking him out of the crowd of five hundred, thanks mostly to the dimly candlelit St. Mark's Cathedral, and the intrusive videographer's bright lights on a stand that glared out most of her view of the guests on one side of the church.

It was sheer will that kept down her two-brownie lunch as she stood in front of the church as her best friend got married. Don't be the maid of honor that pukes on a wedding day, she told herself whenever the brownies seemed to want to reappear. A couple of "you can do this" mind over matter affirmations seemed to do the trick.

After the ceremony and what seemed like a million staged photos in front of the altar, she finally felt safe as she climbed into the white Lincoln sedan. Camille's father had hired a fleet of cars to take the wedding party from the church to where the reception was being held.

"Hey there, Abbey," TJ poked his head in the back of the Lincoln. "I guess I'm riding with you." TJ had a head of unruly brown curls that framed his freckled boyish face. He was long and lean, resembling Ichabod Crane with stick-like appendages. He was having a growth spurt—so his mother proudly said—growing three full inches since the first time he tried on his tux eight weeks earlier. "Scooch over," he said, as he planted his gangly frame in the back seat next to Abbey.

At first, the two of them sat there in awkward silence until TJ broke the ice. "Abbey!" He said, flapping his hand in front of his face as if he was trying to get fresh air.

"What?" Within seconds, she knew what he meant. The smell of someone passing gas was undeniable. "TJ, it wasn't me," she said.

"Yeah, right. Heard that before." TJ had an impish way about him. Abbey assumed he was very popular in school. Probably the class clown.

"So, Abbey," TJ turned to her and flashed a bright smile that displayed a mouthful of braces. Thomas John Ritter III was the product of Camille's father and his second wife. He was one of those overly self-assured privileged preteens who wouldn't give Abbey the time of day unless she was his half-sister's best friend. Camille loved TJ. She grew up always wanting a sibling, and when her parents divorced, less than seven months before TJ was born, she got her wish.

"Yes, TJ."

"What did the grape say when it was pinched?"

"Um, I don't know."

"Nothing. It just gave out a little wine. Get it? Wine."

"Yes, I get it."

"Funny, huh?"

"Sure." She turned her head so he wouldn't see her eye roll.

"Do you want to hear more, cuz I got them."

Before Abbey could respond, TJ said, "What do you call a bear with no teeth?"

"I don't know, what?" Abbey played along in a good-natured way, not letting on that she finally knew what hell felt like.

"A gummy bear." He wrapped his lips around his teeth and moved his jaw up and down for emphasis.

Abbey leaned forward until she was close to the driver's ear. "Are we there yet?"

The driver gave a slight chuckle. "No, ma'am. About fifteen minutes more." Abbey leaned back in her seat. "You know what, TJ?"

"What?"

"I didn't get much sleep last night. Do you mind if I close my eyes for a few seconds?"

TJ seemed satisfied with this request. He took his phone from his pocket and scrolled on social media.

Abbey closed her eyes. She wasn't tired. She just wasn't in the mood for the banter of a prepubescent telling jokes like it was open mic night.

Once the back seat of the Lincoln was peaceful, Abbey calculated what would be an acceptable amount of time before she could flee for home. She decided that the cake cutting would be the earliest; although, feigning a headache may get her out a little earlier. Her best plan had her leaving before any dancing. The last thing she needed was to be sitting alone with a full dance floor—or worse—watching Jax dance with someone else.

The sedan pulled up to the main entrance of the Delaware River Yacht Club at six fifteenish. The sun was still bright in the sky on this early summer evening. TJ got out of the car first and made a grand gesture with his long, skinny arm. "After you, my lady," he said.

Abbey took the hand that he offered and got out of the car. She stumbled slightly on the pebble walkway, knowing full well if she fell, her weight would take him down with her and they'd be piled in a heap at the entrance as the rest of the bridal party's cars pulled up. Gripping his arm so tightly that TJ said "Ouch," Abbey managed to stay standing. Once she was on steady ground, she said "Thank you" and let go of his hand.

"You have been most gracious." He bowed before scurrying inside.

The Yacht Club's main entrance resembled a stately manor, with wooden doors that stood nearly eight feet tall and with shellacked wooden oars as handles. Once inside, Abbey noticed a plaque of all the club's current members. Tom Ritter, Camille's father, was now the club's president.

Just inside the crowded foyer, a white-gloved server greeted her with a tray of tall, thin tulip-shaped crystal flutes filled with pink champagne, each with a single raspberry sunken to the bottom. As she took a glass from the tray, she raised it up in a toasting kind of way and said "Cheers" to the server. She turned away, took a sip, and allowed the champagne's bubbles to tickle her nose and throat. Before walking away, she turned back toward the server. "On second thought," she said, and took another flute from the server. "It's for my sister," an excuse she used to get a second candy bar when trick-or-treating at a house that gave out something she liked.

With a champagne glass in each hand, she turned to walk toward the Admiral's Room where the reception was to be held and within seconds of entering the crowded room, she accidentally bumped into the back of a man, spilling half a flute down the back of his pale blue linen jacket. The man turned around. His look of shock soon turned into a bright smile. "Abbey?"

"Jax!" She gasped.

The ghoster looked like he was seeing a ghost.

Of all the hundreds of people crowded in this small—albeit very stately—room, she managed to bump into the one person she was trying to avoid. She quickly checked for the exit and realized it was too late to run.

"Are you thirsty?" he said with a laugh and nod to the two drinks she was carrying.

"Yeah. I wasn't sure how long the bar line was." She smiled nervously. "Better to be prepared."

"Make sense to me."

Abbey motioned for him to turn around so she could see the damage she had done to the back of his jacket.

Jax turned around so that his back was facing her.

"Oh, dear."

"That bad?" he said, turning back around.

"I'm sorry, it looks like I got you good." Abbey still had a champagne glass in each hand. "Do you know where I can put these?" she said.

"Here." Jax took the drinks from her and walked over to a nearby marble endpiece. And Abbey followed.

"I am so sorry. I think I ruined your jacket. Here." She pulled a tissue from her purse.

"Don't worry about that," he said. He waved a dismissive hand. "It's probably too hot for a coat, anyway." He took his jacket off and folded it over his arm. In doing so, he turned his body just enough for Abbey to see the back of his white oxford shirt.

Abbey gasped. "Oh, no!" She put her hand up to cover her gaping mouth. As if it were possible, his shirt looked worse than his jacket.

"Oh well," he said. He tried to contort his body in a way to see his back, but soon gave up. "It'll be fine." He flung his jacket over his shoulder. "C'mon, let's go outside and see if this will dry off."

He took her hand and they serpentined their way through the throng of people in the Yacht Club's foyer until they made it outside. Jax walked over to a wooden bench that was in the well-manicured grounds in the center of the circular driveway. He laid his jacket off to the side of the bench. Abbey sat down and then he sat close, but not too close to her.

During a long awkward silence, Jax stared mostly at his feet. He finally looked up.

"Look," they both said in unison.

"You go," she said.

He cleared his throat. "I'm not sure what to say."

"The truth works." *Here we go.* She braced herself, not sure she wanted to hear the truth.

He took a deep breath. "I like you."

Her heartbeat returned to a normal rhythm. "But?" she managed to say.

"No but. I like you...a lot." He shifted his posture so that he was facing her. He breathed deeply. "In the interest of full disclosure, my old girlfriend—" he corrected himself. "Former fiancée, Elle, reached out."

Just hearing the words fiancée and Elle in the same sentence made Abbey's stomach turn. "I see." Abbey looked away to hide her disappointment.

"No, it isn't like that."

"Like what?"

"It's not what you're thinking."

She crossed her arms. "So, tell me what I'm thinking." Abbey's candidness surprised even her. Every fiber in her being wanted to get up and walk away.

"She asked me to consider getting back together."

"Then it's exactly what I was thinking."

"Okay, fair enough." He rubbed his forehead. "I told her 'No,' and she left. But she got in my head, I guess." He sighed. "I got scared."

"Of?" Now, she was more confused than ever.

"I was afraid of getting into a new relationship so soon after breaking up with Elle."

"So, the ghosting was intentional?" Abbey bit her lip hard.

"Yes."

With his response, her emotions abruptly shifted to hurt.

"No. I don't know. Maybe." He reached for her hand, but she pulled it away. "Abbey, I love spending time with you. The FaceTimes—" He smiled. "I always hung up and wanted to see you. It didn't help that we lived so far apart."

"You should have told me." She muttered when she wanted to say so much more. She wanted to scream at him. Damn him for leading her on.

"Of course, you're right." He sighed. "I'm just a dumb guy. I was ready to let you go."

Her temple throbbed. This was torture. "Okay then, so, take care." She stood, intending to leave while she still had her dignity. But she felt an arm tug her back down to the bench.

"I get it, you don't want to have to come to Maryland to see me, and I can't just take off and go to Philadelphia without first making plans for my mother's care. Believe me." She emphasized her words. "I get it."

"That was true." He put emphasis on the word was. "But Skip changed my mind."

"Skip?" *What did he do?*

"I was talking to Skip a few days ago. You know, I told him how much I like you, but I was unsure that I could make it work because of the distance thing."

She nodded and waited for him to continue.

"And he said—and I'm quoting— 'Abbey's the real deal.'"

"He did?"

"Yes. And he said, 'They don't come better than Abbey.'"

Skip said those things? About her? Abbey smiled slightly out of embarrassment, but mostly because his words were so flattering to hear.

"And it got me thinking." He looked deep into her eyes. "That's what I want. I want the real deal." He placed a soft hand on her cheek. "I want someone special like you."

She looked up at him. He seemed sincere. "You do?"

"Yes, that's what I was trying to say. Admittedly, not very well," he muttered.

She stared at him to see if his expression changed. It did not.

A curl came loose from the bobby pin clip on the side of her head. Jax slowly reached for it, and she let him. He tucked it behind her ear.

"I'm asking for you to give us a try." He looked deep into her eyes. "Trust me," he whispered. Cupping her cheek, he leaned forward.

Just then, TJ appeared a little out of breath. "There you are," he said. "Camille says they're going to introduce the wedding party, so we gotta go get in line." He offered his arm to Abbey.

"I'll be there in a minute," she said.

"Okey dokey," he said before turning and sprinting back into the building.

Abbey turned back toward Jax and shrugged. "My date." She smiled.

"Oh, I see I have some competition."

"Yes, if you like to tell really bad jokes, then you have a lot of competition."

He laughed as he reached for her hand and took it in his. This time, she let him.

As much as she wanted to sit there with him, she didn't want to keep the rest of the wedding party waiting. "I guess I should go." She let go of his hand and stood. "See you in there?" She pointed to the Yacht Club.

He winked. "You bet you will."

After the entrée course—filet mignon, medium rare, and a twice baked potato perfectly swirled and put back in a salted and crisp skin, Abbey looked around to see if she could catch a glimpse of Jax. He had been sitting with Skip's college buddies—table number twelve—a rowdy group that clanged their wine glasses with their knives about every ten minutes to encourage Skip and Camille to kiss. Once the bride and groom obliged, Table Twelve would stand up and shout "Woot, woot, woot," while twirling their napkins.

She noticed he wasn't sitting there anymore. She craned her neck to get a better look around the room when she felt a tap on her shoulder. Turning around, she smiled.

"Hey there," he said, in a particularly sexy way.

"Hey there."

He pulled out the chair next to her and sat down. As much as she wanted him to sit there, she instead said demurely, "That's TJ's seat. I think he's in the bathroom."

"Was," Jax said confidently. He motioned to Table Twelve.

Abbey looked back and saw TJ sitting with the college buddies. Table Twelve clanged their glasses with a knife. With TJ leading the call, they cheered, "Woot, woot, woot," and waved their napkins.

"Best twenty dollars I've ever spent," Jax said.

"Um—" she bit her lip. "I hate to tell you, but I think he would have moved tables for free."

"Yes, he seems to be in his element." He laughed. "They like to tell bad jokes too."

The band leader tapped on his microphone, which let out an unpleasant high-pitched screech. This caught everyone's attention as the room grew hush. Except for Camille's and Skip's first dance, the band had been pretty much lying low by playing quiet, unrecognizable soft background musak with hushed cymbals and low but sultry bass rhythms. "We have a request," the singer said. "Abbey, this is for you."

Abbey looked at Jax and mouthed "Me?"

He reached for her hand and said, "And now, the second best twenty dollars I've spent tonight," as the band launched into "All You Need Is Love."

Jax led her to the center of the dance floor, which by now was filling up with other guest who were dancing to the familiar Beatles song.

At first, she was self-conscious, not sure of how her body would look shimmying and rocking from side to side like a bowl full of hot pink Jell-O until he took both of her hands and raised them high above her head, squeezing them tightly while they rocked rhythmically together. She felt tingles everywhere as his energy entered her body like a lightning bolt.

Soon, the crowd was singing along to the chorus in what was a perfect anthem for a new marriage. No doubt, the song meant more to her than anyone else in the room.

At the end of the song, he leaned in close enough for only her to hear. "That was fun," he said. She couldn't agree more.

There was a long, awkward silence while the guests on the dance floor awaited what song was next as it would determine if they should stay or go back to their seats.

The slow, rhythmic drumbeats and twangy guitar chords that followed were familiar to Abbey—a song her father proclaimed the best love song ever written—Springsteen's "Tougher Than the Rest." It was a song her father would play often. When she was a little girl, she would gently put one foot on top of each of his while they'd sway back and forth. "Listen to the words, Abbey," her father would say. "That's the kind of guy you want—one that will stick around—one that loves *you* for *you*." He would sing them to her, harmonizing with the record, and she would listen, taking in every word while dreaming of that wonderful man. During the harmonica solo part of the song, her father would spin her around and around while she squealed with delight until she became so dizzy she couldn't stand without assistance. Songs with memories etched in her mind and heart meant the most. And now, the band was tempting fate by creating a new memory for her.

But Abbey didn't want to assume anything that wasn't there yet with Jax. She turned and slowly started to walk toward her seat. An arm tugged her back. She spun around and looked Jax deep in the eyes and smiled. He pulled her close, his arms fitting snuggly around her waist. She wrapped her arms around his neck and rested her head on his chest. Her heart aligned with his as they kept equal time with the steady bass drum. He smelled amazing—soapy and a tinge of a sweet but musky cologne with a hint of champagne on his breath—and unfortunately still lingering on his shirt.

When the band got to the first chorus, he leaned in even closer and sang sweetly the words in her ear—words she knew by heart and had dreamed about a man singing to her forever. She hummed along with him, not caring if she was off-key. In his arms, she felt safe and warm—and even a little small. She was overcome by joy. Her head was buzzing, and her heart was full.

Her chin nuzzled against his chest as he whispered, "Can I ask you a favor?"

Her mind was saying, "You can ask me anything," while she tried not to get ahead of herself. Words were stuck in her throat and head. Instead, she managed a slight nod.

"I know this is short notice," he said.

"What is it?" She encouraged him while she went through a likely scenario in her head—spend the night with me? Cringe, too soon, and she hadn't really *prepared* for that outcome by trimming what had become a thicket of overgrown hair *down there*. Again, best not to get ahead of herself. "Go on," she said, while contemplating her response.

"So, I have this thing." He pulled away a little, so they were eye to eye as they continued to sway back and forth in time to the beat. "I'm being honored at a banquet the Chamber is putting on later this month. Would you—" He didn't even get the rest of the sentence out.

Relieved, excited, and exhilarated, she blurted, "Yes!"

He laughed a little when he said, "Yes? You don't even know what I was going to ask you to do." His dimples punctuated his smile. He leaned in and wrapped his arms around her tightly again, whispering in her ear, "Would you give me the honor of being my date for the dinner?"

Without hesitation, she replied, "My answer is the same. Yes, of course."

During the harmonica solo, Abbey became that carefree little girl that danced in her living room many years ago. Without inhibition, she took Jax's hand and twirled. He caught her on the second spin and pulled her close again.

18

"Magda!" The door to the dress shop slammed with a thud as Abbey let it go.

Like the Wizard of Oz, Magda, the diminutive dressmaker, appeared from the mysterious room behind the lime green velvet curtains. "What is this commotion?" Magda asked. She walked toward Abbey.

"I'm sorry." Abbey tried to catch her breath. She used her hand to wipe sweat from her brow that had formed after running three blocks from the bakery. She wanted to make sure she arrived at 10 a.m. on Monday when the store opened. "I need you," Abbey managed to get out in between gasps for air.

Magda seemed confused but intrigued. "Come." Magda summoned Abbey with a bony pointer finger to follow her as she walked over to the where the dressing room was. "Sit," Magda said, as she pointed to a white rattan chair. Even though she stood an inch or two under five feet, Magda had a commanding presence. Abbey did as she was instructed.

Magda loomed over Abbey, making her appear larger than her tiny frame. She put a hand on Abbey's shoulder. Her eyes, magnified by her reading glasses perched on the end of her nose, resembled two blue-gray shooter marbles. "So, what is it? The wedding was okay, no?"

"No. Yes. No, it was fine. It has nothing to do with the wedding. The dress was fine. Actually, the wedding was good." Abbey felt herself blushing a bit.

"I'm listening." Magda did not let up on her stare.

"My boy..." Abbey couldn't say that Jax was her boyfriend. She feared giving what they had a title would jinx it. Yes, that was weird, and yes, a bit neurotic. "At the wedding, this guy I know invited me to a fancy dinner."

"Oh," Magda said with a raised eyebrow as she removed her hand from Abbey's shoulder.

"He's the guest of honor. And, well, he's asked me to be his date. I need a dress."

Now both of Magda's eyebrows were raised as was her chin. "I see." Magda bit her bottom lip. "This dinner, when is it?"

"April eighteenth. A little less than two weeks. The invitation says cocktail attire." After Jax texted her the invitation, Abbey had read it over and over so many times, the words were etched in her head.

"Less than two weeks?" Magda pursed her lips. "It would be a challenge."

As Abbey expected, it was a lot to ask in a short amount of time. She started thinking about a Plan B. These days, her closet was full of leggings and T-shirts that could stand the dusting of flour and an occasional smear of batter. The dresses she wore when she was an architect were at least twenty pounds too small. The same twenty pounds she had planned to lose when she started her diet in February. As was too often the case, she regretted not being able to stick to a diet. Maybe the black dress she'd worn to dinner with Henry? Yuck. That dress was cursed with bad juju. Darn it. Ordering something new online was risky. Chances are it wouldn't get here in time or wouldn't fit. She could run to the mall and in a fury, try on anything in her size with a small glimmer of hope that something wouldn't make her look matronly or like she was wearing a burlap sack meant for potatoes. Abbey stood up. "Thanks, anyway."

Magda put a firm hand on Abbey's shoulder and forced her back into the chair. "I accept challenge."

"You do?" Life and hope reentered Abbey's body. "Oh, Magda, thank you. Thank you."

Magda put that bony pointer finger up. "Wait here," she said. She went to the room behind the lime green velvet curtain and reappeared with a sketch pad and zippered pouch like the kind school kids used to put their pencils and erasers in. Magda pulled up a small wooden stool and sat in front of Abbey. She unzipped the pouch and looked inside before taking a black pencil out.

Magda stared intensely at Abbey, shifted her gaze away for a second and then turned her head back towards Abbey. Magda tapped the black pencil against her mouth before saying, "Beautiful red hair goes well with some colors and not so well with others." Magda studied Abbey some more carefully. "Skin like porcelain doll. Voluptuous breasts," she said, cupping her own breasts. "These things we must highlight." Magda put the pencil to the pad and furiously sketched, switching out pencils from the pouch now and then. She occasionally peered up at her subject and then returned to focus on her drawing.

After what seemed like an eternity, Magda turned the sketch pad around. Abbey carefully studied the drawing. As she did, she smiled. Her silhouette was outlined in soft, sensuous strokes and a swath of red curls framed her face. The dress Magda drew was a violet-colored lace off the shoulder with short cap sleeves, a deep plunging neck, tight bodice and a short flaring skirt that fell just at the knees. Abbey, the pencil drawing, was beautiful, like a Rubens painting that earmarked beauty from centuries ago.

"Well?" Magda said very matter-of-factly.

"Do you think you can make me look like that?"

"This is you. That's how you look." Magda thumped the sketch pad. "I just make the dress."

Abbey stared at the sketch a little longer. She reached for the sketch pad. Once she had it in her hands, she hugged the drawing close to her chest. "I love it," she said.

"Okay then. We must get to work," Magda said with a wink. "Dress like this usually takes two-three months, not two-three weeks. But I can do it. Magda is magician, remember?" Magda's eyes twinkled as she spoke. Abbey assumed she loved a good challenge.

Abbey's mood suddenly shifted to one of worry. This was starting to sound expensive. She hadn't even thought about how she was going to pay Magda. There typically wasn't much money to spare—certainly not extra money to spend on frivolous things like a custom-made dress. Abbey cleared her throat. "I should have asked this first, but how much will this cost?"

Magda clicked her tongue a few times. "I tell you what. I do you a favor, you do me a favor. In a couple weeks, is my birthday. Big one. Seventy-five," she said with pride. "I am having party for me. You can make me cake. I will make you a dress."

"Really?" Abbey loved the idea of this barter solution.

"Yes, really. I taste your cakes. Wonderful. Delicious. They are work of art. Just like a dress."

Flattered and relieved, Abbey reached her hand out, and Magda shook it firmly. "Deal," Abbey said.

• • •

Abbey arrived home shortly before six.

When she walked into the house, she found her mother and Betty in the living room. Betty stood up. "How was your day, Miss Abbey?"

"We were busy." She rubbed the back of her neck, trying to

ease the stiffness. Nearly eight hours on her feet were taking its toll on her body. The day flew by because she had transported her mind to the banquet less than two weeks away.

Betty walked toward the door. "I'll see you tomorrow." She waved to Millie.

"Betty, before you go. Can you stay with my mom for a few extra hours on April eighteenth? It's a Saturday, and I've been invited to a dinner that starts at six—in Philadelphia. I would have to leave here no later than four to catch a four thirty train, and I should be home by midnight, I think."

Betty frowned. "Oh, no, Miss Abbey. I'm sorry. April eighteenth is the weekend of my family reunion in Delaware. Remember, I told you, I cannot work Saturday or Sunday that weekend."

And she had. For some reason, Abbey hadn't realized it was *that* weekend.

"I'm sorry, Miss Abbey. Maybe your sister can do it."

Maybe. As much as Abbey didn't like that idea, it was a possibility. Penny stayed with their mother so that Abbey could go to Camille's wedding, but ever since they had the argument where Penny pointed out that a long-distance relationship would never work, for many reasons obvious to Penny—the most obvious was that it would impact, well, mostly Penny.

"Thanks, Betty. I'll figure it out. See you tomorrow."

"Bye Miss Abbey. Bye Miss Millie," Betty said as she walked to the front door and left.

Abbey felt a little deflated, but she wasn't ready to declare defeat. Maybe Penny was the best second option. As much as she didn't want to hear "I told you so" from her sister, it was an annoyance that she was willing to put up with because the reward was worth it.

She turned her attention to her mother. "I'm going to go make us some dinner." This wasn't entirely true. She wanted to call Penny, but not in front of her mother.

Millie nodded a faint approval before turning the TV up louder as the Jeopardy theme blared through the room.

Abbey walked into the kitchen. She took in a deep breath and let it out slowly. Why did calling her sister cause her so much anxiety? Her throat grew tight in a not-so-subtle metaphor on choking on humble pie when she heard her sister answer the phone.

"Hey, Pen," she said.

"Yes." Her sister's curtness was less than warm.

"Can you do me a favor?"

"What do you want?"

What came next had to be worded exactly right. "So, I was wondering if it would be at all possible . . . I mean, I know you are busy—very busy. But the guy from Philadelphia ...."

"Uh-huh."

"Well, he's asked me to be his date for a dinner where he's being honored."

"Yes, and . . . "

"And, well, I was wondering if you could stay with Mom. On April eighteenth so that I could go to the dinner." Abbey crossed her fingers as she spoke and whispered "please, please please."

"Hmm." Penny did not hold back her sarcasm.

"Betty can't. It's important, Penny, or else I wouldn't ask."

"Oh, Abbey, you know I'm not one to point out when I'm right."

Abbey rolled her eyes. It was so not true.

"But I think we had this exact conversation when you told me about—what's his name."

"Jax."

"Oh, that's right, Jax." There was a smugness to her voice. "The fact is, I can't. Kayley has a birthday party that day."

"Can't Doug take her to the party?"

"No, he can't. He will be taking care of Brandon."

"Can't you drop her off, and he can pick her up?" Abbey started pleading in her head even though she could tell the direction the conversation was going.

"Abbey, you can ask me twenty different ways. The answer will be no every time. I'm sorry. My family comes first." Penny's voice was stern, as if she was scolding a child.

"Maybe you can give it some thought and let me know tomorrow." Abbey knew she sounded desperate. With her options slowly dwindling to none, she was pulling out all stops.

"Goodbye, Abbey," Penny said, before the call ended.

Abbey was beyond disappointed. Only two people other than herself had ever stayed with her mother for any length of time: Betty and Penny. She thought long and hard about solutions. Who could she trust? Caroline would, of course, be at work because Abbey couldn't. So, that leaves her out. Camille? Nope. She and Skip would be on their belated honeymoon in Greece. Charlie? That thought actually made her laugh. She pictured herself calling him up. "Hey, Charlie, can you sit with my mom while I go on a date with another guy?" That played out like a bad teen movie plot.

Maybe a Granny Nanny service? She had looked into such a service a few months earlier and found them to be very costly and unreliable.

Abbey put her head in her hands. This was getting too complicated. She was a true believer that the universe sends signs—some that are loud and easily decipherable, as was in this case. But she didn't want to give up and call Jax, not just yet.

She opened the cupboard and took out a bag of potato chips. After opening the bag, she took three chips and shoved them all in her mouth. And then followed it with another handful. The salty snack slowly calmed her down.

Above the sound of crushing chips in her mouth, Abbey heard "Who is Huckleberry Finn?" The sound of her mother playing along with her favorite game show.

Amid the cacophony of crunching chips and a blaring TV game show, a plan formed in Abbey's mind. She became deep in thought, thinking this option through before deciding it might just work.

19

On the afternoon of April eighteenth, Abbey tried to calm her nerves. Her hands shook visibly as she stepped into the dress that Magda had created for her. She zipped the dress up and walked to a full-length mirror. Seeing her reflection, she immediately felt comforted. The rich, silky fabric hugged and caressed the curves of her body in a way that made her feel pretty and even a little bit sexy.

Since the wedding, things had been good with Jax. With each passing day of the good feeling, Abbey slowly let down her guard. Even though tonight's dinner would be the first time they'd seen each other in two weeks, they had spent the time in between flirting for hours on FaceTime and dreaming out loud. He made her feel special and desirable, telling her frequently that he couldn't wait to see her. They shared their thoughts on how to make a long-distance relationship work and agreed communication, trust, and respect would be key components to their plan.

He also shared that he was seriously considering buying a place in Baltimore's glitzy Harbor East neighborhood to be closer to his new commercial real estate venture. That meant he would be splitting his time between Baltimore and Philadelphia. *Take that, Penny!* She triumphantly said to herself upon hearing the news.

She looked at her watch, three fifty, ten minutes before the car that Jax was sending for her would arrive. She had originally planned to take the train, but Jax would have none of that idea. He insisted on using his company's driver so that she could ride to the event in style. No schlepping on the train for her this time, and she was grateful.

After putting on some dark cherry-colored lip gloss, she tucked the tube in her purse for later touch-ups. One last look in the mirror. Abbey stared at a face she barely recognized—one with sparkling eyes and deeply dimpled cheeks. For once, she thought she looked as good on the outside as she felt on the inside.

She walked into the living room and over to her mother sitting in her usual spot. "Okay, I'm going to head out now." Millie looked up, nodded, but, as usual, said nothing.

"Where's your phone?" Abbey asked.

Millie searched her pocket until she produced a flip phone—one that one been Abbey's many years ago. Millie held up the phone.

"Good. Okay, let's practice. Until Caroline gets here, what do you do if you need something?"

Millie opened the phone and stared at it briefly. She looked back up at Abbey. "Press number one," she said. Her voice was full of confidence.

"That's right, that will call me. But only call if you really need something. Don't call me if you don't know the answer to a Jeopardy question. Caroline will be here about six, after the bakery closes, so you will only be alone for two hours. Okay?"

Millie nodded again.

"All right. I'm leaving." Abbey turned to walk toward the door.

"Abbey?" Millie called in a faint voice.

Abbey stopped dead in her tracks, her shoulders slouched a little, fearing what her mother had to say. She turned around and faced her mother. "Yes, Momma."

"You look beautiful," Millie said.

Abbey felt a lump form in her throat. She had never heard her mother say that to her. She had often heard her say, "Penny's the

172

pretty one, Abbey's the other one." Her mother's words covered her like a warm blanket, and it felt so good. Abbey smiled. "Thank you, Momma. I'll see you later tonight," she said, before walking out the door.

• • •

The sleek black Cadillac Escalade pulled up to the Engineer's Club of Philadelphia at exactly five fifty-eight. She thanked the driver and stepped out onto the red carpet that covered the club's entrance. Standing at the top of the short staircase leading to the club's door was Jax.

He waved before walking down to greet her. "There she is," he said, as he walked toward her. When he reached her, he kissed her lightly on the cheek. "You look amazing," he whispered in her ear.

"Thank you. So do you," Abbey whispered back.

He stepped away from their embrace. "Lawrence, Jackson Lawrence," Jax said, tugging at the tips of his bow tie and doing his best Bond impression.

Abbey laughed. Could it be real that this handsome, sexy, funny guy was hers?

"C'mon. Let's go inside. There are some people I want you to meet." He took her hand and intertwined his fingers in hers, and they walked up the stairs to the entrance together.

When they got to the entrance, Jax reached for the door. He held it open with one hand while gently placing his other hand on the small of her back.

Abbey had a good nervous feeling—one of anticipation, but also one of joy. It felt like those scenes described in books and movies, with actual butterflies doing a happy dance in her head and stomach.

They walked through the club's foyer and into a grand

ballroom.

"Whoa," Abbey said out loud, and accidentally.

Jax smiled. "Pretty spectacular, huh?"

With ornate gold mirrors and crystal chandeliers that reminded Abbey of her French class's senior year trip abroad, and Versailles in particular. The ballroom was set with a stage in the front of the room and round tables sprinkled throughout. Jax guided her to a table near the stage with a reserved sign posted high on a metal prong.

"This is us," he said. On each place setting was a folded program with Jax's picture on the cover underneath a banner which said, "Philadelphia's Chamber of Commerce Man of the Year— Jackson Lawrence III."

Abbey picked up the program. It took a moment to let it all sink in. That cute guy, the man of the year, was her cute guy. "This is so cool," she said.

A tiny woman and an older version of Jax appeared next to them. Abbey knew his parents would be there, and just like that, before she could panic, they were there.

Jax kissed his mother on the cheek and then shook his father's hand.

"You must be Abbey," Jax's mother said with an inviting smile. Barbara "Bunny" Lawrence resembled her nickname. She had a little nose and brown almond-shaped eyes. Her white hair was cropped short in a stylish pixie cut that emphasized her earrings with the biggest sapphires Abbey had ever seen—that is, until she looked at the matching gem in a ring on Bunny's left hand.

Even though Abbey knew his parents would be there, she was not ready for this moment. Meeting the parents has to be one of the top ten scariest situations that life could offer. At this point, Abbey wished she had an option to choose one of the other nine.

174

"Nice to meet you," Abbey said, reaching her hand out to Bunny.

Bunny took Abbey's hand in both of hers. Her expression was kind. "So nice to meet you, too," Bunny said. Abbey immediately liked her. It was comfortable enough for Abbey to breathe a little easier.

"Hi, I'm Jack," Jax's father said, reaching his hand out to Abbey. The elder Jackson Lawrence had jet-black hair with gray around his temples. He was very tanned, likely from his daily golf ritual that Jax sometimes tagged along on. He shook her hand firmly. He let go and slapped Jax on the back in a playful way. "Mother and I are so proud of you. Our boy, man of the year! This is big for JPL. You can't buy this type of good press."

"Thanks, Dad." Jax returned the pat on the back.

Bunny turned toward Abbey. "So, Jax tells us you are quite the baker."

Abbey was pleasantly surprised that Jax really had told his parents about her. "Yeah, I enjoy it even though it's my job."

"I look forward to tasting some of your treats someday." Bunny's nose twitched a little in a bunny sort of way.

"I bet you'd like my carrot cake," Abbey blurted without a filter. She closed her eyes and instantly regretted what came out. It was too late to put those words back in. She opened her eyes slowly when she heard a chortle of laughter from the Lawrence clan.

Bunny smiled. "Jax said you have a wonderful sense of humor, and he was right. Besides"—her eyes grew wide— "I love carrot cake. Why, doesn't every bunny?"

Abbey laughed. "Oh, good," she said. "Because—all jokes aside—I do make a good one. The trick is grinding up the walnuts along with shredded carrots."

Bunny nodded. "Sounds wonderful. I look forward to trying it."

"Hey, there, Lawrences!" A tall woman with brassy blond hair in an updo poked her head between Jax and his mother.

"Elle!" Bunny turned to embrace the woman. "How are you?"

Did Bunny say Elle? Abbey had a sinking feeling this was *the* Elle. She looked her over. Tall, check. Blond, check. Thin, check. Oozing of money, check, check, check. Ugh, it was *the* Elle.

"I'm good. And you?" Elle said.

"We're doing well. So nice to see you," Bunny said.

Jax looked flushed. "Hello, Elle," he said with a faint smile.

"What, no hug for me?" Elle said as she wrapped her long arms around Jax's neck. She finished the embrace with a kiss on the cheek that left a pink lip print. When she pulled away, she said, "Oh, did I do that? Here, let me." And she did that thing that mothers do, licked her fingers and rubbed the smudge off.

Jax pushed her away gently. He gestured to Abbey and said, "Elle, I'd like for you to meet Abbey Reilly. My girlfriend."

Did he just say what she thought he said? Girlfriend? Girlfriend! The words echoed in Abbey's head like plucked strings on a harp. Until now, Abbey had been hesitant to put a label on what they had. "So nice to meet you," Abbey said as she extended her hand toward Elle.

Elle extended her hand and gave Abbey's a halfhearted shake. "Elle Franklin Thompson. So nice to meet you." When she said her name, she over pronounced the "le" at the end, making it sound more like an "la." It was the same way Abbey remembered her eighth-grade French teacher said the phrase "Elle est la?" while calling roll at the beginning of class.

Elle turned her attention back to Jax. "So, how have you been?"

"Good. Busy," he said.

"Same here. I just reached one hundred ninety-four thousand subscribers on Instagram, and I have close to that on Twitter. As my dad would say, 'She finally found a way to get paid to shop.'"

"Someone pays you to shop?" Bunny was clearly intrigued.

"Well, sort of. I get products sent to me in the mail, like clothes and makeup, and then I post pictures of me wearing or using the products."

"That's great," Jax said. "Two hundred thousand followers. That's impressive."

"Two hundred thousand?" Jax's father sounded like a mynah bird. His smile was the same as his son—broad and displaying perfect white teeth.

The elder Lawrences seemed giddy to be catching up with Elle, and the same sentiment was there in reverse. It was as if Abbey wasn't even there. She studied Jax's expression carefully. She could not tell if he was engaged in the conversation or not, and this worried her more than a little.

"Hey, I've got an idea, how about I post a picture on Twitter and Instagram of Philadelphia's Man of the Year?" Elle took her phone from her cute little pink sequence purse and handed it to Bunny. "Mom, do you mind?"

Did she just call her "Mom"? Before Abbey could react, Jax called her over. "C'mon. I want you in this too."

Abbey walked over to Jax, and he put his arm around her with Elle leaning in close on his other side.

"Okay, on the count of three," Bunny said. "One. Two. Three." Bunny took the phone down and peered at the results. She handed the phone to Elle. Elle viewed the photo and nodded.

"Good," Elle said. "Now, how about one with the four of us?" She pointed to Jax, Bunny, and Jack. "For old time's sake. Here, Addie. Would you mind?" She handed her phone to Abbey.

Abbey peeled away from Jax's embrace. As she did, he let his hand linger ever so slightly on her back. She wanted him to say something, anything—more specifically, she hoped he would say "That's not necessary" or just "no," but he didn't.

She stood in the same spot that Bunny did. "Okay," she said. "On the count of three." She looked through the camera lens at four perfect specimens of inherent fine genetics. Like the old Sesame Street song about one object not belonging with all of the others. In this group of five, it was easy to pick out the one that did not belong. Abbey quickly snapped the picture to not prolong her feeling of being uncomfortable.

Abbey's attempt to hand the phone back to Elle was met with, "Could you do one more?"

Elle then pulled Jax closer, leaning in a little more. She was nearly as tall as he was, at least in heels. Her cheek seemed to nestle close to his like the snug fit of a perfect puzzle piece.

The dagger dug a little deeper into Abbey's back. She took the phone back and peered through the screen. Looking up momentarily, she caught Jax's eyes. He gave her a quick wink, the corners of his eyes creasing making him even more handsome. Not sure how to take this gesture, she chose to think positively. He was reassuring her that he knew she was uncomfortable and to just hang in there.

"One. Two. Three." With a click, the image was sent to Elle's phone and etched into Abbey's memory.

Abbey handed the phone back to Elle. "Thank you," Elle said. She looked at the photos. "I'll tag you. Are you still @ Jax_Lawrence?"

"Yep."

Truthfully, Abbey didn't even know he was on Twitter or Instagram. She had an account, @TheBakersAbbey, which was linked to her blog. She used it to post recipes and baking tips a few times a week. She hadn't even thought to check for him.

"And does Katie still do your social media? @JPL?"

"Yes, she does," Jax said.

"Okay, I'll tag her, too. I believe no press is bad press."

"Why, I say the same thing," Jack chimed in. "Thank you, Elle."

"Sure thing." Elle tapped Bunny on the wrist. "So nice seeing you, Mom. Don't be a stranger."

"You, too." Bunny placed her other hand on top of Elle's.

Elle broke the twine of hands and turned to Jax. "Congratulations, Jax. You deserve it. I'm glad things are going so well for you." She glanced at Abbey and smiled before walking away.

Even though the scene probably didn't last more than five or ten minutes, it felt like an eternity for Abbey. Long and painful beyond words.

"Shall we make our way to the bar, Mother?" Jack was the first to break the silence. "There's a dry martini with my name on it."

"Okay, I guess we'll catch you guys later," Bunny said before the two walked away.

Jax put his arm around Abbey's waist and drew her near. "I am sorry about that."

"It's okay." She downplayed her true reaction. It felt good that he at least acknowledged how uncomfortable the situation was for her.

"No, it wasn't. I'm sure you have a lot of questions about me and Elle. Just believe me when I say I want to be here with you tonight. Not her."

"I do believe you," she said when it would be more honest to say, "I want to believe you, really I do."

"I can tell my parents like you."

"You can?"

"Yes, look, I know they kind of fawned over Elle. It's just that we dated for so long—years. And then we were planning a wedding. They got used to her being a part of the family. She was like the daughter they never had. But both of my parents also recognized that she wasn't good for me...we weren't good together." His words helped. He was always so good at saying just the right thing at the right time.

"Thanks for that. It means a lot."

"And you mean a lot to me." He pulled her even closer. "I promise, the rest of the night will be better."

"Promise?" Abbey raised her pinky up.

Jax locked his pinky in hers. "Pinky swear," he said.

"Okay, I'll hold you to that."

He kissed her cheek ever so slightly and let his hand linger on the small of her back. "Do you want to get a drink too?"

"Um, I probably should find a bathroom before too long," she said.

He shook his head. "Go right ahead. I'll text you if I move around." He squeezed her hand lightly and smiled.

Abbey made her way to the ladies' room, which was just outside of the ballroom. The brightly lit room contained seven stalls with white shutter-slatted doors. She chose one in the middle.

Underneath the custom-made dress was a layer of confining shapeware that could best be described as masochistic, even if they gave the illusion of an hourglass shape by cinching her waist. The contraption was not easy to get into—she contorted her body in every which way as she eased the tight garment into place. It had well-thought-out snaps in the crotch area so that the entire garment did not need to be put on and off for such a time as this.

In the midst of unsnapping, the bathroom door opened, followed by the laughter of two women. The laughter carried to the sink area in front of Abbey's bathroom stall.

"So, what was it like seeing him again?"

"Pretty great." The voice was familiar. Abbey was sure it was Elle.

Abbey leaned forward so that she could peek through one of the slats, in an attempt to spy on the conversation.

Elle's friend was blond too. She was a little shorter than Elle, but other than that, they could be twins, or even sisters.

"Did you say he has a new girlfriend?" the friend asked.

"Yes." Elle put a fresh coat of lip gloss on and then turned to her friend. "I'm not worried about that."

"Why not?"

"Did you see her?"

"No."

Abbey could see Elle's reflection in the mirror as she filled her cheeks with air and extended her arms in a spherical way to indicate she was talking about a big person. "She's fat."

The friend laughed. "No way!"

"Way! Really fat."

A lump formed in Abbey's throat and tears welled up in her eyes. It was the familiar pain of being judged for the shape of her body. One that had happened too often. One that had made her doubt anyone would ever want her. Deep quiet breaths, deep quiet breaths, she told herself, hoping and praying the torture would end.

"Do you think he actually likes her?" The friend asked.

Elle scoffed. "Don't worry. If he does, he won't anymore."

"What did you do?" The friend's voice was filled with awe and maybe a hint of joy.

"I posted a picture of the three of us on Instagram." Elle took her phone from her purse and tapped an app. "My ex and his new girlfriend." She showed the post to her friend. "I'll let my followers do what they do best—they can be so judgmental. They judge me every day. If they are willing to say I look fat in an outfit, I don't have any doubt what they'll say about her."

"Oh, that's mean," the friend said, but in a sinister kind of way.

"Then tomorrow, or maybe I'll wait until Monday, I'll text him saying how much I enjoyed seeing him tonight. Congrats and all that. I'm sure after seeing me tonight he's probably missing all this." She smoothed her hand down her body.

"You are so mean, and I love it!" The friend handed the phone back to Elle.

"Oh, look. The comments are already coming in," Elle said with glee. "Oh my God, listen to this— 'He dumped you for her?'" She let out a squealing laugh. "Oh, and this one, 'The new GF looks like the purple girl that blew up on Willy Wonka.' Wait. Wait. They're coming in faster than I can read them."

Abbey's feet felt like they were encased in cement. She couldn't move, notwithstanding she would never think of leaving the stall while they were in the bathroom. She swallowed hard and tried to fight back the tears, careful to keep quiet.

"Ha! Oh, my God! This one is the best!" Elle shrieked. "She looks like a purple Fiona. Look. They've added a Shrek meme." Elle and her friend cackled like buzzards devouring carrion.

Abbey put her hands firmly over her ears in an attempt to mute their hurtful words. It really did nothing. Unfortunately, she could still hear.

"Oh, wait, there's more," Elle's voice was cheerful. "We now have hashtags trending—#fatchick, #tradingdown, #PurpleFiona. I love it." Elle gave her friend a high five. "I'd say you should brush off your bridesmaid dress. I think my work here is done."

"How do you know he'll see it?"

"I tagged him."

Abbey closed her eyes. She imagined Jax reading these hurtful comments. It's one thing to feel shame and embarrassment, it's another when you imagine someone else feeling that because of you.

"Oh, look. Look!" Elle's voice got a little higher. "He liked the post! Jax liked the post!"

"Oh, girl, you've got him."

He liked the post? He liked the post? He liked the post. All hope left Abbey's body, even though it had already dwindled to a very tiny bit.

After washing their hands and drying them off, the two women left the bathroom.

When she was sure the women were gone, Abbey sat for a minute or two, fearing they would return. Briefly, she was transported to a time when she was in middle school. In the locker room getting ready for gym class, she carefully tried to dress and undress with the locker door shielding her fleshly body until one day Sheila Shannon yelled, "Hey there, Peppa!" The nickname stuck through middle and high school. She had no idea that mean girls existed at this stage of her life. But sadly, some things never change.

Abbey sat in silence, still unable to move. She took a wad of toilet paper and wiped tears. There really was no good outcome. The hashtags reverberated in her head. And, to top it off, he liked the post. What did that mean?

She felt her phone vibrate in her purse. He was probably wondering what was taking so long. She needed to pull herself together. She took the phone out and closed her eyes. Just when she thought things couldn't get any worse, she was wrong. There were seven missed calls from Caroline and one text that read *Call me ASAP.*

20

"Your mom fell." There was a bit of urgency in Caroline's voice.

"What? Is she okay?" Abbey asked.

"I don't know. When I got here, I found her on the floor. I'm not sure how long she was there. An ambulance is on its way."

"Ambulance?" Caroline's words were the "two" in a one-two punch of an emotionally traumatic evening. Still seated on the toilet, Abbey slumped in place. She rubbed her forehead as it pulsed. Her heart thumped like a bass drum as she pictured her mother helplessly lying on the floor. "How bad is it?"

"She's bleeding." There were muffled sounds on the other end. "Pretty bad."

"Oh, no!" The floodgates opened and tears rolled down Abbey's cheeks. "What? Where? What happened?" Her voice shook as she spoke.

"I'm not sure. I think she tried to get up, fell and hit her head on the end table."

"She hit her head?" Abbey managed to say in between sobs. This was bad. Very bad.

"Yes, she has a gash on the side of her face, just near her eye. I think it's pretty deep by the amount of blood on her and the floor."

Abbey tried to gather her thoughts, which were racing in a rapid-fire, staccato way. She should have been there and not here in Philadelphia. She should have never left her alone. "My poor mother," Abbey cried.

"She's really confused—more than ever." There was sincere

compassion and worry in Caroline's voice. "She doesn't know who I am and is convinced I'm trying to hurt her. Pretty combative. She keeps swatting me away and calling for you. Ouch. Hold on." Caroline's voice became inaudible briefly. Abbey could make out a few words— "Millie" and "Stop." And then she heard nothing at all even though the call had not been disconnected.

Still in the bathroom stall, Abbey stood. She shifted her weight from side to side. Come on, Caroline. She pleaded in a whisper for Caroline to rejoin the call. This was so predictable and all because of her stupid, selfish plan.

Shortly thereafter, Caroline rejoined the call. She was obviously out of breath. "Abbey, the EMTs are here. I've got to go."

"Okay, I'll be there as soon as I can."

"Okay, I'll text you updates."

"Thanks." Abbey ended the call and sat back down on the toilet. Tears streamed down her cheeks. She took a wad of toilet paper and blew her nose and dabbed her eyes. Then she balled her hands into fists. She pounded the walls of the stall before putting her head in her hands and collapsing into a fetal position. The day had started out with so much promise and now was ending in disaster.

After taking in a few very deep breaths, she stood. She quickly realized her knees were a little wobbly. She steadied herself with a hand on the side wall of the stall as she opened the door. She looked around. No one else was in the bathroom. She went to the sink and splashed water on her eyes swollen with tears.

She emerged from the ladies' room and saw Jax standing across the hall. He was leaning against the wall in a kind of nonchalant way. His smile quickly faded. "What's wrong?" He approached her, wrapping an arm around her shoulders and drawing her near.

Abbey nestled her head in the crook between his arm and shoulder. "My mom..." she got out in between sniffles.

"What?" He pulled away and grasped her shoulders. "What happened?"

"My mom fell."

"What? Oh, no. Is she okay?"

Abbey shook her head. "I have to go."

"Of course you do. Let me call Ron and have him bring the car around." Jax led Abbey to a marble bench that was near the entrance to the Engineer's Club. "Sit here." He walked away to a more secluded area. After a brief phone conversation, he turned his attention to Abbey. "Ron will be here in a few minutes."

Jax guided her up with his hand and helped her down the stairs and to the curb outside of the entrance. Shortly thereafter, the Cadillac Escalade pulled up. Jax opened the car door and helped Abbey into the back seat. "Keep me posted," he said.

"Jax, I'm sorry. This was supposed to be your night."

He touched his finger to his lips. "No 'sorry' necessary." He shut the door and waved as the car pulled off.

Once Abbey was in the car, she felt all the energy leave her body. She dabbed her eyes of an occasional tear. The mental image of her mother lying helpless on the floor was torturous. Her phone pinged with a text from Caroline. *We're on our way to Howard County General.*

OK. On my way. Should be there in about 90 mins.

After giving the hospital's address to Ron, she settled back into the soft leather seat of the SUV. Ninety minutes seemed like an eternity. It was a long way. On the way up, she couldn't wait to get there, now on the way home, she felt the same way. And now that she was in a helpless state of limbo, the whole evening felt like a painful nightmare that she couldn't wake up from.

With her phone in her hand, she first checked to see if Caroline had sent her an update. She hadn't. Her mind shifted to the horrible scene in the bathroom. The crisis with her mother distracted from the hurtful comments of Elle and her friend. A self-confident Abbey would have marched out of the bathroom stall and punched Elle in the face or at the very least confronted her. That moment had passed and the Abbey that stood up for herself only lived in her dreams. Elle's almost two hundred thousand Instagram followers were no doubt laughing right now. There was nowhere to hide from that. Her humiliation was out there for the world to see.

For some reason that could only be described as masochism, she wanted to see the carnage for herself. She opened the Instagram app and typed in Elle in the search field. This search quickly gave way to a slew of Elles, none that looked like the Elle she was looking for. She was about to give up when she thought to search for Jax—Jackson_Lawrence, she recalled him verifying his moniker when Elle asked. She could get to Elle's post from Jax because she was sure Elle tagged Jax.

Bingo. The search yielded several photos of her sweet, cute guy. The latest was the picture Elle posted earlier. Before clicking on the post, Abbey hesitated. She wasn't sure why she was compelled to do what she was about to do. Dig the knife in deeper, she supposed. Make the wound irreparable. It was karma, and she deserved to suffer.

Based on the post, Elle's Instagram's name was El_La_La. *So pretentious.* Nothing if not predictable. Abbey clicked on it, and even though every voice inside her told her not to, she fell deeper down the rabbit hole.

Reading Elle's IG page, Abbey's eyes widened. Elle—or El_La_La—had more than one hundred posts in the month of April alone. On quick calculation, it was about six a day. Lots of poses in jeans and sweaters with brand name hashtags in the post. While she was scrolling through Elle's various posts, a new post popped up. It was a photo of Elle with her head on Jax's shoulder. The post read: "Congratulations to Philadelphia's Man of Year!" and Jax was tagged again. Abbey's heart sank to a depth she didn't know. She recognized the table's centerpiece and fine crystal ware. Elle was seated at the banquet table next to Jax where Abbey was supposed to be. Elle's swoop in to reclaim what she missed seemed complete.

Abbey threw her phone, and it hit the padding of the back of the driver's seat before landing on the floor next to her.

"Everything okay?" Ron looked in the rearview mirror as he spoke.

"Yeah. Thanks." Tears welled in her eyes for what seemed like the umpteenth time. She looked out the window to gain a sense of where they were on the long stretch of I-95 between Philadelphia and Baltimore. A road sign for Maryland House indicated they were about an hour away. On the sign was a giant picture of fried chicken in waffles dripping in butter and maple syrup. "You know you want it," the sign taunted.

"Ron," she said.

"Ma'am?"

"Can we—" She interrupted her own thought mid-sentence. "Never mind." Turning to food was not the answer this time.

• • •

When Abbey got to the hospital, it was just before nine. Caroline was sitting in the waiting room. "I'm sorry, Abbey." She stood as Abbey ran in.

They hugged long and hard. "How is she?" Abbey asked.

"She's okay. They got her calmed down by giving her a shot of something. I think she's sleeping. She's there." Caroline pointed to an area behind closed doors. "They're going to keep her, at least for tonight. Maybe even a few days."

"Thanks, Caroline, for calling the ambulance and staying until I got here."

Caroline waved her off. "Of course. I just feel bad that you had to leave Philadelphia." She stroked Abbey shoulder. "How was it, by the way?"

"Oh, it was okay."

"Just okay? I'll bet it was more than okay. You look so pretty. That's such a good color on you."

Abbey shrugged. "We can talk about that later. I should go see my mom. Thanks again. I'll let you know how things turn out here tonight." Abbey turned to walk toward the ER receptionist.

"Um. Abbey?" Caroline said, her tone had shifted to one that was more serious.

"Yes?" Abbey turned back toward Caroline.

"She's here. Penny."

Abbey got a sinking feeling inside, as her head filled with the expected shrill screams of her sister's accusatory voice. She had rehearsed telling her sister on the phone in a way that downplayed (or maybe forgot to mention) the fact that she'd left their mother alone. "Oh," Abbey said.

"I'm sorry. When I couldn't get a hold of you, I panicked."

"It's okay, you did the right thing."

"Just be prepared. She's pretty mad." Caroline winced.

"Thanks, Caroline."

"I've got the shop covered tomorrow. You take the day off."

Abbey nodded, but she really just wanted to leave with Caroline—walk away from it all. It would be easier than facing her sister with her "How could you? You promised Dad." As Penny's judgment played in her head, each syllable jabbed a little deeper than the one before it. In this case, Penny would be right to yell.

The receptionist directed Abbey to go to ER bay number two.

Bay number two sat directly across from the nursing station. A thin blue curtain on overhead tracks separated it from the twelve other bays. The ER was noisy. Loud and frequent pulsating beeps echoed throughout the room like a symphony warming up.

Once she swung the curtain, Abbey saw her mother tucked into a hospital bed wearing a hospital gown and a gauze bandage taped above her cheek, close to her eye. Both eyes were closed, and her mouth was wide open. Machines and their rhythmic noises assured Abbey that her mother was just sleeping and not something more ominous.

She went to her mother's side closest to the bay entrance and put her hand on top of her mother's.

Penny sat on the other side of Millie's bed. She looked up from her phone. Her eyes narrowed and grew dark. "Don't even," she said with one hand raised.

"I'm sorry." Abbey didn't know what to say. In all honesty, if Penny had done what Abbey just did—irresponsibly leave their mother alone—Abbey would have trouble forgiving Penny.

"I don't know what's wrong with you." Penny growled. "What were you thinking? I told Dad you were too irresponsible."

Penny's dagger was deep. Bringing up their father was a new blow. Did her father think she was too irresponsible? Abbey looked at her sister in disbelief.

"That's right. He and I had a discussion before he asked you to come take care of Mom. I told him it'd be a big mistake. I told him you were too selfish and of course, I was right."

It was more than Abbey could take. "Shut up, Penny!" she said in a raised voice.

Penny raised an eyebrow. And she had a look of disdain.

"Do you think I don't feel bad? Of course, I do. That's the

difference between me and you. I have a conscience."

"Oh, really? St. Abbey has a conscience. Whoop-de-do." Penny mocked. "Oh, wait. Here. Let me give you a medal for that." She crossed her arms. "You are really unbelievable. You want to know the reason Dad picked you to take care of Mom? It's because you're a loser. You've been right all along. You're a loser." She stared at Abbey unflinchingly.

"And you are a self-centered, egotistical, high maintenance..." Abbey's head was filled with things she wanted to say to Elle hours earlier. A volcano of emotion erupted inside Abbey as she spewed words without a filter. "Mean girl. You're nothing but a mean girl." Abbey didn't recognize the person she had become or the words she was saying. "You're despicable. I hate you."

Penny's expression said it all. Abbey had touched a nerve.

A nurse came into the bay. "You two have got to keep it down or else we'll only allow one of you at a time to visit," she said, shifting her gaze between the two women like a teacher breaking up a schoolyard brawl.

"No worries." Penny stood and picked up her purse from the floor. "I'm leaving."

"Penny. Don't. I'm sorry." Abbey was often on the receiving end of hurtful words, and she knew how badly words could wound. She reached for her sister as she brushed by.

"Don't touch me," Penny said, jerking her body just out of Abbey's reach. The edge of the curtain flew up like a wave in a tsunami as Penny walked out.

"Are you okay?" the nurse asked.

"Yeah. Sibling stuff."

The woman nodded in a way that meant she understood completely.

Abbey went to the other side of her mother's bed and sat in the chair that Penny had used. She leaned forward and rested her head on her mother's chest. She heard her mother's heartbeat in tune with the machine next to her bed. It was a warm and vaguely familiar feeling to lie next to her mother. She breathed in the smell of her mother's body against the freshly washed hospital gown. Tears flowed like they would never stop. In between sobs, she said, "I'm so sorry."

A frail hand lightly stroked Abbey's hair, and it instantly calmed her—just like it had many times before. For the first time in many years, the roles reversed back to their original state as mother comforted daughter.

21

"As we age, our bones can become brittle, and a fall can easily cause a break." A doctor with a salt and pepper goatee and a few strands of gray hair combed over his balding head pointed to an X-ray on his iPad. His lab coat read "Ernest Millian, M.D., Chief of Emergency Medicine" embroidered in blue script.

Abbey rubbed her eyes. She checked her watch. It was seven in the morning. She had spent a sleepless night in the ER bay next to her mother. The gash on Millie's face was stitched soon after Abbey arrived. Then they waited without word for several hours. This was the first update since an orderly took her mother for X-rays more than three hours earlier.

She squinted to see the fracture in the X-ray film.

"Your mother broke her fibula here and here," Dr. Millian continued. "She will need surgery to secure the bones and make sure they heal properly." He used a white pencil to scroll down the screen.

"Whoa. What?" The doctor's words caught Abbey off guard. She thought Dr. Millian was coming in to tell her they were planning to discharge her mother—he'd say something like, "Take her home, give her TLC, chicken soup, wrap her in a blanket and watch her like a hawk." Abbey combed her hair with both hands to move it out of her face in an effort to stall and let the doctor's words sink in. "When will that happen? The operation." She diverted her eyes down to her mother. Millie was resting peacefully, eyes closed and an occasional rumble of a snore.

"We'll operate later today. Dr. Williams, the orthopedist on call, should be here within the hour to examine your mother. I sent him a copy of the X-rays." He put his iPad down on top of the medical supply table next to her mother's bed. "We have her leg in a soft cast to protect it until she has the surgery." He took a pair of rubber gloves from a box on the table and lifted the bandage on Millie's cheek.

After inspecting the wound closely, and touching the bruised area around the wound, the doctor said, "Sutures look good. We'll leave them in for about ten days." While changing the dressing on the wound, he said, "Miss Reilly, your mother is a lucky lady. The wound on her cheek could have easily been a few inches to the right, and that would have likely caused damage to her eye or even loss of sight."

Dr. Millian's rubber gloves made a snapping sound as he removed them one by one. He balled them up before throwing them in the waste bin. "We're going to be moving your mother out of the ER and into a room on the fifth floor sometime this morning. I'm sorry she had to spend the night down here in the ER, but we simply didn't have any beds." He picked up his iPad. "I'd like her to stay here a few days to recover."

Again, the doctor's words seeped into Abbey's brain in a slow way like an old-fashioned record player on low speed. "So, she'll stay here for a few days and then be able to come home?"

The doctor shook his head. "I am suggesting your mother go to rehab after she recovers from the surgery—say, Tuesday or Wednesday, depending on how well she does."

"Rehab?"

Dr. Millian looked very serious. "Yes, for physical therapy. She'll need intensive rehab to build her strength and help her learn to put weight on the broken leg. If she doesn't get physical therapy immediately after surgery, there can be muscle atrophy." He had read Abbey's mind correctly when he added, "Muscle atrophy is when the muscles begin to deteriorate. Once that happens, recovery is much more difficult."

"How long do you think she'll need to be there...in rehab?"

"I'd say six to nine weeks."

"Weeks?" *Nine Weeks?*

Dr. Millian nodded. "Your mother is pretty frail."

Abbey had to agree, but it didn't make his words easier to hear.

A youngish woman with shoulder-length brown hair entered the ER bay.

"Oh, hi, Lucy," the doctor said. "Thanks for coming. Miss Reilly, this is Lucy White, the hospital's social worker."

Lucy's smile exhibited a slight overbite but otherwise perfect teeth. She carried with her a thick black binder clutched tightly to her chest.

Abbey returned Lucy's smile, but with less intensity.

"I've asked Lucy to come here to discuss care options for your mother," Dr. Millian said.

"*I* care for my mother," Abbey said.

"Miss Reilly, if I may," Lucy spoke up. Her voice was nurturing and motherly. "No one is saying you don't take care of your mother." She took a pamphlet out from the front pocket of the binder and handed it to Abbey. "We want to make you aware of options."

Options? Abbey did not like the direction the conversation was headed.

"This is Sacred Heart in Catonsville. They have a lovely memory care unit that would be good for your mother."

Abbey took the brochure and scanned it. It looked like a college dorm for senior adults—all attractive, smiling and with it. The brochure showed pictures of smiling silver-haired men and women dancing, playing tennis, and playing cards. There wasn't one person who looked like her mother—a hollowed-out shell of the woman she used to be. She darted her eyes between the pamphlet, her mother, the social worker, and the doctor. "Thanks, but I think we're okay...my mom and me." She reached her hand out to Lucy, trying to give her back the pamphlet. But Lucy did not take it.

"Did Dr. Millian tell you your mom will need rehab after the surgery? Well, she can do rehab at Sacred Heart, and they have a long-term care unit as well." She cleared her throat. "That means she can live there."

"Are you suggesting my mom move there? For good?"

Lucy nodded. "Yes. I know the admissions director there very well. They have room, and I think it'd be perfect for Mom."

Abbey sat straight up and directed her comments right at Lucy and said, "She's my mom, and you don't even know what would be perfect for *my* mom."

"True. I don't. I only know what we've seen in the last twelve hours. Miss Reilly, if it were my mom...if my mom fell and broke her leg, my first concern would be for her safety. At Sacred Heart, she will be safe. Just hold on to the brochure. You don't have to make a decision today. When the time comes, you know you have an option."

Abbey folded the brochure up and tucked it in her purse. "I'll give it some thought."

"That's all we're asking you to do," Lucy said. "Who knows, she may get to rehab, make some friends, and want to stay. The decision will be easy if that happens."

Feeling defensive, Abbey said, "My mom has a wonderful caregiver—Betty. She takes care of my mom when I'm at work. I've arranged so that she's never alone." She shifted her gaze down, realizing the obvious falseness of her claim.

"Miss Reilly, no one is saying you can't take care of your mother. What we are saying is maybe it's time your mother gets skilled nursing care from people experienced in dealing with residents who have cognitive deficits."

Cognitive Deficit. Those words were always a sucker punch. They were talking about her mother—the once vibrant, funny, active woman was now diminished to a diagnosis that meant limited mental capacity. Abbey reached for her mother's hand again and squeezed. Millie hadn't moved or even opened her eyes during the entire conversation. She wasn't sure what Millie understood, if anything. There was so much Abbey wanted to say to these two strangers. She wanted to tell them about her mother. That she once was a very active, sharp woman who liked to take risks. A woman who would shrink at the thought of her independence being stripped away. That what she was doing was because she loved her mother and she worried that putting her in an assisted living facility would be a dreadful experience for her. It was clear from the look on their faces that these two thought they had the situation figured out—a feeble-minded mother and a daughter in way over her head.

"And, Sacred Heart has a wonderful activities program. They do weekly arts and crafts and play all sorts of games. It will give your mom an opportunity to make friends. When your mother is up to it, you and she can take a tour, see if she likes it." Lucy sounded like a cruise director.

Abbey said nothing. It was totally out of the question for many reasons—the least of which was there was no way she or her mother could ever afford such a place.

"All right. Well, while Mom's in here recouping, give it some thought," Lucy said.

"Thanks, I will," Abbey said without looking up.

Abbey let go of her mother's hand and adjusted the blanket she had wrapped around her bare shoulders. She was still wearing the purple dress that was specially made for the night before. Such a beautiful garment, so carefully crafted and fitted. While smoothing her fingers over the fine lacy fabric of the skirt, she let out an audible gasp. Magda's birthday cake! In exchange for the dress, she'd promised to make Magda her birthday cake. Magda would need it in two days. In the sudden wake of her mother's accident, it had slipped her mind. But a deal was a deal. To bake and decorate a cake for fifty people would take the better part of six hours. Abbey usually allowed a day to bake the cakes and a day to decorate. Before her mother's accident, Abbey had planned to bake the cake today and decorate it tomorrow. Magda would probably understand if she told her she couldn't do the job, but Abbey really didn't want to let her down on such short notice.

"Why don't you go home and get some rest?" Dr. Millian said. He was good at picking up signs from weary relatives.

"Oh, I don't know if I should leave."

Dr. Millian nodded. "We'll call you when your mom is settled into a room. Once she has her surgery, I suspect she'll sleep a good bit—probably well into the night. Please, Miss Reilly, go home. You will be no good to your mother if you don't take care of yourself."

• • •

Abbey went home, showered, changed, and checked in on Figaro. About 10 a.m., she headed to the bakery. Caroline was waiting on a customer, otherwise the bakery was empty. Abbey went in the back. Within seconds, Caroline appeared.

"What on earth are you doing here?"

Abbey shrugged. "I need to make that cake for Magda."

"Oh, well, I could do that."

"No, I got it. It was my barter arrangement." She'd cleared it with Caroline when she'd made the deal with Magda. She'd bake the cake in the bakery—where she had everything that she needed—to pay Caroline back for the ingredients she'd use, she would work an hour for free. "Besides, I could use the distraction." Abbey took two ten-inch, and two eight-inch round cake pans from the cabinet. She was going to make a two-tiered red velvet with rich cream cheese swirled rosettes topped with a blingy seventy-five in rhinestones.

"How's your mom?"

"Okay. They are going to operate today on her leg."

"Operate? Oh, dear, I didn't realize it was that bad."

Abbey nodded. "Yeah, that bad. She broke her fibula." Abbey pointed to her shin. "She'll be there for a few days, and then they want to move her to rehab. Some place called Sacred Heart in Catonsville." She sprayed the cake pans with cooking lubricant. After dusting them with flour, she banged each cake pan hard on the cooking surface to get the flour to settle evenly.

"Oh." Caroline's eyes lit up when she said, "Sacred Heart." She giggled. "A few years ago, I dated a fella that lived there. It's pretty nice." She blushed. "One time, they had a Valentine's Day dance and oh..." By now, the giggle was giving way to a laugh.

"What? What happened?" Abbey said while searching the pantry for the Dutch cocoa powder and occasionally looked over toward to hear the rest of the story. After she found it, she measured a half of a cup and sifted it into a large bowl.

Caroline was now in full-hearty laughter mode. "I...they..." Caroline stammered. In between syllables, she clutched her chest and let out an occasional snort.

Abbey stopped what she was doing and looked straight at Caroline. "Okay, now you got me. What happened?"

Caroline wiped her eyes. "They named me the Valentine's Queen, and I didn't even live there." She let out a long sigh, as if she were deep in memory. "As I said...nice place." She punctuated her response with another round of giggling.

"Sounds like it." Abbey had no trouble picturing Caroline winning a beauty pageant at a senior living facility where she didn't even live.

"I think I still have the crown and sash. Miss Sacred Heart 2017," Caroline gave a mocking beauty queen wave.

"Good for you, your highness. My mom will probably go to rehab there for a few weeks. And they want me to think about moving her there for good." Abbey went back to making her cake. She measured three cups of white flour from a large bin that sat just underneath the baker's block where Abbey was working. She used a butter knife to scrape off excess flour on the large measuring cup. Baking was an exact science—a little excess here, a little excess there could throw the recipe off. A two-tiered cake would take six more cups of flour. She calculated in her head the appropriate adjustments to the recipe.

Caroline, composed by now, changed her demeanor to serious. She looked straight at Abbey and said, "Is that such a bad idea?"

"Yes, it's a terrible idea." Abbey sifted the flour into the same bowl with the cocoa powder.

"Is it?"

Abbey looked up from the mixing bowl. Caroline couldn't be serious, but from the look on her face, she was just that.

"Abbey, why would it be such a bad idea to move your mom to a place where she can have friends?" Caroline leaned in very close to Abbey. "And so that you can be freed up to live your life."

"I am living my life."

Caroline stared at Abbey with very sympathetic eyes. "You've got this exciting thing going with Jax. You don't need to be tied down with the responsibility of your mother."

Without a word, Abbey returned to the task of making a cake for Magda.

"You never told me how the dinner was."

Abbey groaned.

"That bad?" Caroline made a stink face.

"That bad, but only worse."

"Oh, dear."

Abbey told Caroline the whole story. She left nothing out. Caroline's reaction indicated how much her heart ached along with Abbey's.

"So, she was sitting next to him after you left?"

"Yeah." Abbey took her phone out and tapped on Instagram and scrolled to the photo. "Here." She handed her phone to Caroline.

Caroline looked very carefully at the image. She bit her bottom lip and said, "This doesn't mean anything." She handed the phone back to Abbey.

"Maybe. Maybe not." Abbey shrugged. "I've done a lot of thinking between now and then, and I've come to the realization that Elle is better suited for him."

"What? What do you mean? Hogwash. I've only met Jax a few times, and I sincerely doubt that he would want to be with such a manipulative, mean person. When he hears the truth about the horrible things she said and did to you, I know he's going to jump out of his skin to protect you. Any man would."

"Would he? Will he? Why should he? It's just that I don't think I should ask him to do what I'm not willing to do myself."

"What do you mean?"

"I can't accept myself, not in this body. Why should he?"

Caroline's look slowly turned from shock to compassion. "You know, you are right. Why should he accept you when you can't accept yourself?"

"I'm glad you finally see things my way."

"But you can start by accepting who you are," Caroline continued. "You are an amazingly smart and talented person. You have the biggest heart. And those are the things that matter the most." She tapped a finger on Abbey's chest near her heart. "Start here. Give yourself a break. You'll be surprised how life-changing that can be."

"I don't even know how. All my life, I've been judged by my weight. People see this"—Abbey gestured with her hands toward her body— "before they see this," she said, pointing to her heart.

"Well, they are wrong. Have you ever thought about that? They are just plain wrong. Here, I'll show you." Caroline took her own phone from the pocket in her apron. "What did you say was Elle's Instagram account name?"

"Caroline, what are you doing?" Abbey tried to reach for Caroline's arm.

"You'll see. Ol_la_la or something like that." She scrolled until she said, "Here we go. El_la_la." She curled her lip in a sneer.

"Caroline. What are you doing?" Abbey's heart raced. "Caroline, please don't embarrass me anymore."

Caroline stopped. She looked directly at Abbey and said, "I would never embarrass you. It's time someone tells it like it is." Caroline waved a hand dismissively. "You trust me, don't you?"

"Most of the time, yes, I do. I'm not so sure now."

The keyboard on Caroline's iPhone clicked as her hot pink manicured nails typed.

"Caroline, please don't. Don't make it worse." Abbey's pleas went unheard.

After what seemed like an eternity, Caroline stopped typing. She studied what she typed and said, "Perfect." With one hit of the button, the deed was done. "Here, see for yourself." Caroline handed her phone to Abbey.

Abbey was terrified about what she was going to read. She took Caroline's phone and scanned it. Caroline had tagged one of the more awful comments on Elle's post of the picture of her, Jax, and Abbey. Once Abbey started to read Caroline's post, her nerves instantly calmed, and tears welled up in her eyes.

My dear friend, TheBakersAbbey is not only a talented baker but the most kind-hearted person I know. I feel bad for those of you who felt the need to have a laugh by making fun of her beautiful body. But I don't feel bad for her. She's perfect! (eggplant emoji)

Abbey was in awe. Caroline always knew the right words to say on every occasion. "Aw, Caroline, that's so nice."

"I mean every word."

Abbey looked at the post again. "Eggplant emoji? Is that because of my purple dress?"

"No, that's Insta-speak for 'go F yourself.'" She gestured using the universal hand gesture. "Take that!"

"Um, actually, I think it means that's what you want to do to them. The rest of the post is so sweet. Thank you for saying that, but you'd better fix the eggplant thing." Abbey handed the phone back to Caroline.

"Oh, dear, here, let me edit it." Caroline's eyes widened and brightened. "I think you're going to want to see this." She handed the phone back to Abbey.

The post was liked ten times, now fifteen, now twenty—hearts were adding up fast. A comment from @Ragdoll_75 appeared.

"Yesss!" it said. One from @Royal51378 said: "She is beautiful." @LuverGurl posted the pulsating hugging heart emoji. @Shero347 posted: #PurpleFionaIsPerfect. Abbey looked up from the phone and straight at Caroline. The painful memory of last night was starting to ease, replaced by a feeling of acceptance that she had never felt before. "Thank you, Caroline."

Caroline winked. "Nobody puts Abbey in a corner."

22

Abbey got to the hospital a little past four, twenty minutes after she got the call that the surgery had been a success. A receptionist gave her the room number for her mother on the fifth floor. The door to her mother's room was slightly ajar. Abbey tapped lightly on it before entering the room.

"Come in," an unfamiliar voice responded on the other side of the door.

Abbey entered the room. Millie was in a bed closest to the door. A curtain divided the room in half and blocked the window. Muffled laughter came from the other side of the curtain.

Millie was awake and sitting up. A woman dressed in pink scrubs adjusted the pillows that helped to prop Millie up.

"Hi," Abbey said. "I'm her daughter." She pointed at her mother.

"Nice to meet you. I'm Clare, the nurse in charge tonight."

Clare was probably in her mid thirties. She had sandy blond hair tucked in a messy bun held up by a claw clip. "You've got good timing. She just woke up." She tucked a blanket around both sides of Millie. Picking up the call button, she handed it to Millie. "Okay, Mrs. Reilly, if you need something, just press this red button. If you feel any pain, hit this. Are you comfortable?"

Millie nodded.

"Good."

"You know my mom doesn't always remember things," Abbey said.

Clare turned her attention to Abbey. "Yes. Don't worry, we'll take good care of her." She turned her attention back to Millie. "I'll be back shortly to check on you, okay?"

"She likes to watch TV." Abbey felt like she was dropping her kid off at daycare for the first time. "She really likes Jeopardy."

Clare smiled. She placed a hand lightly on Abbey's shoulder. "She'll be fine."

When Clare left the room, Abbey took a seat next to her mother's bed. Millie smiled broadly at her daughter. "The doctor said things went well today," Abbey said.

"Oh, good," Millie said. "Are you here to take me home?"

"No, not today."

Millie frowned. "Why can't I go home?"

"You will soon. Just not today. They put a rod and pins in your leg. You need to heal."

Millie looked down at her leg, which was covered in blankets tucked neatly under the mattress. She looked back up at Abbey. "Rods and pins? In my leg? Why'd they do that?"

"You fell, remember?"

Millie shook her head. "No."

The curtain separating the two beds swung open and an older black man emerged, he was wearing a brown tweed blazer, pale pink bow tie, and porkpie hat. Abbey appreciated his style. He was dressed more for a Sunday at church than a visit to the hospital.

"Bye, Frannie," he said with a wave. He leaned heavily on his cane as he walked. "I'll be back tomorrow."

Millie used her hands to raise herself a little further up in the bed. "Bobo?" she said as he neared her half of the room. "Bobo, is that you?" A light that Abbey hadn't seen in her mother in years returned to Millie's eyes.

The man stopped. He placed a hand above his eyes and

squinted. "Who said that?" He walked toward Millie's bed and stood next to Abbey. "I haven't been called that in more than thirty years." His face creased into a warm smile. "Millie? Millie Reilly? Why, I'd recognize those brown eyes anywhere. But how on earth did you recognize me?"

Millie tapped the top of her head.

"Oh, yes, the chapeau. Of course. I guess I didn't realize it was such a trademark. What are you in here for?"

"She fell and broke her leg," Abbey said.

"Oh, dear. Must have been a bad fall." He rubbed his face in the same place where Millie's bandage was. He then turned toward Abbey and said, "And you must be...no, you can't be Abbey. The last time I saw you, you were oh, about this big." He reached his hand about two feet high.

Abbey stood. "Yes, I am Abbey. I'm sorry, you are?"

"I'm Bob Boone. Or Bobo." He removed his hat and tipped it toward Abbey along with a slight bow. "Your parents were band-mates with me and my wife." His eyes had a youthful spark as he spoke.

"My parents were in a band?" This was news to Abbey. Never in all the time they spent as a family did the name Bobo or word "band" ever come up.

"Yes. Many moons ago." Bobo chuckled. "Is Mickey here?" Bobo looked around the room.

"No, unfortunately, he isn't with us anymore."

"Oh, I'm sorry about that." Bobo shifted more weight to his cane.

"Here, take my seat." Abbey moved away from the chair and the older man sat.

He took Millie's hand. "So, how long has it been, friend?"

Millie shook her head. "I'm not sure. My memory is not so

good."

"Let me see." He rubbed his gray beard with his fingers. "Gloria and I decided to stay in California in 1990." His fingers tapped lightly on his chin.

"How is Gloria?" Millie had come alive again.

"Oh, she passed. It's been about five years now. Bout the same time I moved back here."

"You're nearby?" Abbey asked.

"Yes, got me a place at Sacred Heart—the senior community up the road a piece."

"Sacred Heart?" Abbey said. "Do you like it there?"

Bobo smiled as he nodded. "Oh, yes. I do. When Gloria passed, I stayed with my son Joe for a little while, but then I had a stroke. Had to learn to use the whole damn right side of this old body, and I started to forget things. I didn't want to be a burden on my son and his wife, so I got my own place. It's great to be independent, well, sort of. At least I'm not in anyone's way."

"My mom may go there for rehab."

"You don't say." He turned his attention back to Millie. "The Sacred Heart choir can use a good alto." He squeezed Millie's hand tightly. "Millie Reilly, I can't believe it's you. How have you been?"

"Okay, I guess," Millie said.

"She has—" Abbey started to say, before she was interrupted by Millie.

"How is Gloria?" Millie asked again.

Abbey gave Bobo a knowing smile, and he smiled politely back.

"She passed, Millie. I miss her terribly, as I'm sure you miss Mickey."

"Where's Mickey?" Millie said.

"He's gone, Momma."

"Oh, okay. Will he be back soon?"

Abbey shook her head. "No. He's not coming back."

Millie frowned and turned her attention back to Bobo. "Do you still have the peach?" she asked, with the light returning to her eyes.

"What? The peach?" Bobo's rich laughter filled the room. "No, got rid of that after we settled in California. Great car. Oh, Millie, I haven't thought about that car in years. Did we have some fun in it or what?" He took a handkerchief from his blazer pocket and dabbed his eyes and wiped his nose. "I haven't thought about the peach in ages."

He turned toward Abbey. "The peach was my '68 Volkswagen van. We called it the peach because it was orangish." He rubbed his chin a bit. "Thinking back on it, it may have been rust."

"I loved the peach," Millie said.

Bobo nodded. "I did too. We spent a lot of time in that van driving to gigs."

Gigs? Abbey was learning something about her parents for the first time. "Forgive me, Bob, but this is all news to me," Abbey said. "So, what kind of music did you play, um, with my parents?"

"Us, we were a Beatles cover band mostly, although your dad wrote some original songs. We called ourselves Her Majesty—a song off of *Abbey Road*. I sang, your daddy played the guitar. Your mother here could get down and dirty with the bass." He mimicked plucking the strings of a bass guitar and added "Dooby, doo, doo doo" in a rich baritone voice.

Abbey mouth gaped open. She turned to her mother. "Why didn't you and daddy ever tell us any of this?"

Millie shrugged. "I thought we did."

No, this Abbey would remember. "Why did you stop touring?"

"Your parents were going to be parents." Bobo winked as he

smiled.

"Me?" Abbey pointed to herself. "My mom was pregnant with me?" She looked at Millie. "You gave it up to have a family?"

Millie nodded, although Abbey wasn't sure Millie knew what she was agreeing to. All those times growing up, Abbey thought her parents were these carefree spirits, and she resented that they provided little stability. She was starting to believe she had been wrong about her parents all along. What if the choices they'd made hadn't been selfish at all? Knowing how much her dad loved music, she imagined it must have been a difficult decision to abandon the dream to start a family. Why didn't he ever mention it? Maybe he was disappointed in himself. Or maybe he didn't want Abbey, or Penny for that matter, to feel the heavy burden of the blame.

"Little Abbey Rose," Bobo said. "I can't get over what a lovely young lady you've turned out to be."

"Tell me more," Abbey said. "About your time in the band... with my parents."

Bobo's face lit up. "Well, back then, let me see, I put an ad in the Pennysaver looking for a lead guitar player. I can play, but I mostly sing. And your daddy shows up." Bobo, still seated, leaned forward on his cane. "Man, I thought the dude was homeless." He laughed. "He was painting houses then, so he had paint in his hair and this scraggly beard. But the dude could play."

Abbey remembered listening to her father strum his guitar quietly and hum while she and her sister played in the backyard. He always seemed at peace when he had the guitar across his lap.

"He starts off with the opening riff from *Revolution*. And I tried to keep up. I think that day we jammed for three or four hours. And I remember saying to myself, it don't matter what he looks like, I found my guitar player.

"First, we played a few places around here—small joints,

really hole-in-the-wall bars. I think one place paid us in beer." He laughed. "And then we actually got good enough to go on the road. He was dating your momma then, and he didn't want to leave her behind." He gestured to Millie. "And we couldn't afford to bring her with us, unless she was part of the band. So, he taught her how to play the bass." Bobo chuckled lightly. "She picked it up pretty quick, even though I don't think she could read music at the time. But could she sing—"

He closed his eyes as if he were listening to a sweet melody. "But I'm sure you know that."

Abbey did. The memory took her to a wonderful place when Millie would tuck her into bed by singing her to sleep. She'd wrap her arms around Abbey and stoke her hair as she sung *Starry, Starry Night,* or sometimes *My Girl.* And Abbey would lay her head on her mother's lap and press her ear against her belly so that she could feel her lungs fill with air and her diaphragm contract. Abbey hadn't heard her mother sing in years.

"We added Gloria on drums and backup vocals. And, with me on lead vocals and rhythm guitar and occasionally keyboards, as they say, we found our groove." He had a very satisfied smile as he reminisced.

"How long did you guys do this? Your band? How long were you together?"

"Let me see." Bobo stared up. "Three, four years if memory serves me. Being on the road was tough."

"Oh, it was?"

"Yes, sometimes we'd go weeks without a gig. All four of us living in one hotel room, eating canned chili—which I have never eaten since." He raised an eyebrow. "But it was also fun. No, it was exhilarating at times. You know when you do what you love and you're good at it." He nodded. "Yeah, that feeling of really getting it right."

He sighed. "When your momma told us they were going to have you, I think all of us were relieved." He smiled. "It was time we grew up."

"What'd you do after the band broke up?"

"Our last gig was near Sacramento, California. Gloria and I liked the West Coast so much, we stayed there. I got a job in advertising. And your mom and dad moved back here," Bobo said. "We had fun, didn't we?" He leaned forward, inching a little closer to Millie. "Oh, Millie Reilly, you've made my day."

Millie smiled. "And you, mine. Wait till Mickey hears. He's going to be so jealous."

Bobo gave Millie's hand another squeeze. He looked at his watch. "What's today?"

"Sunday," Abbey said.

"Pot roast night. I best be going. Besides, my ride is probably cursing me downstairs. But spending time with you will make it worth whatever curse words I hear." He stood. "Will you be here tomorrow?"

"I don't know," Millie said.

"Yes, she'll be here for probably three days," Abbey said.

"Okay then, Miss Millie, I won't say goodbye. I'll say *à bientôt*." He tipped his hat again. "See you tomorrow. Bye, Sis." He waved to the woman in the bed next to Millie. He then turned his attention to Millie. "And Millie, you behave now." He winked as he walked away, or sort of shuffled. He whistled the melody of The Beatles' "With a Little Help from My Friends," interjecting a few words here and there, his deep, rich baritone voice filling the sterile room. He timed his step so that his cane struck the floor in perfect rhythm to the beat of the song. A second after he left the room, he popped his head in and sang "help from my friends," holding the last note of the bass line of the song for a few seconds.

Millie clapped and said, "Bye, Bobo. See you tomorrow!"

"You betcha," he said before he disappeared entirely.

Abbey sat back down in the chair. "Do you remember being in the band, Momma?"

"Oh sure. Your dad thought we'd make it big." She laughed. "Of course, that wasn't the case." She smiled and started to sing the same song Bobo had just sung, her shoulders shimmied as she sang. "That was how we closed our set each night."

"Tell me more."

Millie looked confused. "About what?"

"About Her Majesty—your band."

"What band?"

"Your—nothing." Abbey took the bed's remote. "Why don't you get some rest?"

As the head of the bed lowered, Millie settled back. "Abbey," she said. "Are you here to take me home?"

"No, Momma. Not today. Soon. Soon."

"Okay." Millie closed her eyes and drifted off to sleep.

Abbey reached for her purse, which was on the floor next to the chair. While searching for her phone, the brochure for Sacred Heart caught her eye. She took the brochure out of her purse. Caroline and Bobo's words played in her head. She looked at her mother. Would her mother be better off in a place that specialized in caring for those with dementia? A place where there were people her own age? She put the brochure back into her purse and pulled out her phone.

All afternoon, people had liked Caroline's post, and many of those likers had started following Abbey's Instagram page. Abbey shook her head in disbelief. In the few hours since Caroline had come to her defense, Abbey's Instagram followers had grown from one hundred and twelve to nearly five hundred and counting. The recipes she had posted in recent days were being liked and comments such as "Looks so yummy" and "Can't wait to make it" appeared in her feed.

23

"I love it!" Magda clapped as she spoke. "Is beautiful. Thank you. Thank you." She wrapped her tiny arms around Abbey so tight Abbey could barely breathe. Magda's petite stature definitely masked her strength. "Artist. True artist," Magda whispered with her voice cracking.

There were tears in Magda's eyes as she broke the embrace.

"When my friends ask where I get cake, I shout, 'Abbey! The best baker in Maryland!'" Magda then added, "My friends, they throw parties—lots and lots of parties to raise money for this charity and that charity. Prepare for many new bakery customers. Lots, I tell you."

Caroline emerged from the back of the bakery. "Did I hear lots of new customers?"

"Yes!" Magda said. "I am sure. This girl." She pointed to Abbey. "She is best. Truly best. I've been to fancy patisseries on the Champs-Élysée, dined at White House with the Clintons—I even had dinner with a Russian leader who I remain nameless." Her pencil-thin eyebrow arched when she said the last part. "Nowhere have I seen such magnificent cake."

Abbey blushed. "Aw, thanks, Magda." Abbey had to admit she was proud of the cake. In fact, she considered it the best she'd ever made. Two tiers stacked in perfect succession. The top tier was adorned with gold numbers seven and five. No sags, dips, or Leaning Tower of Pisa. No, not this one. Covered in crisp, large white rosettes made from rich cream cheese frosting accentuated with gold leaf here and there, it could grace the cover of any baking magazine. It was perfect—a true feat, given all she'd been through in the past few days filled with distractions and worry about her mother.

"Well, you certainly have outdone yourself. It's a beauty," Caroline said. "Here, let me get a picture of the two of you standing next to it for Sweet Caroline's Instagram. My grandson says we need to post more often. 'Social media is what sells,' he says." Caroline took her phone from her apron. "Face this way." Caroline pointed toward the side of the bakery where she stood. The cake looked grand, centered perfectly on one of the small round café tables. "I want to get some of the bakery in the shot."

Abbey stood behind the cake, so that it was blocking her body from the camera lens. Magda stood next to Abbey. The cake was nearly taller than Magda, so Caroline directed Abbey and Magda to move to either side of the cake so that no one was hidden.

"You know what?" Abbey said, stepping away. "It's your bakery, Caroline. Why don't you get in the photo with Magda?"

"What? No." Caroline protested with a shooing hand motion. "Get back in the shot. You made the cake, and you should be very proud of it. Show off a little."

Abbey did not move. There was still too much pain from the comments on the photo that Elle posted on Instagram. Even though Caroline had protected her like a momma bear would protect its cub, Abbey wasn't ready to have a photo taken and posted on Instagram or anywhere else for all the world to see and comment. "Caroline," she said. "I really don't want to."

Caroline frowned, but then softened into a motherly look of concern. "Don't let them win," she said. "Now, chin up." Caroline lifted her own chin as she used her hand to direct Abbey back into position.

218

"Caroline, please," Abbey said, knowing she sounded whiny.

Caroline shook her head in an "I know what's best" kind of way. "It will be fine," Caroline said reassuringly. "The people that follow the bakery are nice. They love cakes and cookies. Not mean-spirited know-it-all bullies that hide behind a computer keyboard."

No amount of protesting would talk Caroline out of her way. "Okay," Abbey said. She returned to her place next to the cake. She took a deep breath and forced a smile.

"On the count of three," Caroline said, lifting her phone so it captured the cake, Abbey, and Magda. Abbey felt a strong yet bony arm pull her in a little closer. This move shifted Abbey's body so that it was directly behind the cake—where she wanted to be—and Abbey was grateful. Of course, Magda knew about Abbey's insecurities—she had a front-row seat.

"You are beautiful and make beautiful cake," Magda said in a near whisper. "Be proud."

"Three," Caroline said before a flash indicated the photo was taken.

Caroline looked at the photo and seemed happy with what she saw. "I'll have my grandson tag you two."

"Very good then," Magda said. "I'll take photos at the party, but we need to get cake there first." Magda attempted to lift the cake. Abbey had put the cake on a twelve-inch by twelve-inch pressed wood board that was one-inch thick. She had also covered the bottom of the board with nonskid contact paper so that it wouldn't slide around in Magda's car.

"Here, let me help you take this to your car," Abbey said. She lifted one side of the board, and Magda lifted the other side. "Okay, now, careful. Careful," Abbey said. Transporting a decorated cake always made her heart stop. It was a delicate act, somewhat akin to walking on a tightrope—one misstep could mean disaster. It wasn't uncommon to have an icing mishap—a smudge here or there caused by a finger slip, or, even more frightening, a layer shift. Those things could be fixed in a way that few people would notice by redoing that section or gently nudging the shifted layer back into place with steady hands.

"I'll be back in a second," Abbey said.

Caroline raced to get the front door for them. "Happy birthday, Magda!"

As Abbey and Magda walked slowly toward the bakery entrance, Abbey was on high alert—hypersensitive to any missteps. Once, a four-tiered wedding cake had the most unfortunate fate—even though each layer was being transported in separate boxes. While helping a bride's mother carry the cake to her car, Abbey stepped wrong on a tree root protruding through the old sidewalk, in great need of repair, tripped and fell right onto boxes containing the bottom and the top layers, flattening three days of work in mere seconds. The mother of the bride rushed to help Abbey, and in the commotion, dropped the two boxes of cake she was carrying. There was icing in her hair, cake in her ears, eyes— well, pretty much everywhere. Later that day, she even found cake in her cleavage and inside the cups of her bra.

Caroline had saved the day by convincing the bride and her mother to serve layer cakes in several flavors—which turned out to be whatever was in the bake case that day—by saying she'd read on bakery industry blogs not serving a traditional wedding cake was becoming a new trend. She may have stretched the truth a bit. The article said that giving guests an option was trending, but it also said that the selection should include a traditional wedding cake. Thankfully, the bride's family had been friends of Caroline for eons. So, they agreed to the trendy option. Caroline sweetened the deal by returning the five hundred dollars the bride had paid the bakery. The crisis was averted.

When Abbey returned to the bakery, she was relieved the cake made it to the back of Magda's van without a mishap. And that Magda had the forethought to bring a small wooden pallet to put the cake on and keep it from shifting while in transport.

"You must feel awfully proud," Caroline said.

"You know, I do."

Caroline's phone let out a flurry of pings. She retrieved it from her apron. Her eyes widened as she inspected the screen. "Oh, you've got to see this."

Abbey walked over to behind the bake case to where Caroline was standing. Caroline thrust her phone into Abbey's face. Sweet Caroline's Instagram page was up on the screen with a new post of the cake. "Sweet Caroline's makes everything sweeter." The post read. Hearts flew across the screen in rapid succession as people liked what they saw.

"Aw." Abbey hugged the phone to her chest.

"I think you've found your calling," Caroline said.

"Yes, maybe." Abbey nodded.

The bakery front door opened, and a woman dressed in white linen palazzo pants and a crisp cotton candy pink chiffon blouse with a pussycat bow walked in. Her perfect complexion, highlighted ashy blond bob hairstyle, and eyes the color of the water of the Caribbean were instantly recognizable. "Elle est la," Abbey gasped and then immediately felt sick. Here? At Sweet Caroline's— the bakery where Abbey just happened to work? Not to mention it was about one hundred miles away from @El_La_La's posh neighborhood that she frequently shared in her Instagram posts. Surely she wasn't here because she read Yelp reviews.

24

Elle approached Abbey. She had an air about her—walking with her chin held high as if she was being carried by a chariot of privilege. "Hello, Abbey," she said with a voice and demeanor just as snooty.

"Hi, Elle?" Abbey did not attempt to hide her surprise or confusion. There was a long and awkward silence as the two women stared at each other like dogs meeting for the first time in a dog park—and one dog has a known propensity to bite. Finally, Abbey had had enough. "Philadelphia's a long way to come for a cookie. But have to admit, you made a good choice, cuz they are worth it." Abbey said in a half-hearted attempt at humor and a full-on effort to break the silence. "Chocolate chip or peanut butter?" She pointed toward the cookies in the bakery case.

Elle did not return the witty banter volley. There was no hint of a smile nor playfulness when she said, "No. I came to talk to you."

"Me?" And just when she thought the moment couldn't be more awkward, it took a dramatic turn to "surreal town."

"You came to talk to me?" Abbey repeated her question in disbelief.

Elle nodded.

What on earth? Abbey quickly recapped the encounter they had over the weekend. The entire evening flashed before her eyes—Elle, so nice and sweet to her face, but mean and nasty behind her back. What had she come all this way to talk about? They had only one common denominator: Jax. Oh dear, Abbey's mind jumped to a bad conclusion. Something must have happened to him. But would Elle come all this way to tell Abbey Jax was hurt, or sick, or God knows what? Abbey looked at Elle again to try to assess what this was all about. Elle looked the same as she did on Saturday—stiff and emotionless—only with less makeup. She did not look as if she was here to tell Abbey that Jax was sick, injured, terminally ill, or—Abbey closed her eyes—dead. Yes, she went there. She kept her gaze on Elle even though she feared the response. "Is Jax okay?"

"Jax?" Elle seemed unfazed by the question. "He's fine."

Good. Fine was good. But it was the way she said "fine"—it sounded so personal and intimate. Was Elle here to claim victory? Had she gone to Jax and wooed him back, just as she said she was going to do? Would she come all the way from Philly to gloat? During the brief encounter that Abbey had with Elle, that did seem plausible. Abbey looked Elle up and down, eyeing her rival. Was she ready to hear what Elle had to say? "Does Jax know you're here?" She managed to utter.

"No. This has nothing to do with him."

Phew! A feeling of relief swept through Abbey. Maybe Elle was here to apologize. Maybe Jax had told her she had to apologize. Yes, that must be it. Abbey felt a swoon building inside. That thought endeared him to her even more. The tension in Abbey's neck and shoulders eased up slightly. "Okay," Abbey perked up and smiled. She hadn't expected an apology, but she could do this. "Go ahead," she said.

"Well, I'm afraid *we* have a problem."

We? But the tone in Elle's voice was referring to the royal "we." Abbey braced herself as the tension in the room overtook the sweet smell of freshly baked chocolate chip cookies. Her neck and shoulders stiffened back up and her smile faded. Elle seemed nervous, shifting her weight from side to side while standing in a sort of model-like pose with one hip jutting slightly forward. Abbey decided to hear her out. "Go on."

The corners of Elle's mouth bent upward ever so slightly in what appeared to be an attempted smile. "Do you mind if we sit? These shoes may look good, but they really pinch my toes." Her eyes drifted downward to her feet and a pair of pointy pink stilettos covered in scales from some sort of exotic reptile.

"Sure. No problem." Abbey gestured to the empty table that was the nearest to them. "Please, go ahead." She followed Elle to the table and sat next to her.

Caroline hadn't left the room. She stood near the entrance to the kitchen. She cleared her throat in a loud and obvious way. Looking directly at Abbey, she said, "Everything okay here?"

Abbey nodded. "Yes, thanks. I've got this." *I think.*

"Okay then, I'll be in the kitchen if you need me." She turned to walk toward the kitchen but stopped just before entering. Turning back around, she said, "You know, these beads aren't soundproof." She cocked her head toward Elle. "Just saying..."

Abbey sat back in her chair. Her foot tapped lightly on the table pedestal. She worried Elle would sense the terror inside her. She had never sat down across from someone who had hurt her so badly. Usually, she did whatever it took to avoid that person. In high school—where bullying happened a lot—she'd take a different route or even change classes to avoid her tormentor. In the fifteen years since high school, she realized nothing had changed as she sat paralyzed in the bathroom stall as Elle and her friend laughed at the "Purple Fiona" hashtag and other insults. Since that night, she wished she would have burst from the stall and confront them. If Elle was here to apologize, she'd listen. Hopefully, it would lessen the shame and embarrassment that she still felt.

"I'm here because I need your help," Elle said. "I didn't have your phone number, and I remembered you had a baking blog, so I looked it up. I found a picture and name of this place in one of your posts. So, I came here."

Need your help? Could Elle be here to ask for a cake? Abbey quickly talked herself out of that scenario—there were plenty of good bakeries between here and Philadelphia. No, that couldn't be. Need your help. Need your help. The words echoed in Abbey's head. "Okay." Now she was fully intrigued. "Help with what?"

Elle smiled that same smile as before. "I'm in Instagram jail." She laughed a little bit. "Because of a post that included you." She shifted her gaze so that she was staring directly at Abbey. She seemed so sincere. "Do you know the one I'm talking about? It was a photo of you, me, and Jax."

Of course, Abbey knew the post all too well. "Yes, sure. Go on," she said.

"So, I guess some of my fans..." Elle's eyes darted down. "Well, how do I say this? They posted some unkind comments about you." She clutched a hand near her chest in that way that mocks a heart attack. "I get so many comments to my posts—thousands—that I can't read them all."

Abbey knew Elle was deflecting. Maybe she can't read them all, but she did read those horrible ones—out loud.

"So, some of your fans complained," Elle continued. "They contacted Instagram and asked that the post be removed. Cyberbullying is what they called it. Squeaky wheel, I guess." She rolled her eyes, demonstrating her true feelings as any hint of sincerity left the room. "I refused because it wasn't me who said those terrible things." She softened her tone. "And I do think they were terrible things that they said. But you see," she turned back to the business at hand. "I get paid per like. That post blew up. I think there were close to a hundred thousand likes. My highest ever.

So, because I wouldn't remove the post, my account has been suspended for at least thirty days. Maybe longer."

Good. For the first time in her life, Abbey felt vindicated. Her fans—the sweet people who check out her blog and commented on recipes she'd post were protecting her from this modern-day villain who used social media like a sword. She beamed at the feeling of being so loved and supported by her fans. Then she became suspicious. "You said my fans complained. I didn't. I'd say our situations are quite similar."

Elle's smile seemed forced. "Yes, but it seems you can fix mine."

"How can I fix it? I'm not the Instagram police."

"No." Elle's laughter sounded condescending. "Of course you aren't. But, based on my research, if you reach out to Instagram and tell them that you know me..."

"But I don't, not really."

Elle shrugged as if it were semantics. "And that I never meant the post in a mean way."

Um, but you did. Abbey bit her lip as emotions built inside. *Don't cry. Don't cry.* She said nothing to Elle while she tried to calm down.

"Maybe I'm not being clear." Elle talked to Abbey as if she were a child. "You *do* realize posting on Instagram is my job."

Abbey nodded. Her feelings of shame and embarrassment shifted to anger. Anger at Elle's insistence that she did nothing wrong. And anger because Elle was being so dismissive.

"I doubt you could go for thirty days without getting paid from here." She looked around the bakery. "What if someone posted a negative review—said your chocolate cookies were stale." Her tone had become syrupy, and she shook her head as she spoke. "And we know that isn't true. That wouldn't be your fault if you lost business because of one person's negative comments."

Anger simmered inside of Abbey like a cauldron. She swallowed hard. "It's not the same."

"What?" Elle cocked her head as if she didn't hear correctly.

"I was in the bathroom," she said, her voice cracking a little.

"What?" Elle now looked shocked.

"I was in the bathroom...in a stall when you and your friend were talking." By the look on her face, Elle was recollecting that very moment.

"Oh. You were?" She pursed her lips together. "I see."

"Yes." Anger soon gave way to a swell of courage that seemed to come from nowhere. Because of the support felt from her fans, and Caroline's continuously cheerful words, Abbey had the courage to tell Elle the truth. "I may seem like just some fat girl—someone who deserves the ridicule because I lack self-control when it comes to eating—but what is underneath all of this"—she pinched a roll of skin on the side of her waist— "is a person. A real person. I have feelings."

"Of course, you do." Again, with the fake smile. "I know that. Thank you for sharing." Elle reached across the table for Abbey's hand, but Abbey did not give in. Elle pulled back her hand and said, "So, now that we've cleared that up, I have a number here for Instagram."

She can't be serious.

Elle took her phone from her dark brown hobo-style bag covered in the Louis Vuitton logo. With long, square fingernails manicured in a perfect French style, she swiped a few screens.

Abbey thought carefully. The easiest course of action would be to do what Elle was asking—reach out to Instagram, say there was no harm, no foul, and let Elle be on her way. But the truth tugged at her. If she did that, she would bury her real feelings like she had done every time she was bullied in the past. She couldn't change the past, but she could stand up for herself now. "We've cleared nothing up," she said.

"Oh." Elle looked away from her phone and directly at Abbey. "I thought we had."

"No, actually, the opposite happened. I think you are being condescending and dismissive of me. And my fans were right. What you did was bullying."

"What *I* did?"

"Yes, I heard you and your friend laugh."

"What? No. You think we were laughing at you?"

"Yes! You were. I know it. And it was mean."

Elle's lip curled in a smirk. "What do you want from me, Abbey? The post is out there. I can't take it back. What happened, happened."

Abbey straightened her back. She looked Elle straight in the eyes. "I want an apology." She started thinking simultaneously as she spoke. "Yes. I want you to go on social media and apologize." She could see the gears churning in Elle's mind.

Elle's clear blue eyes turned dark and steely. "You are more cunning than I ever gave you credit. Apologize? On social media?" She huffed. "That would be career suicide."

"Maybe you'd gain more followers."

"What? People like you? I'm not that pathetic." It was obvious Elle was used to getting her way.

Abbey did not back down. "I stand by my request. Take it or leave it."

Elle stood. "Maybe a month off would be a good thing. A vacation would do me good. I'll see if a certain someone we both know would like to take a trip. We did love the French Riviera, and it's fabulous this time of year."

"Get out!" Caroline emerged from the back of the kitchen like a lioness protecting her cub.

Abbey stood too. She pointed to the door. "Yes, please leave."

"Oh, you don't have to tell me to do that." Elle walked toward the front door. Before leaving, she turned and said, "You know..." Her voice was full of indignation. "He was just using you."

"What? Who?"

"Jax. He was using you—to look good—for the awards ceremony. Jackson Lawrence, Philadelphia's Man of the Year, no longer a playboy—a most kind and compassionate man who sees the beauty of a person on the inside." Her tone was mocking.

Abbey felt a gut punch.

"He told me all about it when I went to see him on Sunday. He even admitted that breaking our engagement was a big mistake. And he wanted to take me back."

This couldn't be true, could it?

The feeling of being punched in the gut now felt like a knock-out. And Abbey felt nauseous.

"It was Bunny's idea, really." Elle's laugh was like a Disney villain—more like a witchy cackle. Elle seemed to be enjoying this, like when a cat toys with its prey.

"Bunny?"

"Yes, Jack too. They actually came up with the plan." She smirked again. "Did you really think that they'd welcome someone like you—a frumpy, no class baker from the middle of nowhere—into their family? A family that can trace their lineage back to the Mayflower? Don't be silly. They thought having a"—she cleared her throat— "um, I'm sorry, what's the correct term? Big girl? Is that PC?" She shifted her gaze and her stance. "No. Plus-size. Yes, that's it. They thought having a 'plus-size'"—she used air quotes for emphasis— "girl on Jax's arm at the dinner, one that would be photographed, would help his image. They are big on appearances—the Lawrences, that is." She looked Abbey up and down. "Just not your kind of big."

The thought of Jax and his parents sitting around calculating how they would set her up was too much to bear. "GET OUT!" Abbey gritted her teeth as she spoke. She walked to the front door and held it open.

Abbey wanted to throttle Elle and her smug attitude. Of course, now it was all making sense. She was silly to ever think that someone like Jax would be interested in someone like her. Elle laid it out so clearly. She had been too swept up in the feeling of hope that she was blind to reality.

"Gladly," Elle said as she left the bakery.

Abbey slammed the door so hard the jingle bells nearly fell off. She walked swiftly into the kitchen.

Caroline followed closely behind. "You don't believe all that hooey, do you? About Jax?" she said.

Abbey took her phone from her apron. She pulled up his contact information. Her fingers flew over the keyboard as she typed. Her heart was in her throat and her eyes welled with tears. She didn't care if there were typos or punctuation errors.

"What are you doing?"

Abbey continued to type.

"Abbey, don't do something you may regret. Get his side of the story first," Caroline pleaded.

Abbey hit send. "Too late for that. I am tired of being made a fool."

The jingle bells at the front door of the bakery indicated a customer had entered.

"I got this," Caroline said. "Why don't you take a break."

Abbey's phone pinged. It was a text from Jax.

25

"It's from him, isn't it?"

Abbey nodded.

Caroline looked concerned.

"Go ahead," Abbey made a shooing motion to Caroline. "Get the customer."

Caroline slowly left the kitchen, turning around and checking once to make sure Abbey was okay.

Abbey waited before peering at her phone screen. When she did, his text read: *I got your text.*

She wasn't sure how to respond. Before she typed something, he sent another text. *Got to admit, kind of confused.*

Abbey's text to Jax earlier was very clear and simple. It said, *Don't text or call me ever again.* She contemplated a response or whether to say nothing at all. Three dancing dots on her phone screen told her to wait.

Did I do something wrong????

Four question marks? Kind of nervy of him. Um, where should she begin? She thought carefully. *I had a visit from Elle,* she typed.

Elle????

Again, with the four question marks. Point made. *Yes. She told me everything.* She erased the period and added four exclamation points. Two can play the punctuation game.

Everything????

Abbey swiped her phone away from the text app and pulled up Safari. She typed "How do you block a person from texting?"

in the search engine. While she carefully reviewed the instructions, her phone pinged with another text from him.

I feel the need to explain.

She quickly typed. *There's no need. Really.* And hit send. She held her finger on his contact information and selected BLOCK THIS CALLER before deleting their conversation history.

When Caroline came back into the kitchen, she made a detour right to Abbey.

"Okay, what'd I miss. Don't leave anything out."

Abbey paraphrased Jax's text to Caroline—inserting tone wherever she thought appropriate.

Caroline made her stink face. "That could mean anything— not necessarily admitting to those horrible things she said."

Abbey tilted her head and gave Caroline a look that said, *Really? You can't be serious.* "What's that phrase—he 'doth protest too much, methinks'? I mean, four question marks."

Caroline frowned. "What difference does it make how many question marks there are?" Her eyes grew wide to make a point. "What did you say back?"

"Nothing. I blocked him." Abbey walked into the front of the bakery and Caroline followed. She bent down to inspect the bake case. She stood back up. "Okay, changing the subject, we are low on chocolate chips, and I'm thinking of trying out this pecan bar recipe I saw on Baking TV. Oh, and push the Black Forest Cake. What we don't sell today, we'll have to trash."

"Why don't you want to hear him out?" Caroline protested.

"I don't need to feel humiliated all over again. No, thank you. Been there, done that, and have the T-shirt."

"Maybe it won't be like that. Maybe..." Caroline raised a hand in a "hear me out" stance. "Maybe—just maybe—he actually does have feelings for you. And—"

Abbey stared at Caroline. "Caroline, don't. I'm not in the mood for a 'you're awesome...any guy would be lucky to have you' kind of speech." Her tone was sarcastic and mocking. "The truth is, I was stupid to think that someone like him would be interested in someone like me."

"I agree."

"Excuse me? By the way, I'm asking with four question marks," Abbey said sarcastically.

"Funny. But in all honesty, I said I agree because you do need to change. Not your body. I think you're perfect, and one day, curves will be in—trust me. But you need to change your attitude. How can you expect someone to love you when you don't even love yourself?" Caroline crossed her arms. "I ask that with five question marks."

"You don't know what it's like—"

"To be you? You think I don't know what it's like to be you? Look at me." Caroline gestured to her ample figure. "I was you. I *am* you. Do you want to know what the difference is between me and you besides about forty years?"

"You are confident. I'm not." Abbey said.

Abbey wiped down the top of the bakery case. The morning rush appeared to be over and there'd be a few hours of lull until midafternoon.

Caroline shook her head. "Do you think I've always been this way?"

"Yes."

"Well, you're wrong. When I was in high school, I had very low self-esteem."

Abbey continued to clean spraying some cleaning fluid on the glass enclosure that held the baked goods. She imagined Caroline was always the life of the party—popular cheerleader-type who wore short skirts, lip gloss that smelled and tasted like bubble gum, and bleached her hair with Sun-In.

"In high school, I was a big girl. A little bigger than I am, but back in the sixties—when everyone looked like Twiggy—I felt like an elephant."

Abbey stopped wiping the glass.

"I was so self-conscious I didn't want to go to school."

Abbey hung on Caroline's every word. She had no idea Caroline knew what it was like to be a pariah—to feel like an outcast and have people say mean and terrible things about the way she looked. All of Caroline's gentle coaxing and prodding to be more confident not only came from a place of compassion, but also from experience.

"Every Monday, I'd tell my mom I've got cramps, or a headache—I just couldn't face the teasing. It wasn't long before my mom caught on, and she sent me to a therapist."

"Did you go?"

Caroline nodded.

"What'd the therapist say?"

"He said, 'You teach people how to treat you.' You know, if you don't respect yourself, then why should anyone else?'"

Abbey had heard this before—many times. But she had never actually seen it work. "So, what'd you do? How did you learn to, well..." She cleared her throat. "Um, like yourself more?"

"It's easier than you think. The first thing I did every morning was an affirmation. I'd stand in front of the mirror and recite, 'You are beautiful.' And 'You matter.' Then I was changing the loop in my head."

"That worked?" Abbey was skeptical.

"Yes, eventually I believed it. That's when things changed for me. I think I may have gotten a little too cocky." Caroline appeared to stifle a giggle. "My senior year, I ran for Homecoming Queen. And you know what? I won! No, I wasn't the stereotypical beauty queen. I was curvy and fabulous." Caroline accentuated her hips with her hands. "My opponent hurled the usual insults— 'She's fat. She's ugly.' You know that stuff. And it didn't matter. You see, I didn't let her fat shame me. It turns out, I was very popular with the boys—for reasons I won't go into." The statement was accentuated with a flirty wink. "I think I had more than double the votes. When they announced me as the winner, my opponent's mouth fell open. I just smiled, and said, 'I guess they wanted someone beautiful on the inside, too.'"

Abbey thought about what Caroline was saying. Years of being bullied by peers and even strangers had taken its toll. She felt shame whenever she looked in the mirror. She felt shame whenever she got on the scale. She felt shame whenever she shopped for clothes. Her internal monologue was sad and self-deprecating, and it played loudly on an endless loop.

"You are worthy of love and being loved. And if it isn't the judge, Charlie, or Jax, it will be someone so special and wonderful. But you have to love yourself first."

There was a brief pause before Abbey said, "I'll try."

Caroline made a heart shape with her two hands. "You can do this," she said. "I know it."

A short, balding middle-aged man entered the bakery. He was a stranger in a town where Abbey thought she knew everyone.

"Good morning," Abbey said, turning her attention to him.

He approached the bakery case. "Hello." He bent down and adjusted his glasses to get a better look at the display. "What's this?" He pointed.

"It's a key lime cake. Lime chiffon with lime curd and graham cracker crumble in between the layers and coated with a torched

Italian meringue."

"Mmm. Sounds good. I'll take a slice."

"Will that be for here or to go?"

He looked around the empty bakery, appearing to size up the seating situation. "Here."

Abbey took the cake out of the case and cut a slice slightly wider than three of her fingers. She transferred the piece of cake onto a china plate. When she turned back around to face the gentleman, he was bent over, inspecting the bake case again.

"What's your best seller?" he asked.

"Um. Red Velvet." She looked at Caroline for reassurance. Caroline nodded.

"Hmm. No. What's this? Coconut?" he said, pointing to a cupcake dusted with toasted coconut.

"That's a pina colada—tres leches and crushed pineapple sponge."

"Okay. I'd like that too."

Abbey removed the cupcake the man pointed to and put it on a china plate. When she turned back around, she was surprised to see him still inspecting the bakery case.

The stranger adjusted his gold wire-rimmed glasses again. "Is that a brownie?" He pointed to a plate elevated on a pedestal containing six perfectly square and decadent chocolate treats.

"Yes, sir."

"What's the topping?" he asked.

"It's a maple bacon brittle."

"Okay. Give me one of those. And that should do it."

Abbey subtly looked to see if anyone was with him, but the man was alone. Lucky him, she thought, to have such a raging metabolism. Turning around to the counter behind the case, Abbey opened her eyes in an exaggerated way so that Caroline could see. It was pretty rare that a customer came in and asked for three desserts. No, she wasn't passing judgment. He was a slight man. Maybe five foot six and thin. He carried a backpack, but he was a few decades older than a typical college student. She was thrilled to see someone enjoy sweets with careful abandonment. She put the brownie on a plate and picked up a tray to put all three desserts on.

"Would you like something to drink? I can make a pot of fresh coffee," she said, putting the tray on top of the bake case.

"Yes, please. Decaf. Black," he said.

"Okay, you got it." Abbey typed in his order into the iPad. "That'll be eighteen fifty," she said.

He handed her a twenty and asked for a receipt.

"I'll bring your coffee to you when it's ready," she said when she handed back his change and receipt.

The man carried his tray of baked goods over to a table on the far side of the bakery and took a seat.

Caroline tugged at Abbey's sleeve and motioned for her to come into the back room.

Once they were both behind the beaded curtain, Caroline said in a near whisper voice, "I think he's a spy."

"What? Who do you think you are, Willy Wonka, and this is the Chocolate Factory?" Abbey giggled. Even for Caroline, the spy theory was a bit far-fetched. But, from the look on Caroline's face, it was no laughing matter.

"I'm being serious," Caroline said.

"A spy? From where?"

"Perfect Perks. I've heard they want to expand their baked stuff." Caroline paced. "That rat bastard. I smelled something fishy when he asked me out. I should have known it."

"Who? What? I won't ask, but I highly doubt he's a spy. If he is, what's he going to do? Replicate the recipe by tasting things? If that's the case, anyone can do that."

Caroline looked as if she had just thought of something. "You know, I heard someone just made an offer on the old bookstore. I'll bet they're going to put in a bakery and put us out of business."

Abbey wondered if Caroline's imagination had got the best of her.

The two women peeked their heads into the front of the bakery just in time to see the man take a pen and a small notepad from his backpack and put them on the table. He took a bite of the key lime cake and jotted something down.

Caroline and Abbey retreated to the back room. Caroline's eyes widened. "He's a food critic."

Abbey gave it some thought. "You know, I think you're right," she said.

Caroline started pacing again. "Tell me again what he ordered."

Abbey ticked off the items the man bought.

"Good. All things you made."

"C'mon now. Don't say that. You bake just as good as I do."

Caroline shook her head. "No need for flattery now. Okay, so, how old was the key lime?"

"I made it this morning."

"Good. And the brownie?"

"Yesterday, before I left. Why are you so worried? The Yelp reviews from our customers are always really good."

Caroline bit her bottom lip. "Yes, yes, but if he is a food critic, they can make or break you. Word will get out. One bad bite can shut us down."

"What if the review is good, and it brings in new customers?" Abbey put her hands on her hips. "Now, who's telling who to be positive?"

Caroline did not look amused. "Go give him his coffee and while you're there, check to see how much he's eaten," she said.

"Okay." Abbey turned and walked toward the front of the bakery. The beaded curtain clapped together as the beads swung, announcing her entrance. She glanced over at the gentleman. Could he be a food critic? She was both nervous and excited at that prospect. She went over to the coffeepot, which had completed its brewing cycle. The pleasant aroma from a decaffeinated breakfast blend filled the area. She poured the hot beverage into a mug and carried it over to the man.

"How is everything?" she asked.

"Good, thank you."

Abbey put the coffee down and tried not to be obvious while she carefully inspected the table. "Here you go. Let me know if you need anything."

"I will. Thank you."

When she returned to the back room, she huddled with Caroline. "Okay, so he ate almost all of the key lime cake."

"Good."

"Looks like a bite or two from the cupcake."

"Mm-hmm."

"He hasn't touched the brownie yet."

Caroline covered her forehead with her hand. "I'm getting too old for this."

"Has a food critic ever come here before?"

Caroline shook her head.

The jingle bells over the front door indicated the man with an enviable sweet tooth and maybe a food critic had left.

Abbey looked at Caroline. "Well, now, I guess we just have to wait and see."

26

When Abbey got to the hospital later that day, it was quarter to three in the afternoon. Her mother was awake and sitting up in bed.

"How are you feeling?" Abbey asked.

Millie smiled a toothy grin. "Oh, pretty good."

Abbey sat in the chair next to her mother's bed. "So, how was your day?"

"We're getting the band back together," Millie blurted out with an excitement in her voice that Abbey hadn't heard in years.

Abbey raised an eyebrow and said, "Oh, really." She assumed her mother was in one of her usual confused states.

"Bobo's going to get us a gig at Sacred Heart," Millie said.

Just then, the cheerful laugh of a woman came from the bed behind the curtain next to Abbey's mother. "Mm-hmm. Tell her, Millie," the voice said.

Abbey asked her mother, "So, was Bobo here?"

"Yes, he was," Millie said. And then she paused. "I think he was. Oh, I don't know. I can't remember."

"Yes, he was here," said the voice behind the curtain.

Abbey got up and walked toward the curtain. She opened it and found an older woman lying in bed. She resembled Bobo, only her features were much softer. Her silver- streaked hair with several braids framing her face splayed out on the pillow like the sun's rays. The woman exuded style—wearing a caftan covered in brightly colored lemons and limes rather than the drab light blue hospital-issued gown and large, chunky yellow and green bangle bracelets covered both forearms. "Hi, I'm Abbey. Millie's daughter." She waved to the woman on the bed.

"Nice to meet you, Abbey. I'm Frannie. Bob's—or Bobo's—sister." Frannie used the bed remote to prop herself up better, so that she was at Abbey's eye level. "I used to hear him talk about Mickey and Millie all the time. What'd you know? After all these years, it took landing here to meet your mom." She adjusted a pillow so that her neck was supported. "We had a nice visit today—me, your momma, and Bob."

"Is Bobo, I mean your brother, still here?" Abbey asked.

"No, you just missed him."

"Oh, I'm sorry that I did," Abbey said.

"Don't worry. You'll see him again. They're taking your momma to Sacred Heart, day after tomorrow."

"What? Tomorrow?" This was news to Abbey.

"Yes, for rehab," Frannie said.

Abbey felt a little anxious. Every day for more than a year, she had been responsible for everything that happened to her mother. Since her mother had fallen, she had toyed with the "what if" scenario of her mother going to assisted living. The conversation in her mind always ended with uncertainty that it was the right thing. "Okay, I'll talk to Dr. Millian to find out what's going on."

"Don't worry," Frannie said.

Abbey didn't realize her feelings were etched on her face. "I'm not worried," she lied.

Frannie gave her a look that said she knew better. "Now, child, come here." Frannie reached out a hand. Her bracelets clanked together when she did. Abbey walked to Frannie's bedside and put her hand in Frannie's. "Your momma is going to be fine." Frannie lightly shook their hands, emphasizing each word. "My brother loves it there. And he got your momma all excited. He told her they have Open Mic Night, and they could sing together." Frannie's eyes lit up as she spoke. "You should have seen the expression on your momma's face. She lit up when he said that." Frannie stroked Abbey's hand with her thumb. Her ruby red nails were long, but not too long. "Your momma will be fine."

"Thanks, Frannie. I needed to hear that," Abbey said.

"I know." Frannie let go of Abbey's hand. "Your momma's doctors will give you the details, but I think I heard him say three or four weeks—then they'd assess if she needed to stay longer. But the important thing is that the therapy will make her stronger."

Abbey knew Frannie was right. And from what Frannie was saying, they weren't talking long-term...yet. "So, what are you in here for?" Abbey asked.

"Me? Gallstones," she said with an eye roll. "Turns out, they're a real thing. Let me tell you. Painful. Mm-hmm. I've had two beautiful babies—big babies—both over nine pounds. So, believe me when I say I know pain. This. Ooh. I thought I was dying." Frannie clutched her side at a place Abbey guessed was near the gallbladder. "But I'm fine now." Frannie said. The corners of her eyes creased whenever she smiled. "I'll be going home tomorrow."

"Well, I've enjoyed meeting you and talking with you." Abbey turned to go back to her mother's side of the room. "Good luck, Frannie," she said.

"And good luck to you, my dear," Frannie said. "I hope our paths will cross again sometime. You never know. I wouldn't mind seeing Bob and your momma sing at Sacred Heart sometime."

Abbey laughed at the picture in her head of her mother and Bobo performing in front of a group of seniors. She walked back to the chair next to her mother's bed. Millie was now asleep—mouth wide open and snoring loudly. She sat for a minute and thought about what it would mean if her mother did go to Sacred Heart. The rumor had yet to be confirmed, but Frannie seemed like such a reliable source. It was a bittersweet feeling. Even on good days, caring for her mother was stressful. But it was what she *should* do. Family cares for family. Right?

For a brief moment, her mind went to a place where it wasn't her responsibility to make sure Millie was safe—where she didn't have to bathe her mother or make sure she ate her dinner. Could she turn over her mother's care to strangers?

Even if she would allow herself to consider assisted living as an option for her mother, how could they afford it? She could sell the house—it was in Millie's name, but Abbey had the power of attorney. The house was not in great shape, but it was big—nearly three thousand square feet, and it was in a great location. But if they sold the house, Abbey would have no place to live. Her salary at the bakery probably wouldn't cover the cost of a one-bedroom apartment nearby. Maybe get a roommate? She shuddered at that thought.

What was best for her mother needed to be a priority. If that turned out to be Sacred Heart, Abbey would find a way to pay for it—maybe even go back to being an architect. This thought saddened her, and that surprised her. She had always enjoyed being an architect, but not as much as she enjoyed baking. She realized she was passionate about baking. The cake she made for Magda was proof of that. As she had put on the final touches, she marveled at her creation. It was such a rush to feel that kind of pride. She had wanted to run out onto Main Street and drag passersby into the bakery and say, "Look what I did!"

She rubbed her head as it began to throb.

Millie coughed, but did not open her eyes, and continued to snore after a brief pause. Abbey thought she might as well go home, shower, get some dinner, and come back later. As she stood to leave, she spotted a white, business-sized envelope on the table next to her mother's bed. In block letters written in a handwriting that she did not recognize was: For Abbey.

27

The white envelope was secured with Scotch tape neatly lining the edges of the flap. Inside was a folded piece of yellow paper, the kind found on a legal notepad. Abbey immediately recognized the handwriting—it was her father's. No doubt he wrote it using one of his fancy pens that had an ink cartridge and left smudges as his left hand glided over the paper before the ink had a chance to dry.

Stuck to the yellow legal pad paper was a sticky note that read: "Abbey, I got this from your dad a few years back." The sticky note was signed, "Bob 'Bobo' Boone."

She hadn't expected the swell of emotions that came next. She ran her hand over the yellow paper, trying to feel her father's presence. If he were here, he would give her advice about her mother, Sacred Heart, making a living as a baker, Elle, and Jax. He had this way of getting his point across without sounding judgmental or controlling. He had a thoughtful perspective that would methodically weigh all the options. He also made her feel grounded when she worried too much. "The answer is usually not that complicated. Most of the time, it's right in front of you," he would say. That was his way of saying, "Go with your gut and trust your instinct."

She removed Bobo's sticky note, and her father's voice echoed in her head as she read the words he wrote:

December 2015, Happy Holidays, Bobo & Gloria! I hope this note finds you well.

We are all fine here in Maryland. Penny got married last summer. Nice guy, but if I'm being honest, he's a little too serious for me.

He's a lawyer, of all things. Lord knows you and me could have used him that time we got caught with weed during that Missouri gig. Ha! Ha!

I know Penny is happy now. And if I'm being completely honest, she always wanted more than I could give her. So, I am happy for her too.

Abbey thought back to her sister's wedding. There was assigned seating, and Penny put Abbey, Millie, and Mickey at a table near the kitchen with the stragglers she didn't know what to do with—her hairdresser, cleaning lady, and a few neighbors. Penny sat her new in-laws across the room, near the stage, and closest to the sweetheart table. A symbolic gesture of the middle finger.

When they got home after the wedding, Abbey heard her parents argue. Her dad's voice grew loud and cracked with emotion when he said he was no bum. He was the father of the bride. Millie calmed Mickey down in her usual way by helping him understand that they had raised a free spirit in Penny, and for that reason alone, he should be proud.

Abbey returned to her father's note.

*Abbey...*Just seeing her father write her name brought tears to her eyes. The "A" written in perfect Old English, with broad stroked serifs the way he always did.

We did something so right there. Bobo, you'd love her. So amazing. A good mix of me and her mom. She's got my creativity and her mother's compassion and intellect. I have never been prouder of something I created. Proud because of who she is—filled with kindness and goodness — stuff that really counts. Abbey is my masterpiece. I just worry that she doesn't see it in herself.

Abbey put the note down and wiped the tears from her eyes. Of all the grand canvases and murals he created, he thought *she* was his masterpiece. Why didn't her father ever tell her this? Maybe he did, often, but she didn't listen because she was too busy listening to her own negative thoughts in her head. Would it have made a difference to know how he felt? Maybe, maybe not. The self-critical voice was so embedded in her brain, she doubted she could turn it off.

Abbey thought about the end of her father's life. When his prostate cancer had metastasized to his liver, she heard tears in his voice when he called to tell her he knew he had a few weeks—months, if lucky—to live.

"I will be gone soon," he had said. "I'm so worried about leaving your momma." Abbey remembered immediately understanding what he meant. "Don't worry. I'll make sure she'll be fine," she told him.

After that conversation, she quit her job in Philadelphia, packed up her apartment, cried when she told her landlord why she needed to break the lease, and moved back home to Maryland.

Her father lived for only two more weeks. As the inevitable grew near, his piercing blue eyes turned to a dull gray. His love of life and spirit gone—consumed by the cancer that had devoured his body. He was gaunt and winced frequently from pain whenever the morphine wore off. She sat by his bedside and read him their favorite book—*To Kill a Mockingbird*—substituting Mickey for Atticus and Abbey for Scout as he had done when he read it to her as a child. She was near the end of the book when he closed his eyes for the final time.

She often wondered if she should have said something to comfort him as he lay dying so that her words were the last ones he heard and not Harper Lee's.

Reading the note that he wrote to Bobo years before his death somehow gave her peace of mind. She made him proud. That was a good feeling. She held the letter close to her chest, smoothing it with her hand.

The door to her mother's room opened.

She looked up and smiled. "Bobo," she said. "I thought you had left."

"I did. But I forgot my damn phone." He walked over to his sister's side of the room and retrieved his flip phone from the windowsill. "Don't want to miss any calls from my grandkids."

"You'd forget your head if it wasn't on," Frannie said, in a playful way.

"Oh, no I wouldn't. I got my hat." Bobo barked back. He tipped his hat to his sister.

He walked back over to Abbey. "I see you got the note I left for you."

"Yes. Thank you."

"I thought you'd like to hear in your daddy's own words how much he loved you. I remember when I got that note, I said to myself 'she's special.'" He placed a light hand on Abbey's shoulder. "I'm just glad I saved it. We always exchanged Christmas cards until we didn't. And I don't remember why it stopped. Your dad meant a lot to me. I should have kept in better touch with him."

Abbey shook her head. "I'm sure he knew how much you cared for him. The note is lovely, and it means so much. I swear Bobo, I feel him here, with me now. Do you have any others?"

Bobo shook his head. "No, I don't think so. When we met yesterday, I recalled this note. Because of the doodle."

"Doodle?"

"Yes, on the back. I think it's you and him."

Abbey turned her father's note over. And Bobo was right. In the top right corner, taking up about a two-inch square space, her father had drawn what looked like an impromptu portrait of a man—obviously Mickey, shoulder-length salt and pepper curly hair, a mostly gray bushy beard and Lennon-style round glasses, wearing a tie-dye shirt, with his arm around a girl with curly shoulder-length red hair, big green eyes, and an exaggerated smile, dressed the same. A bright sunshine covered the background—it was a rendering of that picture that was tucked in the prized record collection.

She recalled how her father would doodle on anything—carrying a packet of colored pencils to restaurants and make drawings on napkins while he waited for his food. He liked to challenge himself by making the outline of the drawings in one continuous line, without lifting the pencil from the paper. And then use all the colors in the rainbow to color the doodles in.

"I thought it was so beautiful. But my memory isn't what it used to be, and I have downsized, so I didn't mention it for fear it was gone. Lo and behold, there it was in my little shoe box of treasures. Next to a pink rabbit's foot I got when I was a kid. Something told me to save it. And now I know why."

Millie woke up. She rubbed her eyes and yawned. "Is it time for our set?"

Bobo laughed. "No. We've got a couple of days before that."

"Okay, you won't go on without me, will you?"

"What? Of course not. We are a team. Like Sonny and Cher."

Millie smiled. "I like that. I'm Cher." She flipped her hair, mimicking Cher.

Bobo turned his attention to Abbey. "I suppose you heard they're moving your momma to Sacred Heart for some rehab."

Abbey nodded.

"So, I got to thinking, why not have her join me for Open Mic Night for a duet. I'm what they call a headliner in the Great Sage Room," he said with a wink. "So, plan on Friday night at eight. I promise you won't want to miss it!"

Bobo turned and waved to his sister. "Bye, Frannie." He turned back to Abbey. "As much as I'd love to stay here, my Uber is waiting. See you Friday?"

"Yes, sir."

"Good girl. Bye, Millie. I'll stop by when they get you settled at Sacred Heart. The nurses all know me." He had a childlike twinkle in his eyes. "I'm sure they'll tell me what room you're in. Fact is, they find me quite charming."

Even though Abbey didn't doubt that Bobo was a charmer with the nurses, she said, "What's your room number, Bobo? You know, so we have it."

"Apartment 312, third floor, in the west wing."

Abbey tapped the keyboard on her phone and saved it in notes. She reached for Bobo's hand, the one that didn't have the cane, and squeezed it tightly. "Thank you," she said. "For this." She let go of his hand and held up the letter.

"Of course." He tipped his hat and said, "Have a good night, ladies." With that, he turned and shuffled toward the door while whistling "Here Comes the Sun."

28

"It's in the bag, Barry Houdini," a few in the audience chanted in a jumbled attempt at unison. Open Mic Night, a Friday ritual in the Great Sage Room at Sacred Heart, was nearing the end.

The old magician cupped his ear. This caused the crowd to repeat "It's in the bag, Barry Houdini," only slightly louder and a little more scattered. Barry Houdini peeked in the brown paper lunch bag. He coyly shook his head no. Then he stuck his free hand in the bag and felt around in an exaggerated way. The bag made loud, crinkling sounds as his hand thrashed from side to side. When he withdrew his empty hand from the bag, he spread his fingers wide to show there was nothing in his hand. The crowd gasped. Only a mere minute ago, he put a card an audience member drew—the ace of spades—in the bag. Abbey had seen it with her own eyes.

Abbey was impressed—but then again, she always did enjoy magic. She liked to try to figure out the trick—looking carefully for wires, or a sudden move of the hand tucking an object up the sleeve. She monitored Barry Houdini's every move. She was sure she saw him put the card in the bag. She scanned the stage to see if the card had fallen out. It hadn't. *It must be still in the bag*, she thought to herself.

Barry tipped the bag upside down and shook it, revealing there was nothing inside.

"Damn, this guy's pretty good," Abbey whispered to Bobo.

Bobo let out a hearty chuckle that echoed in the room.

"Shhh!" said a woman in the front row with jet black bobbed hair, long straight and blunt bangs, and big, black-framed glasses. Abbey was sure she must have been the inspiration for the costume designer from the Incredibles movie series.

"Former librarian and current Barry Houdini groupie," Bobo said in a voice so hushed, Abbey had to piece together what he was saying.

Once she was sure she got his catty comment correct, Abbey bit her lip to keep a laugh from escaping. "You are so bad," she mouthed. She, Bobo, and her mother were off to the side of the stage in prominent view of everyone. Even though some of the crowd may be hard of hearing, there was no need to draw attention.

The Great Sage Room had a small wooden stage flanked by ramps on either side. Red velour drapes with top swags that had dangling gold tassels framed the stage like a grand old movie theater. Everything was the same as the auditorium in Abbey's elementary school—except for the line of walkers and wheelchairs surrounding the room's perimeter. By the looks of things, the Great Sage Room hadn't been refurbished since the eighties or maybe even the seventies—brown faux wood paneling lined the wall above white painted wainscoting. The guests sat at round tables that doubled as the facility's dining area during the times of 7 to 9 a.m., 11 a.m. to 1 p.m., and 4:30 to 6 p.m. Many stayed in their seats after dinner and waited for Open Mic Night to begin. It was sort of an assisted living version of a sold-out show.

Twenty-four hours earlier, her mother had been transferred to Sacred Heart for six to eight weeks of rehab. They got her settled in a room that she shared with a woman in her sixties who was there for rehab for a broken ankle, and who was on her cell phone at all times talking about what she had for dinner and how cute the physical therapist was.

Abbey had felt a twinge of guilt when she said goodbye to her mother the night before. The confused look on Millie's face had said it all. When Abbey got home, she called the nurses' station to check on her mother. "She's fine. We'll take good care of her," a nurse said in a very calming and nurturing voice. Before Abbey hung the phone up, the nurse added, "Get some rest." That proved easier said than done.

As Abbey lay in bed, her mind jumped from worry to worry. She worried that she was letting her mother down by not bringing her home and taking care of her herself. But then she thought, she's safe, they'll get her stronger, and they are the professionals. When she closed her eyes, she saw her mother's look of confusion. Or maybe it was fear? She's fine, Abbey kept saying to herself. When she was able to reassure herself about her mother's well-being, her thoughts shifted to Jax. By now, days had passed since she blocked him because of what Elle told her. Why couldn't she get him out of her mind? Why was this one so painful? Why did she believe he would be different?

When Abbey arrived at Sacred Heart a few hours before Open Mic Night, Millie was sitting next to her bed in a wheelchair, dressed in an emerald-green sweatsuit that Abbey had dropped off earlier because she didn't want her mother to have to wear the institution-issued gown while performing. Millie smiled broadly when Abbey entered the room. "Did you know it's Open Mic Night?" It felt good to see her mother so happy and looking forward to performing.

Forty-five minutes later, she, her mother, and Bobo were in the Great Sage Room, off to the side of the stage watching an octogenarian magician perform. And it all seemed very normal. What a difference a day can make.

Abbey shifted her attention back to the stage.

"I believe I need the help of my assistant, the lovely Miss Helen, to get this trick right," Barry said. He extended a hand to a woman standing off to his side.

The lovely Miss Helen wore a tiara that sparkled with ruby- and diamond-like crystals. She had short gray hair and was wearing a black sequin dress that fell somewhere midway up her thigh, revealing toned legs through fishnet stockings and shiny black two-inch MaryJane tap-dance-like shoes. Abbey stretched her neck to get a better glimpse of the gold glittered sash the lovely Miss Helen had draped from her shoulder to her waist. Miss Maryland, 1959.

The cool kids from high school are the cool kids in assisted living.

Abbey, her mother, and Bobo sat through a retired opera singer who dressed in a kimono and sang the aria from Madame Butterfly; a ninety-year oldish poet-ish who waxed and waned about his sexual conquests during Woodstock while reciting "The Summer I Loved"; a couple who reenacted the last dance scene from Dirty Dancing—well, sort of—a blow-up doll dressed identically as the woman was used in the lift and twirl sequence. And now, Barry Houdini. Bobo said, for the most part, the acts remain the same week after week. He added with his wry sense of humor, it helps when most of the audience can't remember what happens from one show to the next.

Bobo tapped Abbey on the shoulder. "Get ready. We go on next," he said in a near whisper.

Abbey gripped the handles of her mother's wheelchair and gave Bobo a quick nod.

Barry Houdini flicked his satin cape with dramatic flair. "Okay, Miss Helen, wave the magic wand over the bag."

Miss Helen followed his instructions.

"On the count of three," Barry said. "One, two, two and a half." There were some giggles in the crowd. "Two and three-quarters."

More giggles. "Three!" Barry closed his eyes, reached in the bag, and pulled out a playing card. He opened his eyes to look at the card. A smile flashed broadly across his face. He turned the card to the audience. "I believe this is your card. The old queen of hearts," he said, exuding confidence. The crowd erupted with applause.

Abbey looked at Bobo. "I thought the card was the ace of spades," she whispered.

"Yes." Bobo nodded. "Now he's 0 for 20." Bobo whispered. "We learned the hard way he'll go through the entire deck—all fifty-two cards—until he finds the right one. It's best just to let him think he's got it on the first try."

Abbey stifled a laugh.

Barry and Miss Helen took a bow. "Now remember, I do all the b's—birthdays, bat and bar mitzvahs, barbecues, and baby showers, but if the price is right, I can do other letters of the alphabet too," Barry said. Apparently, Barry was no comedian either. "I'm Barry Hockstein, room 417, east wing, and my lovely assistant is Helen Winslow, room 520, east wing." Barry kissed Helen's hand. "Stop by and visit sometime." He gathered his props—a small black table, a top hat with a stuffed rabbit poking out of it, and an 8×10" tabletop sign that read: "Let's make magic together."

Abbey's stomach got queasy knowing her mother and Bobo were next to perform. It was the same feeling she had the first and last time she performed in a talent show—sixth grade at New Windsor Elementary Spring Showcase. She had practiced her favorite song, *Blackbird*, so often it was embedded in her brain. For the better part of a month, she sang it every morning in the shower, every evening on the walk home from school, and just before bed. But when she stepped onstage, she was overcome with stage fright. She stood in the auditorium in front of her peers, teachers, and parents, and couldn't remember a single word. She felt like a statue with cement legs that wouldn't allow her to run off the stage. She stood there, staring back at the audience. There was an uncomfortable cough or two, and a few giggles. She prayed for a miracle—anything—a false alarm fire drill, an earthquake where nobody was hurt, but she was swallowed up by the earth and spit back out at her home. Most of all, she prayed the words would come.

After what felt like an eternity, a woman with frizzy brown hair stood near the back and started singing the words to the song. When Abbey heard her mother's sweet and soulful voice echo through her grade school auditorium, it soothed her enough to restore her memory and sing along. One by one, audience members stood to join in on what became a sing-along. Even though Abbey finished the song with the help of everyone there, the fear and shame she felt while standing on the stage trying to summon the words that had inconveniently and inexplicably left her brain at that instance never went away.

"Let's give it up for Barry 'Houdini' Hockstein and Helen Winslow," Dave Kendall, Sacred Heart's activities director, said. "And now, it is my pleasure to invite to the stage to close the show, a headliner here at the Great Sage Room, Bob Boone." Dave referred to an index card with notes. "And his friend, Millie Reilly." He led the applause.

Abbey pushed her mother's wheelchair on the stage, and Bobo followed. She locked the wheels in place in front of a microphone on a stand. A sound technician—who reportedly was a resident's college-aged grandson—walked onstage and adjusted the microphone so that it was close to Millie's mouth. He leaned in close to the microphone and said, "Check, one-two-three. Check" and gave a thumbs-up to a man in the back of the room who sat behind a sound board. He then went behind the red curtain and came out with a folded tan metal chair. He unfolded the chair and placed it next to Millie. He again walked behind the stage and returned with an acoustic guitar on a guitar stand and placed them both near the metal chair.

Bobo tipped his hat in gratitude to the technician, who then jumped off the stage and retreated to the back of the room.

He placed a hand on Millie's shoulder. "Now, just like we rehearsed it." Millie put her hand on his, smiled brightly, and said, "Okay."

Bobo sat down. The chair's legs squeaked on the wooden stage floor as he adjusted his position. He laid his cane to his side, in between himself and Millie. Then he reached for the guitar and used a thick leather strap, adorned with embossed peace signs and the initials B.B., to secure it around his body. He played a few chords and listened intently to the notes, adjusting the tension until the instrument was in tune.

"You got this, guys," Abbey said, before walking off the stage.

"Hello, everyone," Bobo said into his microphone. "This here is my dear friend, Millie. Millie and me used to be in a band, many, many years ago." He turned to Millie and winked. "Millie's gonna be with us for a few weeks—maybe even longer. So, I hope you show her as much love as you do me."

The room erupted with applause. One man in the back let out a whistle. "Welcome, Millie," he said.

"We love you, Bob and Millie," said a silver-haired woman sitting in the middle of the room.

"Now, that's what I'm talking about." Bobo strummed the guitar. "Oh, this is gonna sound a little weird, but it's been a long time since me and Millie did this song for an audience. So, if you're moved to clap along, please don't. 'Cause it will mess me up." He laughed in a boyish way.

His words struck panic in Abbey. Why would Bobo choose

a song that he didn't know well? She doubted her mother, in her reduced mental capacity, would be able to remember a song's entire lyrics. Maybe if the crowd clapped along, it would drown out Millie.

Bobo looked at Millie and said, "On the count of three. One, two, three." And his fingers plucked a melody that was familiar, but it was to a song that Abbey couldn't immediately place.

Abbey's heart was in her throat as she stood off to the side of the stage. She'd planned to chime in and save her mother as her mother had done years earlier, but she wouldn't be able to do it if she didn't know the song.

Bobo turned toward Millie and gave a nod. On cue, Millie's sweet, soulful voice emerged and the words to the Beatles' *Yesterday* echoed through the auditorium.

There was no way Abbey could sing along. She was too choked with emotion as her mother sang of a more carefree time. The words that John Lennon and Paul McCartney wrote about yearning for a lost love now had new meaning.

29

Later that night, Abbey had trouble sleeping. It wasn't due to her usual worry or overthinking; it was for a much different reason. Her mind replayed the evening in the Great Sage Room over and over—her mother seemed so happy—laughing and enjoying being around people her own age. It was as if the stroke had never happened. And Bobo, what a spark Bobo had become. There was no denying, the old Millie was back. Maybe Sacred Heart wouldn't be the worst place for her mother after all.

Abbey assessed the situation. How to afford Sacred Heart was of course top of mind. Medicare would pay while she was there for rehab—which could be as long as three months. After that, then what? The monthly costs would be more than she could handle on her bakery salary. She could put the house on the market and go back to being an architect in Philadelphia. With her old salary, she could support her mother and herself. Things would be tight, but she could make it work.

She thought back to her days as an architect. At first, it was so exciting. That feeling of being in a meeting and the first time, having her boss say, "What do you think, Abbey?" Her opinion mattered. She had a knack and a skill for designing buildings, reading codes, and seeing the big picture, and she knew it. There was intense satisfaction watching a building go from plans on flimsy paper to brick and mortar that towered high in the sky. But in those days, there was always something missing. Once, when the team celebrated the completion of a long project, Camille said,

"You must be so happy," but in truth, she wasn't. There was no one special to celebrate with. After the champagne toast at work, she'd later go home alone and unfulfilled.

She thought back to a conversation she'd had with Jax. "Happiness matters," she'd said to him when he was contemplating a career change. Although she never thought she'd say this, baking cakes, pies, and cookies did make her happy. It brought her joy to see the smiles on people's faces when they took a bite of something she created. The smile that came from the intoxicating sweet smell of sugar mixed with butter, flour, and eggs meant that being a baker was more fulfilling than designing buildings.

"Happiness matters," she said to herself. She needed to figure out a way to keep her mom at Sacred Heart and bake for a living.

She got out of bed. The house was dark, and the wood floors creaked loudly as she stepped on each board. She knew what she had to do. Her thoughts were coming clearer with each step she took. She made her way up the old staircase and into the room her parents used to share. The record collection lay untouched since she showed them to Jax about a month earlier. She bent down and ran her hand on the first one—the autographed Abbey Road. Could she really do this? These were her father's prized possession.

She sighed, looking upward hoping for a sign. Was she doing the right thing? The decision was harder than she imagined. She put the record back into the crate, but something blocked its way. She reached into the milk crate and felt the small photo which had become crumbled between two records. She removed the picture of father and daughter and smoothed it with the edge of her hand. The photo taken long ago but so familiar. She ran her finger on her father—outlining him and hoping his good sense would seep into her veins. And then it occurred to her. The two tie-dyed clad figures were the same that he had drawn and sent to Bobo. He must

264

have been looking at this very photo as he wrote the note.

She thought of the letter that Bobo had given to her. She'd often overheard her father saying he'd wished he had Abbey's sensibility and at times, she was more of a parent than he. She *was* his masterpiece. His words rang in her head. His words written for someone else had made their way back to her. She turned back and looked at the records. Confident she had her answer.

• • •

Two hours later, she created an eBay account with the username of AbbeyRose. Each record had been meticulously photographed—all one hundred and forty—making sure there was no glare, and nothing cut off. The ad on eBay read: Vintage Vinyl—A Collector's Dream—**including signed Abbey Road**Selling as a set**no exceptions. She was emphatic about that last part. It was as like she was finding a home for her father's third child.

She paused as she gave serious thought to the price. The autographed McCartney alone should be worth several thousand dollars. She slowly typed a one and then followed it with four zeros. Ten thousand was a respectable price for the collection. And it would go a long way to helping with her mother's expenses. If it was too high, she'd see what offers she'd get, determined not to settle. The albums needed to find a special home—one where someone would take good care of them.

It was nearly dawn when she clicked the link to post the collection. And that was that. There was only time to shower and before heading to the bakery. There was a conversation she wanted to have with Caroline.

30

"You should have seen her, Caroline. She was really happy and alive. More alive than I've seen her recently. And she sang so beautifully." Abbey was still infused with happiness and glowing from the wonderfulness of the night before. "She remembered every word. Every word. It was like she was a new person." She leaned over to assess what was in the bakery case. It was in mostly good shape—not too depleted from the morning rush. Maybe a batch of chocolate chip cookies, some red velvet cupcakes—since they were the best sellers, and maybe a cheesecake. Strawberry. Yes, strawberry cheesecake sounded good.

She stood back up. "After the Open Mic Night, they had an ice cream social—they called it 'Friday is Sundae Nite.'"

"Oh, that's clever. Maybe we can use that here. Brush off the old General Custard." Caroline said in reference to an ice cream machine that stood in the corner of the bakery and hadn't been used since the summer because it was so hard to clean. "I think it would trend well on social media," Caroline said. "Just think of the hashtags."

"Trend well and hashtags. Look at you, using social media lingo. I'm impressed."

"Oh, I can hashtag with the best of them—hashtag Friday Is Sundae At Sweet Caroline's!" Caroline's hot pink nails made a clicking sound as she snapped each word for emphasis.

"Hashtag Friday Is Fundae—spelled like sundae but with an 'F'—At Sweet Caroline's!" Abbey chimed in.

"Hashtag I'm Sweet on Caroline!"

"Hashtag I scream for Caroline!"

"Hashtag Caroline's Now Sweet and Creamy!"

"Okay, you win," Abbey said, catching her breath from laughing. "Although, I'm not sure I want to see what kind of business that one generates."

"Oh, it's great to see you laugh like that. You must feel relieved that your momma is in a good place."

"Yeah, I do. Last night, at the ice cream party, people kept coming up to her and Bobo, introducing themselves, and saying how much they enjoyed the show. I think she made three or four new friends."

"That's great."

"Yes. She seemed very different—but in a good way."

"How?"

"Um, I don't know. Like she was her old self again. And she absolutely loves Bobo. He's so sweet to her. He holds her hand and calms her down like my dad would do. Who knows, maybe there's something there."

"Well, wouldn't that be nice...for both of them."

Abbey let out a big sigh. "But..."

"Oh, here we go again with the worry."

"You know me well. I've got to worry about something."

"What's there to worry about? Your mom sounds safe and in a good place. She's got a great friend in Bobo—maybe even more." Caroline winked. "As you said, she's more alive than she has been recently."

"Yes, I know. That's what I said, and I mean it. I think it'd be a good place for my mom—she'd be taken care of and have friends. I trust Bobo to be my eyes and ears. He'd give it to me straight if something was off. But it may be too soon to tell." Abbey let out a long, slow breath. "She's only there temporarily while she has physical therapy to increase her strength. Six weeks or so."

"And after that? If she's still thriving there, why not let her stay?" Caroline was saying out loud the conversation Abbey had inside her head many times in the past ten hours.

"It's an option, but that place is pretty expensive."

Caroline nodded. "I see."

"She gets social security. Neither one of my parents had a retirement account." Abbey was slightly embarrassed to say that part to anyone, even Caroline.

Caroline nodded. It was one of the things Abbey loved about Caroline. She was such a good listener and rarely judged. Caroline herself did not struggle financially—because of husband number two or four, or a combination of two and four. Even though she lived very well, Caroline never looked down on anyone who had less means.

"The only thing my mom has of value is the house. I can sell it." Abbey paused. "Of course, Penny will go nuts. I think I can deal with that fallout. But there's a part of me that thinks it might be easier for all of us to return things back to the way they were—she comes home, Betty takes care of her during the day while I'm here, and I take care of her when I'm not here." Abbey leaned on the top of the bakery case and propped her head up with her hands.

"Easier for whom?"

"Well, frankly, me."

Caroline's reaction showed she strongly disagreed. "Look, there's a lot to unpack here. The first priority needs to be your mother's safety, right?"

Abbey nodded.

"But a very close second needs to be your happiness. Very close second." Caroline put up her thumb and pointer finger, indicating less than an inch of space in between them. "It's okay to admit it was overwhelming to take care of your mother. You shouldn't be burdened with that." Caroline stroked Abbey's shoulder. "You are young. Lots of life ahead of you. In some ways, you need to think this break is a sign from the universe. You were being run ragged. I mean, really, you couldn't even go to a very special dinner, with a very special someone without dire consequences of leaving your mother alone. That shouldn't happen. You should be free to come and go as you please. Listen to the universe. Take this opportunity to assess both priorities—what would be best for your mother and *you*." She lightly tapped Abbey's chest with her pointer finger. "And you," she repeated.

Abbey knew Caroline was right. The last week had been a blur of mixed emotions—she'd felt so low Saturday after fearing that her mother was seriously injured, feeling the guilt of leaving her alone, reading the hurtful comments on Instagram, and then hearing Elle say Jax was only using her. And, by contrast, she'd felt so much joy last night.

"Okay, now that's settled," Caroline said.

"Oh, I wouldn't go that far. Although you're helping me move the needle in a certain direction."

"I won't tell you what to do unless I feel very strongly. And I feel very strongly about this. Your mom is better off at Sacred Heart, and you are better off with her at Sacred Heart."

"You may be right." Abbey paused. She had actually already headed in that direction.

She sucked in a breath deeply, summoning up the courage. "Caroline," she said.

"Yes."

"I've been meaning to ask you something."

"Oh?"

"Yes, come on. Let's have a seat," Abbey said.

"Oh, dear, this sounds serious."

Abbey led Caroline to a small table nearest the bake case. They both sat down.

Abbey's heart pounded loudly, and her throat felt dry. She swallowed hard. She couldn't believe what she was about to say. "Does the offer to become your business partner still stand?"

Caroline's face lit up. "What?" she said. "I thought you wanted to go back to your job in Philadelphia."

"I did. But now I know my place is here. Thank you for helping me realize that."

Caroline teared up. "I can't tell you how proud I am of you. I would be honored to have you as a partner."

"Thanks," Abbey said holding back her own tears.

The jingle bells at the bakery front door interrupted the business deal. Abbey gasped when she recognized the patron. The food critic who had come in a few days ago was back.

31

Caroline nudged Abbey in the direction of the counter. Abbey smiled brightly, trying to hide her nerves. "Hi." She waved, not exactly sure if she should acknowledge their encounter just a few days earlier.

He smiled back.

"What can I get you today?" she said. "The peanut butter bars are pretty good."

"No, that's not why I'm here." His look turned serious.

"I'm Wiley Renauld." He extended his hand. Wiley was a very slight man, thin and short. Abbey guessed he was probably in his mid to late fifties—but she was never too good at guessing people's ages.

"Abbey Reilly," she said as she shook his hand but withdrew hers quickly so that he wouldn't notice how clammy it was. "Nice to meet you, Wiley."

"Magda said you were the best, and she was right."

"Magda? You know Magda?"

"Yes, I attended her birthday party earlier this week. Magda and I used to be neighbors when she lived in New York. Nice lady. She's told me for months I have to come here to Sweet Caroline's. And, after eating that red velvet you made for her birthday, I wished I would have listened to her and come here sooner."

"That's awfully nice to say. So, you said New York. Do you write for the *Times?*"

"What? No."

"Oh, I see, some other paper in New York. Can I ask when will the review be published?" Abbey asked.

"Review?" Wiley's nose wrinkled like he had smelled something foul.

"Oh, I'm sorry. Is that a bit too forward to ask?"

"What? No. I'm sorry, there may be some misunderstanding." He smiled as he spoke while a look of understanding covered his face. "You think I'm a food critic, don't you?" As the words came out of his mouth, he broke into exuberant laughter. "Of course you do. Oh, dear God, no, I'm not a food critic." He made a stink face again. He reached into his back pants pocket and pulled out a business card. "Here," he said, handing his card to Abbey.

On the card, Abbey recognized the big bold yellow sunshine logo of The Baking TV Network—a cable channel that had twenty-four seven baking shows. A channel that Abbey watched almost obsessively. She handed the card to Caroline who was by now standing right next to Abbey.

"Executive Producer?" Abbey said cautiously.

"Yes, it's my job to come up with new show ideas."

Intrigued, Abbey could barely breathe as she waited for Wiley to get the words out.

"I have an idea for a new show called 'Hometown Baker.' And I want you to audition for it."

"Me?" Abbey reached behind her to make sure the chair was there before she sat down.

"Yes, you."

Wiley definitely had her attention. "You want me to audition for Baking TV?" She repeated the words she thought she heard him say.

Wiley nodded.

"What does that mean, exactly?"

"Well, we'd film you while you bake something. All you have to do is talk to the camera and bake. Give tips—like you do on your blog." He paused. "If the program director likes you after they see the pilot—and I don't see why they wouldn't—then we'd green light ten shows."

He looked deep in thought for a second. "Do you have a social media person?"

"What? No. Just me."

"Hmm. You might give some thought to finding someone to manage your accounts. You should be all over the place—Instagram, Facebook, Twitter." He cleared his throat. "I mean X. I still can't get used to that."

"Me neither," she said.

"I'm not much into TikTok," he continued, "but set up an account there too. You'll want to promote the hell out of what you do. That drives up viewership. I think people will really relate to you because you, my dear, are the demographic. Young women who like to bake. We are trying to increase our twenty-five to thirty-five viewership."

"But I don't look like someone you'd see on TV." She had heard the camera added ten pounds—ten pounds she could not afford.

Wiley looked Abbey up and down. "What's wrong with the way you look?"

"That's what I keep saying to her," Caroline leaned into Wiley but spoke in a voice loud enough for everyone to hear.

"At Baking TV, we are doing a service to provide home cooks ideas. I think the viewers would love you. You're very wholesome and this place"—Wiley looked around the bakery— "would be perfect. We are looking for that small-town, homey feel. But I will tell you, you have to exude confidence in front of the camera. If you don't, the audience will turn the channel." He paused and added,

"Look, I realize not everyone can do this. So, if it isn't for you, then I'll just grab a piece of red velvet cake and leave."

Could she do that? Maybe. She felt at ease in the kitchen and baking calmed her. She looked over at Caroline who said, "I can't think of any baker more talented than you. It gives me chills to think of you on that first day here, shy, and unsure of yourself. You've come so far. Now you bake the pants off me."

"Not true. You taught me everything."

"I have to warn you," Wiley added.

Here it comes.

"If the show's picked up, the pay isn't that great for debut show hosts," Wiley continued. "We can pay five thousand an episode and will contract for ten episodes up front."

Abbey did the math quickly in her head—fifty thousand dollars was a lot of money. She didn't want to get ahead of herself, but if the show did take off, maybe she wouldn't have to sell the old Victorian for her mother to stay at Sacred Heart.

"If the show takes off, the opportunities are endless. Most of our celebrity bakers have product endorsements—cake mixes, and such. We draw from our own talent to help judge competitions on our network, and I'm sure you could get a cookbook deal. Not to mention the revenue it will bring here. I'm proposing we'd do the weekly taping here. Before too long, you'll have a line when you open every morning—not just locals, but tourists."

Caroline's eyes grew wider the more Wiley spoke. "Tourists? Here? At Sweet Caroline's?"

"No doubt. This quaint little place on Main Street in this quaint little town—people will eat it up. Pun intended." One eyebrow arched at Wiley's last comment.

"Caroline, are you sure we can handle the extra people?"

"We'll be fine. The universe has spoken," Caroline said

confidently.

Abbey stood. She straightened her back and squared her shoulders. "Mr. Renauld," she said, reaching her hand out for him to shake. "Let's do it."

32

When Abbey got home later that night, she logged onto eBay to see if there were any bids on the record collection. She secretly hoped there were none because she had become a little unsure if she was ready to give them up.

There was one bid, from a buyer named WaxMan, for the full asking price—$10,000. Her finger hovered over the accept button. If she clicked it, there was no turning back.

Before sending the records off to "WaxMan," she owed it to her father to see where they were going. She clicked on his profile, which was a picture of an old record player—the kind with an arm that would drop records one by one. On his ABOUT section he wrote, "big time record enthusiast." And it appeared he was from right here in Ellicott City. That would make transporting the collection easier.

She had to face it, the records were just things, and things that had collected dust for more than a year. They were no value to her unless she sold them. And she needed money. There was no guarantee The Baking Network thing would be long term. She had to get through the pilot.

Without any more hesitation, she accepted the full-priced bid.

• • •

WaxMan transferred the money and gave her an address that was near the bakery, so Abbey agreed to meet him during her morning break. With the milk crates loaded on a metal luggage rack secured by bungee cords, at 10 a.m. Abbey set out to walk the few blocks to deliver the records to their new owner.

The address he had given her was 234 Main. It was unfamiliar, but then again, she did know Main Street from the businesses and not necessarily the numbers. She wheeled past the Main Street Grille and thought to the night she had dinner with Henry. A lot had happened since then. A lot.

She checked on the milk crates to make sure nothing had shifted as she walked further. The street numbers climbed from one hundred to two.

When she reached her father's mural, still standing because some Good Samaritan had bought the adjacent building, she felt reassured. The number above the door of the adjacent building read 234. The records were going to the new owner of the building that had her father's mural. That was a sure sign. She stepped back, looked at the mural her father had painted many years ago and said, "Look after them, okay?"

She looked inside the building; it was still vacant. So, she knocked on the door—softly at first—and then, using her fist—with a little more umph. She could see a tall, slender figure come from a back room.

As the man got closer, his face was familiar. The distinct droopy brown puppy dog eyes gave him away—WaxMan was Jax.

He opened the door and smiled in a way that indicated he'd been hiding a secret.

Abbey wasn't sure how to feel—shocked, happy, and maybe a little uncertain. "It's you," she said. "You're WaxMan?"

He nodded. He tucked his hands in his jeans pockets. "I guess." He looked rather coy.

Damn those dimples. "So, you bought this place?"

He shrugged. "Yeah, I did." He looked around. "It was something you said to me that night." He looked down at the record collection. "The night you showed me these. You said happiness matters."

She nodded, remembering.

"And I realized you're right."

She was careful not to read anything into what was happening. She pushed her way into the shop, pretending she didn't care when inside, she was dying. "So, I guess these are yours. Where do you want them?"

He pointed to a counter at the far end of the store. He took the cart from her, and they walked together to the back of the store.

Once there, Abbey unstrapped the bungee cords. She reached and grabbed the first milk crate in the opening meant for hands and his hand met hers. "Let me," he said. Their eyes met and for a brief second, she didn't want to look away. She let go of the crate and allowed him to lift it.

"Look," he said. "I not sure what Elle said to you. But I know it must have been bad for you to send the text that you did. And then to block me."

Abbey turned to face him again. "She, um, Elle, said you were just using me," she said kind of matter of fact, playing it cool when that was not how she was feeling inside.

"What? No." He looked confused and a little angry. She had never seen him look this way before. His brow furrowed as his eyebrows knitted together. "Using you? For what? I don't understand."

Abbey breathed in deeply. She looked him squarely in the eyes even though her voice cracked a little as she spoke. "She said that you concocted this plan to invite me to the dinner."

"I don't follow. What? How would I be using you to invite you to the dinner?"

So, he was going to make her say it. "Because I'm, well, I'm—" Getting the words out was harder than she expected. "Because I'm bigger." There, she said it. "I'm—" She cleared her throat. "I'm curvy."

"So?"

"Well, I'm assuming I'm not your type."

"Type? Wait. What?" His brow stayed knitted. He ran his fingers through his hair and tussled it a bit. "That isn't true!"

"She said you were a real ladies' man, and you brought me to the dinner so that the people of Philadelphia would think you're the kind of guy who can see beyond looks to be with someone like me. Because—" *Just say it.* "Because I'm fat." She took in a meditative and cleansing breath through her nose and let it out through her mouth.

"You have to believe me. What Elle said isn't true. It's an outright lie."

Abbey was relieved. Elle's words still stung. But they hurt more because she thought there was truth to them.

He paced. "I'm so sorry. Look, in the interest of full disclosure, she did come over to my house right after the dinner."

Here we go.

"She wanted to get back together." He shook his head. "But I said 'No.' Again." He looked her deep in the eyes. "She can ask me a hundred times, and I'll still say 'No.' You have to believe me." He balled his fists down by his side. "But I will just say this, if Elle is miserable, she wants everyone else to be too. It's one of the reasons I broke up with her. You believe me, don't you?" He reached for her hand.

Abbey was not ready to take his hand yet. She clasped her hands together so tightly her fingers ached. "I know I'm not tall and thin like Elle. And I have this love-hate relationship with food.

I love food, but I hate what it has done to my body. I don't think I can change. And maybe I can't change, because deep down, I don't want to." Then she had what Oprah refers to as "a light bulb moment." "I guess I love food more than I hate my body or the criticism I get for being overweight."

"Oh, Abbey, I don't want you to change. Did I used to be a ladies man? I guess. That was the past. The truth is, I am thirty-five. My priorities are different. I enjoy being with you. You make me laugh and you are so kind and caring. Not many people would have given up a career to care for a parent. That speaks to your character."

He was telling her what Caroline had said for months, but for some reason his words mattered more.

"And smart." He continued uninterrupted. "And talented. I mean—" A smile crept on his face as he spoke. "I don't know anyone else who can design buildings and bake amazing cakes. I saw the cake you made last week. The one that was posted on Instagram. I was like, 'How does she do it?'"

Abbey eased her grip. She breathed deeply. He seemed so sincere. "I never thought you'd be interested in someone like me." She darted her eyes down. She felt him get closer to her, and she let him near, in her space. "And then when Elle came here, what she said played into my insecure feelings about us."

"I won't smear her because that's not the kind of guy I am. I know she's used to getting her own way, but I can't believe she'd come all the way down here to confront you." He massaged the back of his neck with his hand.

"Actually, she had a different reason for coming here."

He cocked his head in Abbey's direction. "She did?"

"Yes. She thought I could help her get back on Instagram." Abbey told him about the Instagram post, the mean comments

Elle's followers had made, and how Elle and her friend seemed to delight in it. Abbey held it together until the end. Recounting the awful comments proved to be what broke the dam of tears.

Jax reached for Abbey and drew her close, and she let him. "Oh, sweetie," he said. "I am so, so sorry." His arms were firm but comforting as he wrapped them around her. She felt his heart beat and her heart chose the same rhythm. He snuggled closer, squeezed her tighter and she wasn't afraid he would judge her because her body was fleshy and soft. This was what it felt like to be in the arms of a man. This is what it felt like to be loved.

He stroked her hair and said, "I think you are the most beautiful woman I have ever seen." Then he pulled her closer and rested his chin on the top of her head. She fit perfectly in that space between his neck and collarbone and felt small while enveloped in his arms with her body pressed against his. "Beautiful on the inside and out," he whispered. His body swayed slowly as he cradled her in his arms like he did the night at Camille's wedding.

She slowly lifted her head until her eyes met his. His deep brown eyes looked like melted Hershey's kisses. Her tears stopped as she felt warmth all over inside.

She wrapped her arms around his waist and breathed deeply.

He leaned in, and so did she. His lips were soft and sweet as he kissed hers lightly at first and then with a little more passion. She moved her arms up to his neck and stroked his hair like she had seen in movies. He started to pull away from their embrace. Abbey cupped his head in her hands, pulled him back in, and kissed him again. He seemed grateful that she did.

They stood in the back of the store, in each other's arms, rocking back and forth to no music at all—just the sound of the hearts of two lost souls that found each other again beating in unison. For Abbey, it was an unfamiliar melody to the most beautiful song she had ever heard—one you play over and over the first time you hear it because you can't get enough of it.

He slowly stepped back and smiled as he did. "You don't know how relieved I am," he said. "When I got your text, I couldn't get you out of my mind. I kept telling myself, 'Don't let her get away.' That's why I came here. To fight for you."

"You came here to fight for me?" She couldn't believe her own words.

"Yes, you. I want to spend time and get to know you better. See if we can make this work. Because I really like what we've had so far. You're real. Genuine. Not plastic and phony. I love that about you."

Caroline was right—she usually was. There was one special, wonderful man out there that would accept her no matter if she was a size six or sixteen.

"Oh, one more thing," he said. He looked through the stack of records and pulled out the signed Abbey Road and handed it to her. "I bought this one for you."

Abbey swallowed hard. He was giving up the most valuable piece of the collection. She flung her arms tightly around his neck and kissed him. "Thank you," she whispered.

33

Two weeks later, the kitchen in Sweet Caroline's Bakery was filled with big, bright lights, three cameras to get each angle, and about a dozen members of the production crew from Baking TV. Thick black cables lined the floor and climbed the equipment like jungle vines. The back of the bakery had been transformed into a television set in a matter of hours.

A short while ago, a tall man of average build, with a dark—almost black—thin mustache, soul patch, and spiked hair with blond highlighted tips, introduced himself as Liam, *her*, yes, *her* show's director. He leaned in very close as he shared with her his vision, outlined with drawings and handwritten notes put together in a white three-ring binder. He said he liked the hometown-y feel of the bakery. He 'loved, loved, loved' Caroline. "She's perfect," he said. "A cross between Marilyn Monroe and Paula Deen." Motioning to a camera operator, he added, "Let's get some shots of her we can use in the opening." He had done research, including reading her blog and social media pages. And he gave her advice on what the network and viewers would look for. "Tell us who you are. Who is Abbey Reilly? Give us a little anecdote—tell a story or two about what got you into baking. Make the viewers relate to you. Make them want to make what you're making."

Abbey listened intently. The last part would be a challenge—not the baking part, but the part about making the viewers relate to her. Before walking away, Liam slapped her on the back, maybe a bit too hard, and said "I believe in you" followed by "You got this, kid." His encouragement helped.

They decided to shoot it all from the island in the center of the kitchen. Abbey did as instructed and premeasured all the ingredients to make red velvet cake—and placed them in clear glass ramekins and bowls on the island's countertop in order of how they would be used.

In between the island and the cameras, Wiley Renauld paced back and forth like an expectant father from an old black-and-white movie. As Executive Producer, he had a lot at stake. It was his job to make sure he produced shows for the network that viewers would swarm to see. Baking TV had invested a lot of time and money—sending the crew and equipment down from New York wasn't a small investment. After the pilot was shot, Wiley and Liam would edit the footage into a twenty-four-minute show (allowing six minutes for commercial breaks) that the network's head of programming would either give a thumbs-up or thumbs-down. Abbey tried not to think about the enormity of it all. "It's just another day at the bakery," she'd said to herself over and over until it was embedded in her head.

Jax walked into the kitchen from the front of the bakery. He had come down from Philly the night before to be her moral support. He winked and flashed his ever so sexy smile. "Looks like they've got everything set," he said, scanning all the cameras, lights, and cables strewn all over the kitchen.

"So, they want me to stand here," Abbey said as she stood behind the island in the center of the kitchen. "Like this, 'Hello bakers, I'm Abbey Reilly and today we're going to make...'" Then she noticed the intrusiveness of the cameras—all three staring down at her. She gripped the edges of the island's countertop for support.

Jax walked behind her and encircled his arms around her waist.

"Don't worry. You got this. They'll love you," he whispered. Then he lightly kissed her neck, just behind her ears.

Abbey wrapped her hands around his. It felt so good to be in his arms. The past two weeks, they had gotten closer. Not a day went by that they didn't see each other or FaceTime. He came down twice to work on getting his record shop open. And Abbey's guard was dissolving a little with each passing day. She felt like a schoolgirl, giddy with excitement at the mere mention of his name. And, finally, she allowed herself to dream. Dream about what a future would be like with this wonderful man who respected and cared for her.

"Sorry to break this up," Caroline said. "But there's a customer out in the front of the bakery who needs to speak with you."

"Me? Now?" Abbey gave Caroline an incredulous look. "Can you handle it?"

Caroline shrugged. "I tried to help her, but she's insisting she speak with you."

"Can she come back later? I'm kind of busy." It was truly the last thing she needed—some customer complaining about a cupcake or cookie just as she's about to share a recipe on camera.

"You know me, I wouldn't have you do it if wasn't important. But I think you need to handle her."

"Okay, fine. Whatever," she muttered as she carefully maneuvered around the equipment labyrinth. When she parted the beaded curtain, her feeling of being annoyed quickly shifted to joy when she saw Magda. "Oh, Magda!" Abbey hugged Magda tightly. "It's so nice of you to come."

"Wiley told me about the show." She put a light hand on Abbey's cheek. "So proud. You gonna do great. I know."

"Thanks. Hope so."

"For you." Magda handed Abbey a royal blue gift bag with

blue tissue poking out. "I make good luck charm."

"Oh, Magda, you really didn't need to do that." Abbey took the bag from Magda and looked inside. She reached her hand in and pulled out a neatly folded dark purple cotton fabric. Magda took the bag so that Abbey could unfold the fabric. It was an apron with Sweet Caroline's logo embroidered in cotton candy pink, and Abbey's name just above the logo. "Oh, Magda! I love it!" Abbey put the apron over her neck and pulled it over her body. She pulled the ties behind her. Something felt different. Yes, this apron's ties were long—long enough to loop around to tie in a bow in front.

"What do you think?" Abbey said, one hand on her hip jutting to the side, modeling the apron.

"You look beautiful." Magda clasped her hands.

"Come on back. We're going to tape in the kitchen. I'd love for you to stay. Honestly, it will calm my nerves."

Magda followed Abbey to the kitchen. "Look who's here!" Abbey said. Caroline approached them.

"Where did you get that apron?"

"I make," Magda said in her deadpan way.

Caroline looked deep in thought. "You know, Magda, your friend Wiley here says if the show is a hit, we'll have tourists. I'm thinking we'll need some Sweet Caroline products. I'll bet aprons would be a hit."

Magda nodded. "We'll talk after the show."

With Magda and Caroline in tow, Abbey walked toward Jax, who had found a place to stand behind the center camera. "Jax," she said. "This is Magda. You've heard me and Wiley speak about her."

"Oh, yes, Magda. So nice to meet you." He shook Magda's hand. "I understand we have you to thank for this."

Magda waved a finger. "No. I plant seed. Is true. But I no bake.

Abbey is baker. Abbey is star."

Wiley walked over to them. "Okay, we're ready for you."

Jax gave her hand a tight squeeze. "Go knock 'em dead."

"You got this," Caroline said.

Magda nodded. "Got this."

"Okay, I guess it's time." Abbey took a deep breath and walked toward the island in the center of the kitchen. She turned and faced the cameras. Her hands visibly shook as she placed them on the counter in front of her. On the counter were all the ingredients needed to make red velvet cake—butter, vanilla, Dutch cocoa, sugar, eggs, flour, salt, buttermilk, and red food coloring. She carefully scanned them, making sure nothing was missing, and breathed a sigh of relief when she did the mental checklist.

"Quiet on the set," Liam said.

"Hometown Baker—Abbey Reilly Pilot, take one," a young man said. He held a digital clapboard, with those same details in front of the camera.

"And we're rolling," Liam said.

Abbey gripped the counter tighter. She shifted her gaze. All three cameras were pointed just at her. Just beyond the center camera, she saw Jax's reassuring smile. "You can do this," he mouthed and added a thumbs-up.

She breathed deeply. Her heart thumped so loudly through her neck she worried that the microphone clipped to her collar would pick it up. Thump, thump, thump. Liam gave no indication that anything was amiss or that her audition was slowly turning into Edgar Allan Poe's "The Tell-Tale Heart." She breathed again, looked straight into the center camera and said, "Hi, everyone. I'm Abbey Reilly, and this is my bakery, Sweet Caroline's on Main Street in Ellicott City, Maryland—near Baltimore. Today, we're going to make one of my favorites, and a favorite of our bakery customers—red velvet cake."

Liam nodded along and said, "Good, good, good," in a very hushed tone. He motioned with his hand for more.

"Now, the key to a good red velvet cake is buttermilk." She pointed to the glass measuring cup containing the buttermilk and noticed her hand was not shaking. She felt the tension in her shoulders ease up. "I use my grandma Nona's recipe."

Liam flashed an "okay" sign with his fingers and added a wink.

"Growing up, my family lived with my grandma. And I used to like to watch her bake." She picked up the bowl that had a stick of softened butter in it and added it to a larger bowl. "You want to make sure the butter is soft enough that it will mix easily with a spoon or spatula."

"Tip time," Liam mouthed.

"Softened butter is much different from melted butter. If you forgot to leave the butter out, no worries. What you can do is put a cup of plain water in the microwave for two minutes or so. Remove the cup, empty out the water, and put a stick of butter in. The steam from the hot water will soften the butter in just a few minutes. Give it a try sometime."

Liam gave a thumbs-up.

She added the buttermilk to the softened butter and mixed the two together.

"I like to bake because it combines science with creativity. I used to be an architect." As the words—used to be—flowed from her tongue, she realized how easy it was to say. "I use the same principles here—science and creativity." Satisfied the butter and buttermilk were thoroughly mixed, she added the cocoa powder. "My dad would ask what's the difference between red velvet and devil's food? Shouldn't a devil's food cake be red?"

Spurts of laugher came from the crew.

"Come to think of it, he had a point." She cracked an egg.

Liam made a grand gesture indicating he wanted her to raise the egg high above the bowl so that the camera could see the yolk and white cascade down.

Abbey did as he instructed and discarded the shell in the trash can next to her. While cracking the second egg, she said, "My parents were sort of nontraditional. Free spirits is the best way to describe them." She couldn't believe she was sharing this information—a fact that had been a source of embarrassment for many, many years—had suddenly become a something she was not only saying out loud to a room full of strangers, but potentially to millions of people. "And my dad had this saying. Every Wednesday, he'd say, life is short—eat dessert first. And that's what we'd do. We'd have cheesecake, pie, cake, ice cream—you name it—before we'd eat the main course. Sometimes—actually, most of the time—we weren't hungry after devouring dessert, so we didn't eat anything else. It's safe to say, on Wednesdays, there were no vegetables."

More laughter from the crew.

"My dad's no longer with us, but on Wednesdays, on occasion, I still eat dessert first."

Baking in front of a crowd and camera was much more enjoyable than Abbey thought it would be. She had a rush of adrenaline bouncing through her body. She felt alive and at peace for the first time in her life. The sadness, fear, and self-consciousness that she felt only a short time ago was gone. She was the same person—the outside hadn't changed at all, but the inside had metamorphosed into a beautiful butterfly.

Life was sweet. Sweet indeed.

Epilogue - Two Years Later

Abbey composed herself and faced the cameras.

"In on one, two, three." Liam used his fingers for emphasis. "And we're back," he said.

"So, after twenty minutes in the oven, your apple tart with a brown butter crumble should have a nice golden top just like this." She used oven mitts to raise the tart just enough for the center camera to get its glistening top covered in pecans, oats, brown sugar, and melted butter. She brought the tart close to her nose. "Hmm. It smells so good. You've got apples mixed with a granola-type topping and the butter and brown sugar give it a hint of caramel. I can't wait to cut it open and have a piece."

After her audition, she negotiated and signed with Baking TV for a trial run of ten episodes of Hometown Baker. Now, two years later, her show was the network's highest rated, pulling in nearly two million viewers during its prime time slot every Wednesday night, and she boasted nearly as many fans in Instagram (ten times the number of followers Elle had, but who was counting). And she was putting the final touches on a cookbook—*Eat Dessert First*— which was scheduled to be released the following spring. She often marveled at how different her life had become. It took a while to believe that she deserved the good life as much as anyone, even if, at times, the good life was exceptionally good.

Soon after Jax bought the building in Ellicott City, he had a long, difficult conversation with his parents and was relieved when they were supportive of his plans to transition out of the family business. He got a small apartment near Abbey, and they began spending time together—like a real courtship. The two spent hours painting and refurbishing the old building until it was perfect. Six months later, For the Record opened its doors to much fanfare—thanks to a write up in the *Washington Post*. The center of the story was the signed Abbey Road album, which now hung in a frame above the checkout counter.

Exactly seven months after the record store opened, on the most beautiful fall day, Abbey and Jax wed. Social media was plastered with pictures of her wearing a princess style dress made of ivory lace and adorned with tiny pearls that Magda had sewn by hand herself. *People Magazine* even ran a small photo of the happy couple along with a blurb and headline that said, "Baking TV's Star, Abbey Reilly, Weds former real estate mogul Jackson Lawrence III in Intimate Ceremony." Sure, there was the expected fallout on Instagram with comments like "What's he doing with her?" She'd hired Penny to be her social media manager. The two sisters had a tearful reconciliation shortly after Abbey filmed the pilot. And it came as no surprise that Penny was quite good at her job at shutting down the snarky comments from trolls that crept onto her feed.

Abbey put the tart on the counter and rubbed her growing belly. She felt the life inside of her move. Boy or girl, she and Jax agreed to name the baby Mickey only after promising Bunny, the second child would be named after a Lawrence family member. She hoped that Baby Mickey would have his or her grandfather's kindness and creativity and grandmother's sweet singing voice and love of music.

"According to my mother, this kid is going to have a lot of hair because I have heartburn all the time," she said while looking into the camera. With her salary from Baking TV and endorsements, Abbey was able to hold on to the old Victorian house and even make the necessary repairs. She had enough money left over to move Millie into an apartment in Sacred Heart right next to Bobo's. And every Friday night, Millie and Bobo followed Barry Houdini as they closed Open Mic Night in the Great Sage Room.

The magician changed up his act. He had a lovely new assistant, Sweet Caroline—whom he'd become smitten with when she'd visited Millie. During one of his recent Open Mic shows, he got down on one knee and pulled a round diamond weighing nearly four carats from behind Caroline's ear and pledged his undying love for her right there on the spot. Three weeks later, he became her fifth (and last?) husband. Although Caroline now lived with Barry at Sacred Heart, she still came into the bakery on a daily basis. She had great fun taking selfies, giving daily tours, and selling souvenirs. Magda's aprons with the long ties were a big hit with the busloads of tourists whose second stop was the little record shop just down the street.

"What goes best with brown butter apple crumble? For me, it's cinnamon whipped cream." Abbey walked to the freezer. Opened it and removed a metal bowl. "I like to chill the bowl for about thirty minutes. That way, the cold heavy cream will whip up faster." She opened the refrigerator and removed a pint of heavy whipping cream and walked back to the kitchen island, all with the watchful eye of the camera crew. "Just pour in the whole pint and whip it at high speed for a minute or two. You'll get some nice tall peaks. But don't over whip it—unless you want butter."

She turned off the mixer. "And when that's done, I fold in a half teaspoon of cinnamon. If you like your whipped cream a little sweeter, you can also fold in some powdered sugar or honey." She added a dollop of whipped cream to the tart. "Nothing says fall better than an apple tart with a rich brown butter crumble topped and with cinnamon whipped cream."

She looked at the digital clock with large red numbers that read 29:55. "I'm Abbey Lawrence," she said. "Always remember, life is short. So, if it's Wednesday, Eat Dessert First."

Liam yelled, "Cut. That's a wrap."

Nona's Red Velvet Cake with Cream Cheese Frosting

2 ½ cups of all-purpose flour

1 ½ cups granulated sugar

1 tsp salt

1 tsp baking soda

1 tsp apple cider vinegar

½ cup butter, at room temperature

1 cup buttermilk, at room temperature

1-2 tablespoons red food coloring, more or less depending on
    how deep you want the color

2 tablespoons unsweetened cocoa powder

2 eggs, at room temperature

1 tsp vanilla

Preheat oven to 350 degrees F and grease two 9-inch cake pans.

In a large bowl, combine eggs, buttermilk, sugar, butter, vanilla, apple cider vinegar, and red food coloring.

In a separate bowl, whisk together the flour, salt, baking soda, and unsweetened cocoa powder.

Add the flour mixture to the egg mixture and mix until all ingredients are well combined.

Divide batter evenly and bake for 25-28 minutes or until a toothpick inserted comes out clean.

Cream Cheese Frosting

½ cup butter, at room temperature
16 oz cream cheese, at room temperature
4 cups powdered sugar
1 ½ teaspoon vanilla
A pinch of salt

In a large bowl, using a handheld of stand mixer, beat cream cheese and butter together on medium-high speed for 2 minutes.

Add powdered sugar, vanilla, and salt. Mix on low for 30 seconds then increase to high and beat for 3 minutes until completely mixed.

Acknowledgments

There are so many people I want to thank who helped me in my journey as an author.

First and foremost, I can't thank the staff at Apprentice House Press enough. I am forever grateful to continue our working relationship. It has been a pleasure to go on this journey together. Thank you to Kevin, Lindsey, Claire, Chris, and Abby for making this book come to life.

To all the readers of my first novel, *New Normal.* Thank you for your comments and supporting me as a writer.

To Dian, I am grateful this process brought us together. Thank you for your friendship and for allowing me to walk this path with you.

To Cari, thank you for your feedback. I wish you much success as an author.

To my editor, Kimberly Hunt of Revision Division, thanks for the thorough and thoughtful editing suggestions early on. You helped me craft a story I am proud of. And thanks for catching the typos.

To Deliah, Susan, and Lisa—my writing buddies—I am inspired by your talent and confidence. Thanks for all the good advice, honest feedback, and the many years of friendship. It's hard to believe how far we've all come since walking into that classroom so many years ago.

To Trice and Megan, thanks for the many years of laughs and

friendship. One day, we will be guests on WWHL! (I'd settle for being the bartender.)

To my dearest friends, Elaine, Joan, Gabrielle, Bibi, and Diane—I know you see yourselves in some of the characters in my books. That's because you have been such an integral part of my life. We've shared lots of laughs and tears. All of you make my world a better place.

To Nita, the sister I choose, thank you for your love and support through the decades. I would have crumbled years ago if you weren't there to provide great advice and a soft shoulder to lean on. We crush it!

To Stephanie and Ari—thank you for continuing to allow me to be a part of your lives.

And most of all, to Kevin—thank you for giving me the encouragement to pursue my dream. And for listening to my half-baked story ideas and providing input. But most importantly, thank you for loving me every day. My life is sweeter because of you! You rock!

About the Author

Michelle Paris is an award-winning Maryland writer who writes about hope with humor. *Eat Dessert First* is her second novel that deals with a serious subject told with a mixture of heartfelt and comedic moments. Her debut novel, *New Normal,* loosely based on her own experience of being a young widow, received First Place in The BookFest Fall 2023 Awards, and was a finalist in the Independent Author Network 2023 Book of the Year Awards Contest. Michelle's personal story of overcoming grief was featured on the front page of the Wall Street Journal, and her essays have appeared in multiple editions of *Chicken Soup for the Soul* and in other media outlets. She is a member of the Women's Fiction Writers Association and the Maryland Writer's Association. Currently, Michelle is enjoying chapter two of her life with her new husband, Kevin, who keeps her from being a cat lady but only on a technicality. For more information, please visit www.michelleparisauthor.com.

Apprentice
House Press
Loyola University Maryland

Apprentice House is the country's only campus-based, student-staffed book publishing company. Directed by professors and industry professionals, it is a nonprofit activity of the Communication Department at Loyola University Maryland.

Using state-of-the-art technology and an experiential learning model of education, Apprentice House publishes books in untraditional ways. This dual responsibility as publishers and educators creates an unprecedented collaborative environment among faculty and students, while teaching tomorrow's editors, designers, and marketers.

Eclectic and provocative, Apprentice House titles intend to entertain as well as spark dialogue on a variety of topics. Financial contributions to sustain the press's work are welcomed. Contributions are tax deductible to the fullest extent allowed by the IRS.

To learn more about Apprentice House books or to obtain submission guidelines, please visit www.apprenticehouse.com.

Apprentice House Press
Communication Department
Loyola University Maryland
4501 N. Charles Street
Baltimore, MD 21210
Ph: 410-617-5265
info@apprenticehouse.com • www.apprenticehouse.com

Printed in the USA
CPSIA information can be obtained
at www.ICGtesting.com
LVHW050532130524
779804LV00013B/869